SERPENTINA

FAITH CONSIGLIO

OCELOT CITY Publishing
New York, NY

Published by Ocelot City Publishing
New York, NY

E-book ISBN: 979-8-218-45924-6
Paperback ISBN: 979-8-218-45925-3

Cover Art by Zohra Julia Mekki
Original cover design sketch (back page) by Faith Consiglio

1

Dark leaves rustled in the forest, their dried tips rubbing against each other like the slow rattle of a snake. Emma paused, a warning echoing in her mind. Since her arrival to the reptile research base on Crete, she had ventured into the palm forest alone each afternoon, wandering deeper each time.

Never enter the forest alone. It was the rule her research mentor emphasized most during orientation. But there was nothing truly dangerous on the island. Hercules had cleared away all the deadly creatures to honor Zeus's birthplace. She smiled, recounting the myth the airport taxi driver had told them. Emma knew, out of all the snakes there, only the cat snake had venom, and it was too mild to hurt a human.

Still, if Dr. Belken discovered her sneaking out at dusk, she might as well kiss a Columbia University recommendation letter goodbye. Yet the forest called her in, beckoning her to explore its ancient grounds.

She stepped over sandy soil, glancing over her shoulder at the wooden stairs and scanning to see if anyone was watching before turning into the trees. She savored a breath. The air was dry and the heat tame, with an endless breeze carrying wisps of sea salt and the spice of wild herbs through the dancing shadows of leaves.

A rustling halted her steps.

Her eyes darted to catch a beige, reptilian tail slipping into the nearby shrubs.

She held her breath and crept toward it, afraid to scare it off. It would sense the vibration of even her lightest step.

She peered through a thicket of narrow, glossy leaves and clustered pink flowers. Her heart pounded, instincts heightened, but she reminded herself that even a bite couldn't kill her.

At first, she didn't see anything. Then scales materialized among the leaves on a thick, coiled body. Only now they were green and pink. She squinted. Was it a different snake, or had it changed?

Its serpentine head emerged through the leaves, forked tongue flickering. She froze.

This was *not* a cat snake.

Images of the other native snakes raced through her mind. She was good at identifying them. This didn't match any. With all the travel to and from the island, she supposed it could be an invasive species. Her heart pounded faster and sweat broke on her brow. It could be venomous. And she was alone.

To her relief, the snake slid through a patch of tall grasses and emerged on the far side. Her eyes widened in disbelief as the scales changed back to beige as it slithered over dried leaves.

She slid a trembling hand into the pocket of her capris, then took a picture with her phone. *A closer one would be better.* She held her breath and stepped again. A dry leaf crinkled underfoot, and the snake's head snapped in her direction. Its eyes flared as they set on her, hungry with anger.

Predator's eyes.

Heart drumming, Emma turned and sprinted back to the base. She burst into the atrium, bending over to catch her breath.

"It appears I have to go over the rules with someone." A voice from the side doorway made her jump.

"Dr. Belken!" She faced her research mentor, chest heaving.

"Do you realize what trouble your wanderings could get me in?"

She nodded, grasping for words to explain herself. When he had warned of dangers, he meant strangers who might prey on a young foreign girl wandering alone. But the forest was gated off for research and far away from the crowded city center, where an occasional pickpocket might lurk among the seaside cafes and street vendors selling figurines of the Minotaur. Emma was annoyed by the warning that a boy her age could go pretty much anywhere without.

"So," he said, his eyes glistening. They reminded her of an owl's, both wise and threatening. "Did you find anything?"

Relief flooded her that she might actually escape this without any repercussions. She nodded, her mouth dry. "A snake," she said. "But I couldn't identify it."

He placed his glasses on. "Where?" he asked. She pointed. "Let's go," he said without hesitation. She lingered, the final traces of daylight now slipping from the sky, and wondered if he'd be insulted if she warned him.

She described the snake's changing patterns as they paced toward the ferns, and she felt a slight relief having him there. His tall, lanky frame didn't offer much security, but surely he could identify the snake. He wouldn't put her in danger, would he?

But when they reached the ferns and searched the underbrush and surrounding trees, the snake was gone.

Or at least they didn't see it.

She quickened her pace as they headed back, recalling how seamlessly it could conceal itself even in daylight, and tensed with each step, poised for it to strike from the earthy shadows.

Emma locked her legs around her friend's shoulder in a jiu jitsu hold as they rolled over their cabin floor the following morning.

"All right, all right," Pria said, tapping Emma's hip. She released her, and Pria wiped long, silken waves from her sticky face. "Can we be done?" she asked. "We have lab samples to go through."

Emma nodded. "Thanks."

Her friend promised she could practice jiu jitsu on her during the two weeks of their trip. Emma never missed a class, and she was so close to getting her black belt she didn't want to fall behind.

"You're welcome," Pria said, as she rested back on her elbow. Emma loved her friend's voice, melodic with a hint of raspiness that gave it texture. "I'm sure it'll pay off to have a friend like you if I'm ever in trouble," Pria added.

Emma smiled, offering a hand to help her friend from the floor. Pria was the only one outside the martial arts gym that Emma felt comfortable practicing with. She was reluctant to try it on her boyfriend, especially after her parents called her sport of choice *aggressive* and suggested barre or Pilates instead.

"So, what did the snake look like?" Pria asked as they walked down the hall.

The mysterious scales flashed in Emma's mind, scales she had stayed up late into the night thinking about, searching the internet for photos to match them. "The back had a diamond pattern," she said, "but its color changed with its surroundings, like a chameleon."

"Are you sure it wasn't just shadows or the sunlight hitting different angles?" Pria asked.

Emma shook her head. "No, the color totally transformed. I've never seen a snake like that." Emma took her phone out and scrolled. "Here, I got a picture." She squinted, then zoomed in. It was the picture of the ferns, the exact spot the snake had been coiled. Only the snake wasn't there. She zoomed in farther, unnerved. "That's weird."

"What?"

"I swore I got it…"

Pria studied Emma's screen, leaning in until her eyes were just inches from it. "I don't see a snake," she said. "Maybe you were shaking so much you didn't aim."

"Maybe," Emma murmured, unconvinced.

Pria shook her head. "I would've fainted. Thank god it didn't bite you."

Emma nodded, shuddering at the thought. It would've been so easy. She thought about messaging Jason to tell him, but her boyfriend was probably asleep—it was five in the morning in Chile, where he was visiting family. With the time difference, and his spotty service in his mom's hometown near the mountains, they kept missing each other. She had almost gotten used to not talking every day like they had in New York. He hadn't been thrilled with her choice to spend their final summer of high school doing a research project abroad. Waking him up with a text about her discovery didn't seem like a good idea. Maybe a picture would help ease the distance, but one look at herself in her phone's camera, with her hair frizzy and green eyes bloodshot, made her put the phone away.

Pria unlocked the door to the venomics lab down the hall. Cages lined the walls holding cat snakes, with their striped gray bodies coiled languidly and pale-yellow eyes that followed the girls as they passed.

Emma began preparing the solvents for the procedure. Today they aimed to isolate the toxin from the cat snakes' mild venom and prepare to purify its various contents. Emma's specific project focused on using the isolated molecules to fight tumor cells. The process was tedious, but she often reminded herself the goal was exciting. They might find a cancer treatment. The venom's disintegrin enzyme had already shown cytotoxic effects on tumor cells in petri dishes.

Dr. Belken was noticeably absent as the girls labored until afternoon. When he didn't make his usual two o'clock check, they set a timer and left for lunch. Outside, the woman who served both as their chaperone and Dr. Belken's secretary was sitting behind a bulky computer monitor.

"Have you seen Dr. Belken?" Emma asked.

She shook her head, her short blond hair immobilized by gel. "He's been gone all day." She leaned in and lowered her voice. "I think he's obsessed with finding that snake you saw yesterday." Then she smiled like it wasn't too serious.

"Really?" Emma asked, her heart fluttering at the thought of seeing it again. Just the idea of the snake allured her.

"Does that surprise you?" Pria asked. It *did*, at least a little. As a high school student, Emma half expected this Ivy League professor to trivialize her claim of finding an unidentified snake. "He's dying to find new compounds to isolate," Pria added. "Just the thought of a new or even out of place species is probably driving him crazy."

He *was* rather over the top. In interviews he'd admitted to injecting small amounts of snake venom into his blood for years, turning himself into a human source of antivenoms. He'd lost funding several times for his questionable methods, but Emma's dream school, Columbia University, still praised his genius. Emma's parents, on the other hand, had scrutinized Dr. Belken for days when she expressed interest in working with him. But they couldn't stop her drive to work on a potential cancer treatment, not after her little brother's diagnosis.

That reminded her. She took out her phone and rang her mom's number.

"Hi, Emma," her mom answered. "Listen, I only have a quick second to talk, but how's it going there?"

"Fine," Emma said. "How's he doing today?"

Her mom's sigh rattled the phone speaker. Danny wasn't getting better. Thousands of miles away, his tiny body was held captive to a ruthless disease, while she, in her parents' minds, was wasting time basking in the Greek sun. *Did she really need to go on this trip?*

She beat out hundreds of applicants in the essay contest to secure research funds from the school district, then read all of Dr. Belken's papers and successfully emailed him to volunteer for his research team. This trip was only a few weeks, but they would've brought the venom samples back whether she went or not. *Was she selfish?* She tried not to let the guilt overtake her and, instead, felt resolved to make this project worthwhile. She held onto the hope, however wavering, that she could find *something*. After all, her grandfather had been born in Greece. Although he had died before she was born, she hoped his homeland might somehow speak to her.

"We're with him now. He's the same," her mom said.

She imagined her parents in their white lab coats, her mom seeing patients and her dad doing lab research, in the same hospital where their son lay fighting the cancer in his blood. He had gone through chemo several times, but this last treatment had been the hardest on him. His doctors were still unsure if it had worked, and it left him more drained, a shadow of the energetic child he once was.

"I'll be back to see him soon," she said, her throat tightening over her words.

"Honey," her mother said. "You should really consider working in Dad's lab. It's very credible, and a lot shorter of a commute."

The guilt deepened.

"His lab's great, but I'm not interested in rheumatology," she said. "And working with Dr. Belken could really help me get into Columbia." She didn't say the obvious, that she wanted to work on a promising cancer cure. Her parents never expected her to actually discover something.

"Yeah ... well, we'll talk about it when you get back." Her mom's voice sounded tired.

Emma's stomach clenched as she ended the call. She rarely saw her busy parents, but when she did, the same topics surfaced. She now imagined their disapproval morphing into outrage if they knew an unidentified snake was lurking in the forest.

"Ladies." Dr. Belken's voice jolted Emma from her thoughts. He stood in the doorway, his disheveled hair and undereye circles hinting exhaustion. "There's something I need to discuss with you."

He paced into his office, and Emma tried not to grimace at the stench of sour sweat. She glanced at Pria who pursed her lips in exaggerated interest, always amused by their mentor's eccentricity.

Dr. Belken rubbed his glasses with a cloth. His brow was deeply furrowed, and he avoided eye contact as they sat across from him. "With this snake out there, unidentified," he said, "I've decided it's safest if we treat ourselves with a general antivenom, prophylactically."

Emma tensed and glanced at Pria, whose face was serious now.

"No thanks," Pria said. "I mean, there's not much of a chance it'll come bite me. I'm not wandering into the woods. And I thought there were no venomous snakes here anyway."

"There shouldn't be," he said. "But a species could've been transported or escaped from somewhere else. And the nearest hospital is several hours away." His voice turned authoritative. "I'm in charge of keeping you safe. I don't know how many of those snakes are out there, and if either of you gets bitten, this would protect you. It's the safest option. I've already injected myself."

Emma spotted the bandage on his gangly arm and relaxed a little.

"But you've already done that to yourself a bunch of times," Pria said, always the more vocal of the two of them. "You probably have some immunity anyway. Who knows what that would do to us." Emma was secretly relieved her friend was standing up for them. She wouldn't even consider questioning him, not a research professor from Columbia. She might have a near-perfect GPA, but a letter of recommendation from him could be her ticket to acceptance there. Maybe Pria had less to lose—she was interested in science, but not Columbia, and had admitted a motivation for the trip was 'to check out the cute guys,' a goal which had gone mostly unfulfilled. But Emma was more concerned with making a good impression, and showing distrust of Dr. Belken's judgment didn't seem like a good idea, even if the injection made her uneasy.

"This is an antivenom, not the venom itself. It isn't dangerous," he said simply. "It's really routine."

Emma considered. He had worked with snakes for *years* and likely done this many times, and she *had* been unsettled since she'd found the snake, watching her step even indoors. A general antivenom would likely cover whatever venom that snake might carry.

"I already got my shot," their chaperone called from the doorway.

"Yes," Dr. Belken said. "She did fine, no reaction. I just suggest you sit for a few minutes afterward to make sure there's no allergy."

"Wow, wait," Pria said. "You didn't say anything about that before."

Dr. Belken smiled a little. "Of course, *any* substance has a slight chance of causing allergy, and this is no exception. But I have antihistamine here in case that happens, not to worry."

"I'll do it," Emma said quietly. Pria looked at her wide-eyed, and Emma was reluctant to meet her gaze. "I think it's the safest," Emma whispered. "That snake looked like it *wanted* to strike." She heard Pria sigh.

"Fine, but I'm passing on this one," Pria said.

"Okay," Dr. Belken said. "I'm only trying to offer protection, so if you change your mind, I have more."

He gestured Emma forward and opened a box of syringes. He attached one to a vial of fluid and tapped the air to the top, pushing until a clear droplet gathered at the needle's tip.

Emma didn't flinch as he prepared to inject. She was thinking about her brother, all he'd endured in that hospital. He'd had more injections in his eight years of life than she'd had in eighteen. She watched a cat snake in its tank at the far corner of the room. He was basking on a rock in the sunlight near the window, his glossy eyes like citrine gems.

The needle pricked her arm, and she grimaced. It seemed to hurt more than shots she'd had in the past, but maybe she had just forgotten their pain. She held her breath as the fluid seeped into her muscle with a slow sting.

It was done. Dr. Belken stared at her arm a second longer than she thought he should have.

"I'm fine," she said, thinking he was waiting for reassurance.

Only when she stood, she wasn't fine. All at once, a sharp, hot pain seared through her arm, and she yelped, clutching the spot. The pain sunk its claws deeper, piercing her bone. She crouched, gasping as it spread to her chest. Her heart began to race.

"Oh my god! What's wrong!?" Pria said, kneeling beside her.

Emma couldn't speak. Scalding heat encased her body, and her hands began to shake.

"She must be having a reaction," Dr. Belken said urgently from somewhere behind her.

"Yeah, no shit," Pria cried.

"Stay calm, it'll be okay," he said.

"What the hell did you do?" Pria screamed, but the sound faded by the time it reached Emma's ears. She shook her head to clear it, but that only made the world spin. The scene before her blurred, distorted as she lost vision. Then everything went black.

2

Muffled sounds and shadows swallowed Emma as she receded from the world. An undercurrent of sirens and torrents of light faded as she was enveloped by a quiet, eternal stillness. Suspended in this void, a deep chill seeped into her core.

A dream started gently, a warm tide rolling over her feet as she stood in an endless night. It was more a memory than a dream, only Emma had never seen this ocean. She peered over dark waters stretching toward a shrouded horizon, until a ray of golden sun emerged, its light catching the water's ripples so they flickered with incandescence.

But the beauty clashed with the striking fear that gripped her heart. Her hands were clenched. When she looked down, she gasped. These were not *her* hands. A gentle breeze blew soft curls across her shoulder and the sunlight illuminated the chestnut and honey amber strands woven through them. This was not *her* hair. It cascaded to her waist where a golden belt cinched the blue, caressing fabric of her dress. Emma's own hair was wilder and rougher than this, and her body less curved.

She was seeing through someone else's eyes. But who was this woman? And what was causing her heart to race with such terror? Danger lurked. Something was coming.

"You can't fight against the sea," a voice bellowed from behind her, so loud it seemed to shatter her eardrums and rattle each bone of this woman's gentle frame. She turned, her pulse throbbing and her fists clenching tighter.

A man towered above her, if she could even call him that. He was more monstrous than any she'd ever seen. A pale, sickening tinge of green vaporized off his skin with a stench of fish and salty grime that churned her stomach. His seaweed-spattered beard and crimped hair meshed together over his thick neck. But it was the look of his sea green eyes that struck her most, with their hungry, gleaming menace. They watched her in a way that made her want to run, set on her like a snake stalking its prey.

"Stay away," she heard herself say, only it didn't sound like her voice. It was beautiful, but like a broken song. He stepped closer. Fabric hung loosely at his waist, and the muscles of his bare chest and legs bulged and twitched as he moved.

Behind him, the shoreline rose into a rocky cliff, and through it she spotted marbled stairs, ascending toward an open temple where incense wafted through white columns. The stairs were off to his side. She could make a dash for them.

"You should be careful," he said, "telling someone as powerful as me what to do."

"I am sworn to Athena," her voice replied, grasping for boldness. "I have sworn my life to her. You cannot touch me."

Athena. The name was at the forefront of this woman's mind. Emma didn't understand. *The goddess?* The woman repeated the name under her breath, a sacred, worshiped name. She was beckoning her. But no one came. Instead, a sickening smile spread across the man's face as he stepped closer, his weight quaking the sand beneath them. His eerie green glow threatened to engulf her.

"I am tired of your refusals," he said. "You have no choice. I will take you. Athena's power is no match for the sea. And *you … you are nothing.*"

Nothing. The words seeped deep, slicing to Emma's heart. Anguish flooded the woman, and Emma felt her burning to fight. But she knew she was no match. If only her desperation could howl over the seas, summon her long-estranged family to protect her, but even they did not come. Her eyes flashed toward the stairs, and she bolted toward them. With each stride, her feet slid in the powdery sand, but the woman's slender ankles and lithe feet carried her with a desperate, surprising speed.

But it wasn't fast enough.

Just as her feet met the cool marble of the first step, a thick hand gripped her hair and yanked her back.

"No," she cried. "Let me go!" He only tightened his grip, pulling her hair painfully from her scalp.

He whispered into her ear, taking a long, savory breath. "Beautiful, as soft as a goddess."

She kicked at him, her efforts futile against his unearthly might. He threw her against the marble steps and, in one movement, as effortless as swatting a fly, ripped her blue dress from her body. Golden beads scattered over the marble. She was jealous of their escape. His body, sticky with salt and slime, pressed down on her, so heavy she couldn't breathe. She knew what was coming. Hot tears streamed over her cheeks, and her panicked heart felt ready to burst.

She shut her eyes.

"Emma?" A voice echoed through her dreams. The darkness swirled again, the void in between worlds.

"Emma?" It came again. It was a familiar one, coaxing her back to consciousness. The woman on the beach faded, and a vague glow penetrated her eyelids.

She squinted. The scene around her materialized, and she jolted at the sound of her name. "Emma!" Pria hovered above her in the fluorescent light, her face contorted in worry. "Emma, are you okay?"

Emma's hands shot to her ears to block the sound. "Why is everything so loud?" she asked. Her hands shook as her eyes darted about the space, disoriented. She was lying in an unfamiliar white bed. There was an IV drip in her arm and a drape hanging beside her. On the bedside monitor, she saw her heart rate surge to 120.

"What?" Pria looked confused before relief flushed over her face. She had dark circles under her eyes, and her thick hair looked greasy. "Thank god you woke up." Pria threw herself across the bed to hug her. At the rush of unbearable heat, Emma recoiled.

"Oh my god. Did that hurt?" Pria looked distraught.

"I'm okay," Emma said. But she felt sensitized to everything around her—the lights were too bright, the sheets too constraining. "I just, I was having the strangest dream," she said. She tried to sit up, and her head began to pound.

"Easy," Pria said, her face straining as she adjusted the pillow for her.

"What happened to me?" Emma asked, distracted by the noise in the hallway.

Pria paled and glanced around. The room was empty except for the two of them.

"What's the last thing you remember?" Pria asked.

When Emma closed her eyes, memories of the nightmare flashed in her mind, so vivid it was hard separating them from reality. And the *sounds* were *so* distracting.

She was on Crete, she told herself. *The snake. She had found that snake. And then the needle. Then…*

"I remember getting injected with the antivenom," Emma said.

Pria grabbed her hand. Again, Emma grimaced at the intense heat of her touch.

"That's it," Pria exclaimed. "Our chaperone and Dr. Belken supposedly had that injection and nothing happened to them. Dr. Belken … I don't trust him."

"What do you mean?"

"He must have injected you with something else!"

Emma winced. It sounded like Pria was shouting again.

"Like what?" Emma asked.

Pria shook her head. "I don't know. I just have a weird feeling about it. The doctors ran blood tests and said there was a reaction in your blood, but not like a typical allergy. Dr. Belken brought in the rest of his antivenom samples, and the lab here said they looked all right. Now they're guessing the sample he injected you with was contaminated by something."

Emma's mind raced. She couldn't make sense of it in that bright, dizzying room. Too much stimulus. Even the voices and alarms outside were unbearable to her ears.

"Why is everyone shouting?" she asked.

Pria shook her head. "No one's shouting. There's some doctors in the hallway, but they're not… Are you okay?"

Emma inhaled deeply, trying to calm herself. "How long have I been here?"

"Three days. You were in a coma." Pria's voice quivered.

"What?" Emma asked, shaken. "*Three days?* How did I come out of it?"

"We're not sure. Maybe your body naturally fought it. Or … it was the flower."

Emma bolted upright. "What flower?"

Pria's golden brown skin was coated in sweat as she glanced around again. "Dr. Belken seemed desperate for something to help you," she said. "He left for a day, and I started to think he abandoned us. Then he came back with this red flower."

Red, Emma thought, how had she known it was red? An eerie thought arose in her mind, like a memory she couldn't quite grasp, of blood droplets over sand and red flowers. But she couldn't place that memory, couldn't tell if it was something she had seen or only imagined, like uncovering a lost dream. Or had part of her mind remained alert through the coma and heard someone talking about this?

"He went to several other hospitals," Pria said, "supposedly asking for any other treatments, and came up with nothing. So he went into one of the tiny villages," Pria continued, "looking for anyone who might know a cure. He said he found a medicinal healer who used herbs." Pria's voice was pressured, and Emma could sense her anxiety. "He described your symptoms, and she said this rare red flower would cure you."

Emma furrowed her brow. "What? I know he's not the most traditional scientist, but isn't it weird for him to resort to *herbal remedies*?"

"Everything about this is weird," Pria said. "But the doctors had no medical options left, so he argued it was worth trying. He said there might be some *ancient knowledge* here."

Emma took a long breath, trying to process the tale. "And how did I take it?" she asked.

"You couldn't swallow it, so they gave it to you through a g-tube. I argued against it, saying he might be poisoning you, but the doctors said you might *die* and it was worth a try." Pria's voice trembled.

"What kind of flower was it?" Emma asked.

"I don't know. Nobody here could tell what it was." She took out her phone. "I snuck a picture of it though. It's dried, so you can't really distinguish anything."

Emma looked at Pria's phone screen, the electric glow paining her eyes. The pale, crinkled red flower could've been anything from a hibiscus to a rose.

"What kind of doctors work here?" Emma asked, knowing her parents would be horrified if they knew any of this. But Dr. Belken wasn't obligated to tell them. She was eighteen. He wasn't legally required to have her or her parents' consent for medical treatment in the case of a life-threatening emergency. Still, considering he had caused that emergency, he could still be in a lot of trouble. "Did he call my parents?"

Pria shook her head. "That's another thing—" she began.

Emma felt the vibration of footsteps approaching in the hallway outside. No, she thought, she *heard* them, right? It didn't make sense that she could *feel* them, yet her ribs seemed to rattle with the steps. A knock came at the door, and it rippled through her body.

Dr. Belken walked in, his usually pale face now sunburned. Beneath the red color, his dark undereye circles were more prominent than ever. He was accompanied by a tan, dark-haired doctor in a long white coat.

"Thank goodness you're all right," Dr. Belken said and smiled stiffly.

Pria glared at him. "I already told her everything," she said.

"Oh?" Dr. Belken said, unshaken. The monitor beside Emma's bed began to beep, a shrill noise that felt like needles to her eardrums. "Then, Emma, you must understand that what happened was a horrible accident. We're still not sure if the antivenom was contaminated or if your body had a paradoxical reaction to it. Either way, I'm so relieved you're better."

That's it? You're a scientist. Don't you want to know how this happened? She turned to the hospital doctor. "Can you explain this?" Emma asked, the beeps sounding louder now.

He nodded. "If you were given antivenom, it could have caused anaphylaxis," he said in a light Greek accent that Emma might have found cute if the circumstances were different. "But this didn't appear quite like that," he continued. "I've never seen someone in a coma from that. And at first your labs actually looked more like a reaction to *venom* than an allergy."

Emma sensed a subtle, uncomfortable shift in Dr. Belken's stance, but it was gone before she could decipher it and so fleeting it might've been imagined.

"You had elevated D-dimers, which can cause clotting," the doctor continued. "And prolonged prothrombin time with low fibrinogen, which can cause excess bleeding. Some other levels spiked, like your albumin protein and then your cardiac and skeletal muscle enzymes. Then, surprisingly, everything normalized, but you still hadn't woken up. We were looking for other causes and preparing to do a lumbar puncture."

It was hard to follow. She squinted at him, trying to focus on his voice through the beeping at her bedside. She turned to the monitor, jabbing a hand to shut it off, but instead sent it rolling back into the wall, still beeping.

"Oops," she said.

"It's okay, I got it." Pria jumped up, glancing somewhat meekly back at the doctor. "Can I?" He nodded.

"What about the flower?" Emma asked him, relieved as Pria ended the alarm.

"When Dr. Belken came back with this flower," the doctor said, "I figured it was a long shot but worth a try if safe. The other doctors and I actually ate some first to test its safety."

Emma nearly laughed, sure it was a joke, but his serious expression convinced her it wasn't. She nodded, her head spinning with the movement, impressed by their dedication.

"It's hard to tell if that was a cure or if this resolved on its own," he added.

Dr. Belken stood beside him, tall and unwavering. "It seems like you might be a good case report for this hospital," he said.

"I'm not interested in being anyone's study subject," Emma said curtly, surprised at her sudden boldness. She had never said anything remotely antagonistic to him. Without warning, the vivid dream flashed before her and her stomach churned. "I'd like to go home now," Emma said. She realized she had missed days of research while in the hospital and hoped she could pick it back up in New York, when everything settled.

"Of course," Dr. Belken said. He nodded and left the room, but the hospital doctor lingered.

"You know," he said, as the door closed. "He shouldn't have been giving you antivenom unless you were actually bitten by a snake. It has risks and wouldn't be worth it if there was no bite in the first place. And it wouldn't really make any sense here because there aren't venomous snakes, but he explained you work in a lab with them."

Emma's head pounded. The fluorescent lights around him made it hard to meet his gaze, and his voice rang so loud in her ears she wanted him to stop talking. But his words seemed important. Dr. Belken had told him they had venomous snakes in the lab. But they didn't. The cat snake wasn't venomous to humans. It seemed he had hidden the real reason he had given her the antivenom to begin with—they had discovered an unidentified, possibly venomous species. Of course, Emma knew scientists could be secretive about discoveries, and maybe since he hadn't actually caught the snake, Dr. Belken didn't want to make such a claim.

Or maybe there was another reason for his secrets.

3

Emma packed her small assortment of cargo pants, shorts, and V-neck tees into her suitcase, her limbs slow and her head groggy as she moved. Her senses had dulled ever so slightly since leaving the hospital, but not enough to allow her rest. Instead, the stimuli in each passing minute drained her.

She thought to call Jason again, aching for the comfort of his voice. She had last seen him the day before she left for Greece, when they celebrated his eighteenth birthday at the bowling alley. Her heart fluttered at the thought of him in his gray T-shirt, flashing his inviting smile after bowling a strike. How could she tell him what happened? How could she explain it in a way that wouldn't shock or upset him? He hadn't been happy about her opting to go on this trip. Imagine what he might say if he knew *this*. She stared at her phone. It would be better to talk in person anyway, when she didn't have to worry about their connection cutting off. And maybe with more time, she could figure out the best way to present everything.

The sun rose higher, and in the heat of the afternoon, Emma slipped under her sheets. It wasn't long before her exhausted mind drifted to sleep, serenaded by the rhythmic hum of cicadas outside. But the peaceful depth of darkness that greeted her gave way to terror as cool marble materialized beneath her body.

No, she thought, *not here, I can't be here.* As the scene brightened around her, she saw the hands of the woman, splayed over marble steps in front of her. Emma was in her body again, seeing through her eyes. Her cheek throbbed where it had struck the stairs, and her breath was heavy with choking sobs. A putrid brine surged through her nostrils, and she heaved, vomiting into the sand, her ribs aching with the effort. Even then, she did not feel free of what tainted her. A pain burned between her legs.

Behind her, the sea lapped at the shoreline beneath the hot indifferent sun. Slowly, she hoisted her body on a trembling arm, feeling some relief that the man was gone. But she didn't feel safe, only exposed in her raw pain. She had barely stood on her shaking legs when the sky exploded with silver light, so bright she shielded her eyes. As the burst faded, she squinted up at the form of an armored woman standing atop a pillar of rock before the temple's columns.

She was a stunning sight, with beaming skin haloed in light. Emma's eyes seared as they met the level of her shimmering feet adorned in golden sandals. The light faded further to reveal stormy eyes framed by a sharp, crested helmet with shining hair billowing out the bottom in waves. Perched atop her shoulder sat an owl, its orange eyes glaring.

Athena. The name formed on the woman's lips, but she could barely speak, her throat raspy from cries. Instead, she joined her quivering hands and bowed.

"You dare try to worship me still?" Athena's voice boomed, so intensely Emma winced.

"I tried to resist him," Emma felt the woman say, her voice feeble. "I didn't want him to touch me."

"You disgust me," Athena boomed, her silver eyes piercing like spears as they narrowed on her. Athena clenched her fists. "Your temptation has defiled this temple, humiliated my name among gods and men."

"Please," Emma felt herself begging, her hands trembling. "Please, forgive me."

Emma wondered what she was begging for. *Forgive what? She had done nothing wrong.* Surely this goddess would show a facet of sympathy, especially after she hadn't answered the woman's cries for her protection.

"Please, I have devoted my life to you," she said. And Emma felt the woman's heart ripping at its core, a heart she had devoted to her goddess, Athena, forsaking any human's touch, the gentle kisses of a sea nymph she once adored, and the chance of having her own family with one of her many suitors. It was love, Emma realized. This woman loved Athena, with a pure, steadfast love that had quenched her loneliness. "I would never dishonor you," she cried.

"Enough! You *have* dishonored me, taken the seed of my rival, distracted by your own beauty." But it was only Athena's beauty that the woman had ever cared about. Her crimson lips, the ones so beautifully rendered by sculpture, now tensed into a fierce line. She had spent long nights in the cool darkness of the temple admiring those painted sculptures, envisioning Athena in the flesh. Now, the hardened hatred on her idol's face poisoned that sacred fantasy.

Athena raised a glowing hand toward the sky, her fingers contorted like ravenous claws. *No,* Emma thought. The owl took flight, its dark shadow passing over her as it circled above.

"I curse you," she shouted, her voice cracking like a whip as she thrust a finger at the woman's cowering frame. Pebbles of rock tumbled from her pillar. "Your beauty is mine to take, and no one will look upon you again."

With that, Athena disappeared in a burst of blinding light. For a moment nothing happened. The woman blinked to recover her sight. Just as the searing burst faded, the sky darkened.

In the shadows near the bottom of the cliffs a loud hissing arose from the sands as dozens of snakes slithered from their crevices. Fangs bared, they writhed toward her.

But something else threatened to reach her first. A wave gathered near the horizon and a gust of cold wind barrelled over her from the sea. Emma was desperate to wake up, but something held her there. The woman leaped up the stairs toward the temple. The menacing wave approached faster, gathering force and height until it blocked out the sky. Below her, a sea of serpents bounded up the stairs. Cold mist eclipsed her skin. Was that better than fangs?

She wouldn't make it. The truth of it registered a split second before the wave crashed, seizing her in a torrent of foam and sea, as if she had no strength of her own, as if she was *nothing.*

It was dark and cold as she twisted in the chaos, a victim to its whims. She slammed into jagged rock and was pulled against shards of coral. Her body whirled as a powerful current jetted her back, deep into the heart of the sea.

She held her breath in the darkness, unable to escape its pull. *You're nothing against the power of the sea.* The words taunted her mind. Was Athena's curse to have her drowned in her enemy's lair?

Just as her lungs began to burn and her eyes dimmed, she felt the current lift her toward the surface. At last, one final surge of water pushed her onto a wet, flat stone.

The seawater drained away as quickly as it had come. Her lungs gasped for air, and her eyes swelled from the sting of salt. It was quiet then, aside from the echo of water dripping into pools among the surrounding rocks. Her battered body seared with pain as she slowly turned in the darkness.

It was a cave, faintly lit by the slightest beam of sunlight penetrating its mouth. She followed the ray as it touched the skin of her hand, and in shock, saw it tinged dark green. Sure it was seaweed, clinging as if in mockery, she tried to brush it away. But as her fingers swept over it, the tinged skin only began to harden.

Emma felt the woman's heart race in terror. Horrified, she watched as the skin morphed into *scales*. She jumped, pain shooting through her limbs. A lock of wet hair fell heavy over her chest, where her once delicate skin had turned reptilian. The curl began to coil as if alive, and like some horrid hallucination, she watched it morph into the form of a *serpent*.

She screamed and struck to get it off her shoulder. But she couldn't escape it. It was … attached. Her shaking hands rose to her head where, instead of her soft golden locks, her fingers met the torsional, polished bodies of serpents.

Her scream echoed through the walls of the cave, unlike any scream Emma had ever made or heard before. And it didn't stop. She thought her throat would rupture and blood would erupt from it.

The sound echoed as Emma awoke to the shrill cry of her alarm, the daily reminder to check if the constituents of her venom samples had separated. But today she wasn't processing any. She lay in bed, afraid to move, covered in sweat. Her heart pounded in her chest, and her hands flew to her head. She was relieved to find her hair tied back in its usual ponytail and was comforted by the feeling, however frizzy it might be. She turned off the alarm and drank from her water bottle. Sitting on her bed, her head in her hands, she coaxed her pulse to slow.

What the hell was that?

After several minutes, she opened her laptop and began typing search terms. As much as she didn't want to return to it, the dream's vividness demanded it. It didn't feel like a typical dream. It was sequential, more like a memory. That woman must be real, she thought, and there was more to her story.

Later that day, Emma wheeled her luggage into Pria's room. Her friend was in bed, clearly exhausted from their time at the hospital. Her full lips were dry and peeling.

"You awake?" Emma asked.

Pria stretched and yawned. "Barely," she grumbled.

Emma sat on her friend's bed, staring out the window at the trees. Their sharp leaves swayed and glistened in the sunlight. She *felt* their rustling, the friction of leaf edges sliding across strips of bark.

Pria propped up on her pillow. "Emma, you look like you're going to faint. Did something happen? I mean, besides what already happened, which is a lot."

"Do you know the myth of Medusa?" Emma asked.

"Sort of. It originated here, didn't it? There's that snake goddess statue in the museum we saw, and the restaurant named after her," she said casually. "Why?"

Emma hesitated. She remembered that statue, the snake goddess clutching a serpent in each hand, created by the ancient Minoans who predated the Greeks and their myths. "I never knew the full story," Emma said. "But when I was asleep, I swear I dreamt it." A chill crept over her skin as she said it, but Pria didn't seem to notice.

"You probably heard it once, when you were little or something," Pria said, seemingly unaffected by something that shook Emma's core.

"I don't think so," she said softly. She had even been angry at herself as she read the myth on her laptop for not studying more mythology before visiting Crete. It hadn't seemed that important compared to her research goals, but now it became a priority. She met Pria's eyes. "I was having this dream while I was in the hospital. And it picked up exactly where it left off when I just took a nap."

"That's weird," Pria said. "But I think it happened to me once after I ate extra spicy food."

Emma tried to laugh, but she was still perturbed.

"I didn't know who I was in the dream, but I wasn't myself," Emma said. "So I started looking up what happened in it and realized it was the story of Medusa that I dreamed about, and I was *her*. She was this young woman, a beautiful priestess worshiping in a temple of Athena. The sea god kept making advances on her but she rejected him to remain pure for Athena, until one day he raped her."

"Yeah, that sounds familiar," Pria said, more serious now. "Are you sure we didn't talk about it before?"

Emma nodded.

"Wait," Pria said softly, her face lined with concern. "Does that mean you were raped in your dream?"

"I woke up before it happened all the way," Emma said, feeling like she might vomit. "But I was there right before, and after too, so I felt it…"

Pria moved closer. "Oh my god," she whispered. She put an arm on her back and Emma tensed at the heat of her touch. "That's horrible." She paused. "How did it end?"

"Like in the myth," Emma said. "She asked for help from Athena, but Athena was jealous that the sea god Poseidon had wanted her, or because Poseidon was her rival, and instead of helping, she cursed her to become a snake monster in a cave."

Pria shook her head. "It's a pretty screwed up one, isn't it?" she remarked. "Why would she punish her? So much for female solidarity."

Emma nodded.

"You don't think it's weird?" Emma asked. "That I dreamed a myth I never knew before?"

"I'm sure it got into your subconscious from somewhere," Pria said, rubbing Emma's back. She wanted to tell her to stop but was afraid to offend her. "Listen, you've been through a lot the last few days. But we're going back home soon. I think that'll help."

Emma nodded and returned to her room with an urgency to research more about Medusa. But the more she read on her laptop, the more questions sprang in her mind, like a whirlpool gathering depth. Why was she alone, and why, born into a family of deathless gods, was she mortal? Why didn't her family help her? And what did Medusa do in between the points mentioned by various poets and historians? Emma both feared a return to those dreams and hoped they might resume to fill these gaps.

Her head swirled as the day turned to evening. She was exhausted but somehow still alert, agitated. It was their last night in Crete, and Emma was eager to get back home, to return to a routine and sense of familiarity. Surely she would feel safer with Jason by her side. Yet the eagerness to see him clashed with her urgency to progress with her research. She hadn't accomplished very much on the trip. Maybe he had been right after all. Maybe her parents had been right too, and it had been a mistake to come here.

As she lay in the darkness of her room, she found herself afraid to fall back asleep. It hadn't been *her* in the dream, she told herself, but somehow, she had felt the trauma like it was her own. Her unease seemed to magnify the sounds around her, the rustling outside, the creaking floors, and the water dripping in the sink. She rolled over and played the cricket sounds on her phone to drown her senses, hoping it could coax her into peaceful dreams, or even better, a dreamless sleep.

Lethargy soon gripped her, and she drifted off despite her fears. This time, the dream started differently. There were rapid images, churning from one scene to the next as if her mind were flipping through an album of memories. There were images of her parents, her brother, and things from the past, like her interview for her research position in her junior year of high school. But they were mixed with snapshots of things she had never seen. There were glimpses of that dark cave she had dreamt of already, then a forest, and people carrying weapons and shields not from her lifetime. There was an urgency to the dream, and though asleep, she seemed aware of her racing heart. Then the images reeled to a halt.

Slain bodies covered the rocky shores of a blood-stained sea. Her eyes scanned inland and found *red* flowers blossoming over sand. At their center stood a man with blood smeared over his hands and arms. It wasn't the sea god from before, but when she looked into his eyes, she saw that similar gleam. He sneered, and though Emma swore she had never seen this man before, when they locked eyes, he was familiar. She gasped as she awoke, her body trembling. Her skin was moist with sweat, and for a split second, she swore it hardened. She scratched at it, and the feeling faded. Maybe she had still been dreaming.

She stared out her window into the black night, where tiny stars shimmered between spiny leaves. A faint breeze carried a chill from over the water, and she could taste the salt in it, even from inside. Her heart was still racing. *Who was that man?* Somehow he felt nearby, like an imminent threat. But that was impossible. She sat there motionless and felt more still than she ever had before. She knew she couldn't fall back asleep. She would stare until the rising sun woke the sky, if only to not see that man again.

4

"Maybe you're having some sort of PTSD from the hospital," Pria suggested late in the morning, as the two dipped pita bread in tzatziki sauce on her bed. "People get that when their life was in danger."

Emma lowered her bread, her eyes fixated on the blanket as an image flashed in her mind. Amy. They were ten years old, walking back from their fourth grade class at their school down the block. Amy was carrying a tiny terrarium with the pet hermit crab she had brought in for show and tell, talking about the shell it had just changed into, when a van crept up the road beside them. Emma shuddered, recalling the sound of Amy's scream when the men grabbed her and Emma sprinted away, shouting for help. It was only when she returned and found her friend's broken terrarium that the reality of what happened settled in. Despite a year of exposure therapy, the nightmares and hypervigilance ensued. Yes, Emma knew what PTSD was.

"What's wrong?" Pria asked, her eyes wide with concern.

Emma stiffened. She had told Jason about it, but saying it aloud was hard. Despite considering Pria her best friend in high school, it still unnerved Emma to talk about it. Maybe she feared that Pria, with her upbeat and matter-of-fact vibe, wouldn't understand. The current

31

situation was different anyway. These nightmares were about someone she had never met and things that hadn't happened to her.

"It's just…" Emma shifted uncomfortably. "This man, I felt like he was after me, like he was looking at me *through* my dream, but I don't know him." As she said it, a strange sensation crept over her skin. It was hardening again.

"One sec," Emma said, and ran to the bathroom. She turned the sink on and plunged her hands into the water.

She swore, for a split second, that she noticed a tinge of green on her skin. She blinked, and as the water ran over her, it was gone. She shut the water off and stared. Could it be the lighting? A reflection from the leaves outside?

Get it together, she thought. *You're fine. Your skin is normal, just a little tanned from the sun.*

"You okay?" Pria called.

Emma wasn't sure. She was lightheaded and her ears were ringing, or was that the sound of the air conditioner or the cicadas outside? The ambient noise seemed to mount into a roar around her, worsening the more she paid attention to it.

"Yeah," she said quickly, steadying her breath to regain composure. *I'm fine,* she repeated to herself, *I'm just tired and need to get home.* Her skin seemed to soften, and the intrusive sounds faded.

"I'm gonna go finish packing," Pria said.

Emma stepped into the empty room, still tense. She slid down into a split, hoping some stretching could calm her before the flight home. She paused at the position she normally fell into but, to her surprise, found she could lower herself farther and farther. It almost seemed limitless. Baffled, she reached an arm upward and began to bend backward, until her hand reached all the way to her knee. She couldn't believe it. It wasn't even uncomfortable. She stretched nearly every day, but this was astounding. Had her body's reaction to the antivenom somehow softened her muscles and ligaments?

Approaching footsteps startled her, and she snapped back into a seated position. She recognized the gait even before she turned to find her research mentor in the doorway.

"Emma?" Dr. Belken's shoulders were more hunched than usual, and beneath his graying hair, the furrow in his forehead seemed deeper. Her pulse sped, and she tried to quell it. It wasn't that she necessarily saw him as a threat, although she had the right to after what had happened, but an uneasy suspicion tinged the air. "Sorry to intrude," he said.

"You're not," she answered, and rubbed her shoulder.

"Are you feeling okay?" he asked.

She nodded, realizing she feared he might see what she saw, these changes that she wanted to ignore.

"Listen," he said. "I hope you know I never meant you any harm. Those days you were in the hospital were the worst of my career. I had only wanted to protect all of us against the potential threat that snake posed. I still don't know what species it could have been. But I've never seen a reaction to antivenom like that."

His words were meant to comfort her, she thought, but they sounded stiff, and the sweat trickling down his temples unsettled her. She sensed his unease. He was nervous, and she *tasted* it, like metal or acid on the sides of her tongue, and the fresh air soured.

"Why didn't you call my parents?" she asked.

"I didn't know how serious it was. I thought it was just an allergy," he answered, so quickly she suspected he had prepared the answer beforehand. "Then when it wasn't, I was busy looking for an antidote. Of course, when I saw you getting better, it was no longer an emergency so I decided *you* could choose to call them or not." His gaze was intent, studying her response. "You are considered an adult after all," he said.

She let the silence linger, sensing the unease beneath his words.

Then she nodded. "Thank you," she said, still wary.

His answer was well crafted, pretending he was handing her power. But she didn't feel any real power. Of course, telling her parents would create trouble for him, so deep he might struggle to crawl out from it with his career intact. She even felt guilty that his research could be risked for her sake, but then bitter at her lack of assertion. She could tell her parents now but held herself back, not wanting to worry them or create trouble for the mentor she wanted to impress. She also had more questions and needed time to craft them. This was beginning to feel like a puzzle.

That evening, Emma wore her noise-canceling headphones as the plane took off to New York. They had helped her relax on the flight there, but now, with her ears so sensitized, they barely dulled the drone of the plane's engines. And it wasn't just the noise. She felt the air friction in the plane around her, as if she were fighting her way through a tornado. Her eyelids drooped with fatigue. She closed them, playing her music until she drifted into tumultuous sleep.

She wanted to know the woman whose eyes she had seen through, to see her fight against that brutal, merciless world. But instead, the bloody image of that same man with the menacing, intrusive stare crept back into her dreams. Even when she didn't see him, his image seemed to lurk, agitating her awake.

As her eyes opened, she caught Dr. Belken glance at her from across the aisle and thought there was something different about his expression. Was it concern, or could it be … suspicion? But of what? She made eye contact for a fleeting second, and he quickly turned away. She couldn't wait to land in New York.

Emma dragged her suitcase toward the terminal exit, her legs weary from the flight. Her body slouched, drained from the plane's sounds and vibrations, as if she'd been around a drilling site for hours. Outside, her eyes fell on Jason, leaning against his parents' Mazda in the parking lot, his skin a deeper bronze than before. Her clouded mind brightened.

She ran to him, leaving Pria trailing behind. Her heart lifted from the recent turmoil as she leaped into his hug. But as soon as his arms were around her, the intense heat of his touch made her skin prickle. She gasped and recoiled suddenly. His amber eyes were momentarily confused as they searched hers, and she tried to hide how startled she was.

"What is it?" he asked, his voice faltering. She forced a smile, trying to suppress whatever that sensation was. It was so intensely warm it felt hard to breathe. *Maybe it's just the New York humidity*, she thought, but it didn't feel right.

"I missed you so much," she said and hugged him again, this time ready for the intense warmth.

The hope that seeing him might soothe her anxiety crumbled as her unease swirled. She didn't know how to explain what had happened on Crete, even to herself. Still, there was something about his presence, his muscled arms around her, that softened her worry.

"I'll let you lovebirds sit in the front, I guess," Pria said, climbing into the back with feigned grumpiness as Jason loaded their suitcases into the car.

Pria ended up talking for most of the ride, which was a relief to Emma, who was still grappling for words. From the driver's seat, Jason reached a hand over to caress her arm. She sensed his eagerness for her and wished she could match it. She smiled at him as he took her hand and forced herself not to let go, despite the uncomfortable amount of heat radiating from his grasp.

She leaned on the window, staring at the buildings and trees passing by. Her brow contorted. The streets were the same ones she had seen a few weeks ago—cracked concrete sidewalks beside apartment buildings, giving way to manicured lawns and shingled houses as they drove—but they appeared changed. The colors were more vibrant. And she seemed more aware of the noises and movement.

"Stop!" Emma shouted suddenly, snapping her head forward.

The traffic light in front of them was green, but Jason slammed on his brakes, just as a car sped through the red light at the intersection.

Jason cursed, his eyes wide in shock. He honked loudly but the other car was already out of sight. "I didn't see— How did you see him coming?"

The truth was, Emma wasn't sure she had actually *seen* the car. There were trees and a fence lining that street, making the visibility poor and the intersection accident prone. *No.* Emma had somehow *felt* it, the vibration. Regardless of how she did it, she knew Jason couldn't have reacted in time if she hadn't shouted when she did. She could feel the racing beat of his heart reverberate in her own chest, like a powerful drum.

"Is everyone okay?" Jason asked, clearly shaken. Behind them Pria clicked her seatbelt in.

"We're okay," Emma said.

Slowly, he started to drive again. It was quiet for the rest of the ride. After dropping Pria off, Jason drove by Emma's house. She got out of the car and collected her suitcase from the trunk.

"Do you want me to come in?" he asked. His smile was just returning. She loved the shape of his mouth, how inviting it was, but she felt restrained.

She bit her lip. "I'm just a little unsettled right now."

"Because of the car?" he asked, sounding apologetic.

Emma had already recovered from that. Actually, she had felt surprisingly calm during that whole incident. When it came down to that moment, she had felt almost serene in her focus. But she nodded because it was an easy excuse to avoid the more complicated one.

"Or is it because of your reaction?" he said.

She was stunned. "What?" She looked at him in alarm.

"The reaction to the antivenom," he said with concern.

Emma froze, startled. There it was, the words she'd struggled to bring up, words she'd never told him. Her skin started to itch. Was she starting to get hives?

"How do you know about—"

"Pria told me," he said.

She furrowed her brow, unsettled that he already knew and that Pria hadn't mentioned telling him. She almost felt … betrayed.

"She called when you were in the hospital. She was so scared for you and didn't know who to tell."

Emma stared at him, speechless.

"I was scared too," he said, his face now solemn. "I thought you were going to call me right away when you got out."

She felt her chest tighten but wasn't sure why it upset her so much.

"I planned to tell you when I got back," she said, feeling defensive now.

She didn't know what to say. She *had* wanted to tell him, when the time was right. But somehow, when he already knew, she didn't want to talk about it.

"What the hell was this crazy, so-called *doctor* thinking?" he said, in the accusatory tone she had wanted to avoid. "He should be fired."

She looked away and didn't respond. She didn't want someone else making decisions for her or for the incident to explode into something out of her control. She didn't want her mentor to be fired. He still contributed so much to science, and she feared backlash from the university she wanted acceptance into. But she wasn't quite sure what she wanted, maybe because she still didn't know exactly what had happened.

"I'm really glad you're okay," he said more softly and tentatively reached for her hand. "Were you scared?"

"It was scary, yeah," she muttered, still unnerved.

"Are you back to normal now though? You feel okay?"

She gulped, thinking about the signs that things were not normal at all. She nodded, but even as he spoke, she could hear the movements of the people on the neighboring street, feel their warmth and smell them as if they were next to her in the locker room. She was adapting to it all, her mind learning to zone things out, focus on his voice, but something was definitely different. She was afraid to confess it, like it would make it real. Maybe things would still return to normal.

"You're so pretty," he said, and she softened a moment. Emma was used to being called many things, but pretty wasn't one of them. The kids at school preferred pale or nerdy when talking about her. But the way Jason looked at her, she really did feel pretty. "But you know, you look different," he said.

She stiffened. "Really?"

"Maybe it's your hair." He timidly reached a hand to touch it.

Her curls were always a bit wild if she didn't tie them back, but now they seemed especially so, barely contained by her hair tie. She figured it was the humidity or the different shampoo she had been using on Crete. She didn't want him to touch it, so she grabbed his hand and rested it on her cheek, leaned forward and kissed him. Even if it had felt forced, the taste of him made her heart flutter. She didn't fight the heat that swelled from it either and, for a moment, let it transport her.

"Are you sure you don't want me inside?" he whispered, and she giggled at the innuendo he seemed unaware of.

"I have to catch up with my parents," she said, knowing they wouldn't be home yet. But as much as she wanted to be with him, there was too much uncertainty, too much she needed to process on her own.

Before leaving, Jason dropped a hand into his jeans' pocket, bringing out a beaded bracelet and slipping it onto Emma's wrist. She smiled at the glossy green stones, interspersed by smaller copper ones.

"I got this to match your eyes," he said, blushing slightly, his smile infectious.

Emma kissed him again before watching him drive away, then lingered there a moment, tracing the smooth beads with her fingertip.

Inside the house she found a welcome note from her mom on the kitchen counter, saying they would be home late and there was food in the fridge. Emma threw her bags on the bed and went to the bathroom, where she let her hair down and brushed it, aggressively trying to tame the frizz. *Why was it so coarse?* Frustrated, she found a pair of scissors in the cabinet and tried to cut away the ends. But when she closed the blades, the hair wouldn't cut, almost like it was made from wire. She pressed harder, opening and closing the blades until the screw popped out. Startled, she tossed the broken scissors aside. *They must be defective,* she thought, but underneath that, there was something undeniable. Things were not back to normal.

5

Emma awoke refreshed from her first restful sleep in days. Her familiar room, with her green desk and cactus plant by the window, felt like a calm exhale. She stared at the ceiling fan, its wooden blades etched like leaves. Maybe it had all been anxiety, she thought, those vivid nightmares. It didn't explain everything though, how she suddenly knew the story of Medusa so well. The echo of *her* screams reverberated somewhere deep in her soul, but they seemed more distant now, like she might escape them after all. Emma didn't have answers to all her questions but decided she should probably take a break from reading about the myth.

And it would help to get back to training and the lab. Her pulse quickened with excitement at the thought of her project. She was eager to see if the disintegrin enzyme from the cat snake venom could destroy tumors in live mice.

Emma walked downstairs.

"Good morning." Her mom greeted her in the kitchen as if she'd been waiting for her. She paused from stirring her coffee to hug Emma, who tried not to squirm beneath the embrace, tense with worry that her mom would notice something different. She was thankful at least for the dim light of early morning.

"How was Crete?" she asked, and Emma was afraid she somehow knew about the incident. It was actually a bit strange to think she didn't know. Then again, there was a lot her mom didn't know about her.

"It was … really nice," Emma said. She thought about Pria, who called her own mom her best friend, detailing their frequent chats over tea. Emma wondered why her exchanges with her mom often felt rigid, even after she had been out of the country for two weeks.

"Did you get a lot of work done?" her mom asked. Emma sensed she was judging the trip. After all, she had claimed any work done there could be done at the lab in New York. Emma hadn't made any true progress in finding anticancer molecules after all, but research was a slow process.

"Actually, I think we may have found a new snake species," Emma said.

"Really?" Her mom began pouring her coffee into a paper travel cup and raised her brows doubtfully.

"Mhm. Well, at least we couldn't identify it."

"Ah, well that's different," her mom said, which annoyed Emma, but she hadn't expected to prove anything to her.

"But it escaped," Emma said. "So we're not sure."

"Why don't you paint it?" her mom said, and Emma smiled. She knew her mom didn't believe she had discovered anything significant, and she hadn't painted in years. It had been more of a middle school hobby. Still, she brightened at the suggestion. She would have to try.

An hour later Emma walked through the summer heat to her martial arts gym, where she changed clothes, embracing the familiar comfort of her thick training gi. It reminded her how she felt playing sports as a child. Free. Before she developed. Before that time in middle school gym class when the teacher scolded her to cover up as her shirt jostled while running and exposed her midriff. At first, it only confused her. But as she grew, Emma shied away from the gym where wandering eyes settled too easily on her. Pria often complimented Emma's perfectly proportioned frame, suggesting she swap her loose tees for something tighter. Emma considered her own body scrawny in comparison to her friend's but was nevertheless unsettled by the reactions it drew—the honking of cars on the street when she ran outside in the summer, the whistles, the persistent gazes. Beneath her gi she felt safe.

She slipped off Jason's bracelet and wound her hair so tightly it pulled her skin taut, then she joined the others out on the mats. Her sensei, Michelle, welcomed her back.

"How was your trip?" she asked, her eyes lighting up.

"Good, hopefully I didn't get too out of shape."

Her sensei smiled. Her high cheekbones and full, slightly upturned mouth lent her a serene elegance, a type of ultimate control Emma wished to emulate, along with her athleticism. She had a crew cut and was a small but compact woman, muscular but not obviously intimidating. Her strength was more subtle. She could easily be mistaken for a weaker person walking down the street. But Emma smiled at how surprised anyone would be if they tried to mess with her.

After they jogged in circles and stretched for warm-up, her sensei matched Emma with a brown belt named John. Emma watched her opponent's legs, trying to decide her first move, feeling a little nervous to be rolling with someone other than Pria for the first time in weeks. A match demanded full attention, but this time, she felt distracted. Her hair, tied back in its usual bun, felt too tight, as if it *wanted* to break free. Her opponent lunged forward, and a second later she was on her back. Refocused, she defended, grabbing for his arm.

She had been scared of losing skill after missing two weeks, but as she moved she felt reassured. The positions came naturally, almost instinctively. Invigorated, she became aware of her own agility and speed. She had somehow become even *faster*.

Before John could react, she had his arm pulled back between her thighs. At first he didn't tap out, and she squeezed, thrusting her hips upward from the floor as she usually did to finish. Only this time—

"Ah!" An agonizing scream left his mouth.

She knew his arm was broken. Each part of the bone that cracked reverberated through her own limbs. It happened faster than she could even control. She jumped back, panicked.

He writhed on the ground, his forearm dangling at an ugly angle. She inhaled sharply. *How did I do that?* Her sensei rushed forward, stopping the class.

Emma tried to step toward him. "I'm so sorry, I didn't mean—" But her sensei waved her off.

Emma was still shaking when the ambulance arrived. The class had been dismissed, but the students were lined up, watching their friend leave.

"I'm so sorry," Emma repeated. Some of the others whispered among themselves and avoided direct eye contact with her. Michelle got off the phone with the boy's parents and told everyone to go home, except Emma.

"Come with me," she said. Emma's stomach knotted further. "We need to talk." Her heart was racing. *How can I explain myself?*

Emma followed her to the back where her portable desk sat in a private, matted room. Michelle motioned for her to sit.

"I'm not a doctor, but I can tell," her sensei began. "His arm was broken. And that's not normal." Her tone was flat.

Emma couldn't look her in the eye. She was right. Emma knew it too.

"Emma, you've never missed a class in five years. Then you go on this trip and come back and this happens. I don't want to tell you you're not allowed back here, but I need an explanation."

Not allowed back here. The words stunned her.

"It was an accident," Emma said, her heart sinking

"You have to tell me. There are all sorts of things out there to try. What have you been doing?"

"What do you mean, *doing*? I haven't been doing anything."

She sighed, her usually smooth forehead slightly creased. "You were never that strong before. Even I might not be that strong," Michelle said. "It doesn't make sense. Did something change?"

Emma hesitated. She felt like *everything* had changed, just when she had hoped it wouldn't.

"I've been drinking vitamin water," she offered.

"Vitamin water," her sensei said, and shook her head. "Look, it's not safe for you to roll with other people—"

"I have to come here, please," Emma cried. "Don't kick me out."

Her sensei studied her face. "What does this mean to you?" Michelle asked. "Why do you come here?"

Emma didn't know how to explain what was going on. She didn't know. But this was something she could answer.

"When I was in fourth grade, I was walking home when a van pulled up and men got out and grabbed my friend. I ran. I could hear her screaming, and I tried to get help. But I was too late. My parents and teachers tried to hide what happened to her. They thought I was too young for it. But I found out. I just … I never want to be caught helpless like that again."

Michelle nodded once. "You were only a kid. You couldn't have expected yourself to know what to do or how to do it." Emma studied the mat beneath her, wondering what shade of blue this was called. "You have nothing to feel bad about," Michelle said.

"I know that." It was true, but she had dreamed of fighting them. And although recently she had dreamed of someone else's struggle, it dawned on her that maybe that was the same kind of fight.

Her sensei took a long, knowing breath, and Emma thought she saw the type of understanding on her face that came only from someone with a similar experience. She felt vulnerable yet safe there. *She couldn't kick her out, not now.* But the echo of John's snapping bones still reverberated through her own.

"It's important for everyone to feel safe here," Michelle said. Emma hung her head. She was right, of course. She hurt her opponent badly. And if it kept happening, no one would want to roll with her, or they might gang up on her for revenge.

"The truth is," Emma said, holding her breath. She felt herself unraveling. "Something happened to me when I was on Crete. I had a reaction to antivenom that no one understood. It didn't make any sense." She was terrified to tell the truth, but the calm, accepting look on Michelle's face coaxed her on. "But now I'm starting to have these … changes. I don't want to admit that they're happening, but today just proves it."

It was true. The last time she had been this afraid to admit something was junior year, when she was unexpectedly captivated by a transfer student with glossy hair and beautiful doe-like eyes. For a time she was confused by how frequently she thought about her, imagining what it might be like to touch her glowing, warm skin. She wasn't sure if it was a crush and knew it would be easier if it wasn't. It would be a lot to admit to anyone, even herself, and it had faded once she started dating Jason. Still, *this* confession felt even stranger.

"Like what changes?" her sensei asked.

"I can hear things far away, before others can. I can sense people coming, sense their vibrations in the ground. And it's like I can *smell heat* and emotions. I know it sounds totally crazy, but—"

"Nothing's crazy," she said and didn't appear baffled at all by Emma's claims.

"I feel like I'm going crazy though. I'm constantly flooded with all these sensations. It's overwhelming. I can't shut it out."

"Then don't," she said, raising her chin resolutely, her face relaxed. "Whatever's happening, don't resist. If this is your new reality, fighting it will only disturb your peace."

She thought about her words, took a breath, and already felt quieter within herself. It was a relief to tell someone, to feel accepted.

"Now, is it really all the time or sometimes more than others?" Michelle asked.

Emma thought about it and came to a realization. "I guess it's mostly when I'm feeling something, like fear."

"When you feel there might be danger," her sensei finished, nodding like she understood. "Emma, this could be an extension of your own instinct, and a powerful tool."

Emma nodded. "It's not just my senses though," she said. "It's strength and flexibility, and it happened *overnight*." She drew in an unsteady breath. "My research mentor said he gave me antivenom, but I think it could've been something else." Emma's voice trailed off. She hadn't even admitted that suspicion to herself. But there it was.

"Listen," her sensei said. "Until we figure out what's going on, I can't let you back in the class."

Emma's stomach sank.

"But I'll train with you," her sensei continued. Emma's heart lifted. "We can test these new abilities, *control* them," she said.

Emma looked up and a smile spread over her face. Relief rushed through her.

"Thank you, so much. I promise, I'll be careful," Emma said.

As she walked home, Emma replayed what had happened. *She had squeezed with the usual force, maybe seventy percent of her ability. How the heck did she break his arm?* She winced, recalling the snapping sound of his joint, then his scream. The pain must have been searing.

Emma was lost in thought as she walked straight through a basketball game. She often walked through that park, named in memory of her childhood friend, and cutting through the court was the quickest route. But today she wasn't paying attention to whether anyone was playing on it, until her senses cut through her thoughts. Something was approaching fast. Emma whirled around, just in time to see a basketball whizzing toward her. She smacked it down, but not before it crashed into her chest, punching air from her lungs. She stumbled as the ball bounced away.

She expected to hear shouts from the players, but they were silent as she caught her breath. There were four of them, and they stood frozen in front of her as the ball bounced away. They weren't looking at her face but rather at her neck and shoulder, where her skin tingled from the ball's impact. She didn't know them and didn't understand their wide-eyed expressions, until she followed their gaze.

Emma gasped when she saw it, her own skin, if she could even call it that. It had hardened into lesions. *No, not lesions.* She reached out a hand to touch it. She knew what it was. She began to tremble.

Scales. They erupted to cover the skin where the ball had struck, green to match the color of the court. They saw it too. She took another glance at their shocked faces, still staring at her as the ball rolled off into the far corner of the court. Then she turned and sprinted home, pulling a scarf from her bag and wrapping it around her shoulders and neck.

6

Emma stood at her kitchen counter drafting an email to Dr. Belken. She needed to get to the lab as soon as possible but didn't want to sound too urgent, afraid to reveal what was happening.

She considered going to a doctor but remembered what they had said in the Cretan hospital. Her lab tests looked normal in the end. Maybe they didn't know precisely what to check for. A doctor in New York might not either, unless she told them *everything*. But then she feared they'd admit her, that she might sound crazy. *Am I? Could I be hallucinating?* She knew of a classmate who had a psychotic break junior year. *Could this be one?* No, she told herself. Those guys on the court had seen it too. The chilling look on their faces proved it.

She picked up her phone and opened her thread with Pria. She paused.

"I can't believe it," she typed, then deleted it. She started again, texting, "I think something's really off," then paused before deleting that too. What was the point? Pria wouldn't have any answers. Besides, she might tell Jason, like she had in Crete. The thought made her tense, and for a moment she considered texting Pria to confront her about it. *Hey, I wish you would've told me you contacted Jason ...* but she stopped herself. She didn't want a fight. Besides, Pria had been scared, not malicious. But

Emma suddenly felt more isolated than ever. School was starting soon. What if she couldn't hide this from her classmates? She wasn't even sure she could mask it long enough to get to the lab.

She needed answers so badly she even wished the dreams would come back, if only to give her some information, wisps that she could latch onto and research. She took a breath and focused on the email in front of her. Her phone rang.

"Hi, Mom," she answered.

"I got a call from John's mother," her mom said. "She says you broke his arm?"

Emma stiffened. "Yeah, during jiu jitsu class. It was an accident."

"Emma, maybe you need a break from those classes." Her mom sounded stressed, with beeping and overhead hospital announcements competing with her voice.

"I *just* took a break!" Emma said, but slowed her breathing. Getting upset made the skin on her neck begin to harden again. "I mean, I worked things out with the sensei."

Her mom sighed. "I know the counselor thought it was a good idea, back when … well, back when you had the trauma. But maybe you're taking this too seriously now."

It wasn't worth trying to explain, and she wasn't ready to reveal the truth. Besides, if Michelle wanted to meet with her privately, it would technically be a break from the class. No one had to know.

"Sure, yeah," Emma said.

"Also, why are you wearing a scarf?"

Emma froze. For a second she didn't understand. Then she looked around uneasily. "How do you see me?" she asked.

"I forgot to tell you, we had cameras installed while you were away. There was an increase in crimes in the neighborhood, and Dad thought it was a good idea."

Emma's body tightened in unease as her mind raced through everything she had done before knowing she was being watched. After rushing through the door, she had been too afraid to check what her skin looked like beneath the scarf. Now she was relieved she hadn't removed it yet.

"What type of crimes?" Emma asked.

Her mom paused. In the background Emma heard alarms beeping. Their shrill tone, though distant, triggered her memory of waking up in the hospital. Emma felt her skin prickle and her stomach coiled. Her mom murmured to someone before answering Emma.

"Some kidnappings," she said, "and thefts. But don't worry, nothing close to us really. It's just a precaution, since we're not around the house a lot. Anyway, aren't you hot in that scarf?" her mom asked again.

"Okay, that's weird, Mom. Spying on me," Emma said. "But the scarf... I think I had some skin reaction, probably from the sun."

"Oh really? What does it look like?" Her mom's voice sounded suddenly interested.

Emma worried she would ask her to remove the scarf for the camera.

"I'll show you later," Emma said. "It's just more like dry skin."

"Well, if it's serious you can go to the dermatologist. Or I can take a sample for the lab."

"No!" Emma said, wishing she had made another excuse for the scarf. "I mean, it's fine, it's already going away."

"Maybe you should get tested," her mom said.

"For what?" The conversation was making her sweat. The last thing she wanted was a random lab testing her blood.

"Well, syphilis is seeing a rise again," her mom said.

Emma almost laughed in relief. "Oh my god. No, it's not syphilis." She wondered if this was her mom's way of asking if she'd had sex. She hadn't but didn't want to talk about it either.

"You know you can catch it in *other* ways," her mom continued. "Some stages of syphilis could be spread from the skin through a simple handshake or other touching."

"Okay, Mom! Thanks!" Emma said quickly. "I'll see you later." In a way she was relieved by the distraction from the bigger secret, that Emma was having an unknown reaction to her research mentor's antivenom.

"Wait," her mom said, and the sudden quietness of her voice made Emma stop. "Danny misses you."

She felt a pang of guilt. She shouldn't have waited so long, consumed by what was happening to her. She should've gone the minute she got back. But was it even safe to go into public? She hung up the phone and ran upstairs. She removed her scarf and examined her skin in the mirror. It looked perfectly normal now, no trace of the reaction from earlier. The color was warm, and when she brushed it with her fingers, it felt smooth again.

To be safe, she changed into a long turtleneck and pants to cover as much skin as possible. The more time that passed, the more she questioned what she had seen. *They couldn't have really been scales. And whatever they were, they're gone now, hopefully for good.*

Her phone chimed with a text from Jason, but she didn't have time to read it. She needed to get to the hospital. She tried to calm her racing thoughts. Maybe she could control the reaction somehow, keep it in check with her mind. *I'm okay. The real one to worry about is Danny, not me.*

The bright light from the window of Danny's hospital room illuminated the smiling dolphins and turtles painted on the walls. When Danny saw her, his drawn face lifted in a smile. Joy congealed with a bitterness that hit Emma's chest. His face was more sunken than a few weeks prior, and his big, hazel eyes had dark circles around them, the kind no child should have. He had lost all remnants of his dark hair, and he seemed smaller than the last time she'd seen him.

"Emma!" he cried, and she saw the energy it took him to say her name.

"How's my favorite brother?" she asked, sitting on his bed and trying to keep her voice steady.

"Good," he said. "Did you bring me something from your trip?"

She rummaged in her pockets for the ouzo hard candy from Greece. His face fell when he saw them.

"I'm not allowed to have those," he said.

"Why not?"

"The doctors need to do a test. I have to not eat before it."

A lump hardened in Emma's throat, straining her voice. "Well, how about I leave them here for after?" she said. Hot tears gathered in her eyes, and she blinked quickly. She didn't want to cry in front of him, to make him sad when he wasn't.

"Did you see anything cool there?" he asked, ever curious.

"I did," she said. "We found a new snake."

"Can I see?" he asked, his eyes brightening.

She smiled and rubbed his leg beneath the blanket. "It got away," she said.

"Draw it!" He pointed to crayons and paper sitting on the table behind them.

"All right." She smiled. "But only if you draw something too."

She handed him some crayons and a notebook from the table, then picked up her own. She stared at the paper, recalling that moment in the woods, alone, when she had seen it. A chill ran over her skin.

"Your hand looks blue!" Danny pointed.

Emma's gaze darted to her hand, where a bluish tinge had emerged to match her crayon.

"It's cold in here," she said and turned away, tilting her paper up to block her skin from him. She took a deep breath, reminding herself she was back in New York, at the hospital, safe. She focused on her drawing. Eventually, the skin turned beige again.

She colored the torsional, scaled body of the snake, trying to detach herself to avoid any further skin reactions. But it was difficult, the details of its diamond pattern and sharp eyes seemed to strike the chords of her heart. The snake was made even more stunningly beautiful by her memory, with scales luminous like stained glass and majestic movements the page couldn't capture.

"What are you?" she whispered, studying her drawing. She took a picture of it. Maybe there was a forum she could post it on. She turned the page to show Danny, but he had fallen asleep, a loose-leaf paper full of angular animals on his lap.

She took his hand and pressed her forehead against it. He felt so delicate and a little too cold. She pulled his blanket up higher then placed her drawing on it, leaving her name with a heart on the bottom of the page. As she stepped into the hallway, the hospital's PA system spurted to life.

"Code gray, five south," the announcement rang. "Code gray five south."

Emma found a nurse standing by the computer.

"What's a code gray?" she asked.

"It's behavioral," the nurse said, not looking up from her computer.

"What does that mean?"

The nurse looked miffed then turned from the computer. "It means a patient's acting up on the medicine floor."

"Acting up?" Emma tensed in alarm despite the nurse's apathetic expression. "Do we need to be concerned?"

"No, they'll call security and restrain him or medicate as needed. Nothing to worry about."

It wasn't reassuring. Emma furrowed her brow at the thought of a violent patient needing to be strapped down and sedated and gently closed her brother's door behind her, hoping none of the code grays happened near him.

Emma studied her textbook again, trying to figure out what the snake had been on Crete. She couldn't narrow her search geographically, since it was possible the snake had been transported from anywhere else. Furiously, she flipped through her book of species, not finding anything that matched. She still had all of Asia to go through though. Her phone rang, and she answered reluctantly, still studying the ridged lateral scales of the Field's horned viper.

"Are you ready to start school tomorrow?" Emma paused when she heard Pria's voice, her stomach tensing.

"I guess so," Emma said. She had been spending most of her time in her room, avoiding as much contact with the outside world as possible. The thought of school starting made her queasy.

Pria rambled about her class schedule, excited they had a few together. "We have English third period, so I'll definitely be counting on your summaries." She laughed. "What about Jason?"

"What about him?" Emma asked. Hearing Pria mention him stirred a subtle anger within her. There was a pause.

"Does he have any classes with us, or you I mean?" Pria asked. *Why don't you ask him,* Emma thought to say, but it sounded too bitter in her mind.

"I'll have to ask him," Emma said, fidgeting with her bracelet. In the past, it was always such an important thing, but now her mind was consumed with everything else. Dr. Belken had responded to her email. He was brief but said she could return to the lab.

"Hey," Emma said, turning a page to yet another snake photo that looked nothing like the one from Crete. "When are you going back to the lab?" It was the first time she'd brought up anything related to their research projects, and she sensed tension in the pause that followed. Still, it might be nice to resume their routine of riding there together.

"I quit," Pria said.

"What?" Emma was stunned. "Why?"

Pria sighed. "It's senior year. I just want to enjoy myself. The lab wasn't really helping me much anyway … and I think Dr. Belken is crazy."

Emma didn't know what to say.

"Let's hang out though, go shopping or something," Pria said.

Nothing sounded so unappealing to Emma. A fleeting thought crossed her mind. What if Pria was just her friend because they worked together? Otherwise did they have much in common? She chased the thought away. Pria had loyally sat by her side while she was in a *coma.* That's more than anyone else had done for her.

"I think I'll be busy this week," Emma said.

"The only busy you should be is with Jason," Pria said, teasingly, but an angry heat throbbed in Emma's cheeks. She had been avoiding Jason and wondered if Pria meant it as a subtle accusation or if Jason had complained to her.

"So, do you have any news to share?"

Emma's stomach dropped. "What do you mean?"

"You know."

Emma realized the gossipy, playful tone Pria was using and sighed with relief.

"With Jason!"

"Oh," Emma said, chuckling. "Nothing new, no."

"What are you waiting for with him?"

Pria's persistence started to irritate her. Her tone now bordered on judgmental. And how did Pria know if she was waiting or not. They hadn't spoken about it in ages.

"It's just … complicated," Emma said.

"Maybe you're overcomplicating it." The enthusiasm in Pria's voice was fading.

"Maybe," Emma said but didn't think so. What could be more complicated than morphing into a snake?

Pria sighed. "You deserve to be happy," she said, and there was a reassuring touch of warmth to her voice. This was the friend Emma knew.

"Thanks. I guess I'll talk to you later," Emma said, but Pria had already hung up.

Emma didn't want to think about school on top of everything else. She wasn't bullied, or at least not as badly as some kids. There were the popular girls who loved to talk about anyone who wasn't part of their clique, murmuring jabs about Emma's clothes or book-stuffed backpack, but most of the time Emma went under their radar, too busy studying or going off to the lab or training. She preferred it that way. When she started dating Jason, the school's rising soccer star, it did spike a wave of unwanted attention, but she remained focused on more serious things, which Jason seemed to love.

Jason. She looked at her phone and saw his text from two hours earlier. She had avoided him for too long, Pria was right to seem surprised.

"Do you want to come over?" he had texted.

She hesitated. What if something weird happened and she couldn't control it? Part of her wanted him to know, but another wanted desperately for things to be normal again. Maybe this would be a good test.

Emma sat on Jason's living room couch, his reggaeton music softly playing in the background. He was telling her about horseback riding through Torres del Paine national park in southern Chile, recounting the sharply peaked mountains and bright blue icebergs. It sounded incredible, but Emma was having trouble envisioning it, her mind preoccupied. Seeming to sense it, he raised the music and pulled her up from the couch to dance.

In the past, this might have made her stomach flutter with excitement, but tonight her skin stiffened beneath his touch, and she feared it might transform again. Only she realized the more worried she was, the more likely the reaction became. So she closed her eyes, relaxed, and let the warmth of his touch spread through her body. He spun her around, and she let her body sway, loosening into his grasp. When the song finished, he looked at her sheepishly.

"Were you mad at me this week?" he asked.

"No," she said, surprised. "Not at all."

There was a long pause, and she knew he must be wondering, *what then?*

"I didn't mean to ignore you," she said. "There was a lot going on, getting back from Crete, visiting my brother, and ... then I broke someone's arm in jiu jitsu class," she confessed, partly to avoid confessing the real reason she had avoided him.

"What?" He raised his brows. "How?"

"I just squeezed too hard I guess. It was an accident of course, and I feel horrible."

"Geez. All right, well I know I can never double cross you." He laughed, holding up his hands. She playfully hit his shoulder.

"Did you get in trouble?" he asked, lowering the music as the next song began to play.

"Well, yeah, I'm not exactly allowed back."

"Oh." He looked concerned for a moment, then his smile returned. "Well, in the meantime if you want to practice any moves on me, there's a few I'd like to try with you."

Emma smiled. "I don't think you could handle them," she said, softly returning his tease as she ran a hand through his tousled black hair. She was relieved to be so calm with him, even just for a moment. The tension that had swarmed her began to fade like a receding wave.

"So are you excited to start senior year?" Jason asked.

Emma's stomach coiled again and she looked away. Her hand dropped to her side. His face, so close to hers, now felt intrusive.

"Actually," she said, "I'm a little stressed." She considered telling him everything, easing into the conversation.

"What's wrong?" he asked.

She studied his face, her mind racing. *Can I tell him?*

"I guess I'm a little worried about going back to the lab," she said finally, purposefully vague.

"You're going back?" He sounded incredulous. "Are you kidding me?"

"I still have a project," she said, stepping back, not expecting that response.

"I know but ... it'd be nice if you could listen to me once in a while. I'm *always* listening to you. I didn't want you to go on that trip, but you went anyway, and then almost died."

She felt her pulse quicken, and the skin on her chest prickled.

"Where is this coming from?" she asked. "Are you mad about me missing Chile? I'm sorry, okay? It was a hard decision to make, but I thought it would be a good one for my future. Do you need me to apologize for that again?"

"Is getting into Columbia really that important to you?" Jason asked. Then he looked away. If the argument escalated any further, she would have to leave before the scales broke out. She regretted bringing up *the future*. A few months ago he had told her he wanted to go to Stanford. The idea of him leaving for California had created somewhat of a rift between them. They had decided to take things one day at a time after that, avoiding the topic. Things had felt better, up until her trip to Crete.

"It *is* important," she said quietly. "But you're right. My mentor put me in danger. I didn't know that was going to happen." She almost told him she wished she went to Chile with him instead, but she couldn't bring herself to say it … because it wasn't true. She was so captivated by that snake, she couldn't imagine not having seen it. "But," she said, "if I have even the slightest concerns about him again, I'll leave."

"And report him?" Jason asked, his voice intense. She didn't like it. It was like he was stealing her control. But she nodded, mostly to appease him.

Jason turned off the music. They sat silently on the couch, facing forward. After a moment he said, "I was just scared, Emma, really scared that something happened to you. And … I don't know what I would do if I lost you." He turned to her, and she met his deep gaze, her heart softening.

"I would've been scared too," she said and held his hand, welcoming its firm warmth. In the back of her mind she felt angry at Pria again for calling him while she was unconscious, setting them up for this fight. But it wasn't really her fault. *She* was the one keeping secrets. And now, any thought of telling Jason the truth, the extent of her scaly reaction, only felt further away.

"You know," he said, smiling. "There are some really good research labs in Stanford."

"There are." She nodded and smiled back. *He wanted her with him.* Maybe she could consider California. But she didn't want to be far from her brother. Still, she let herself revel in the warmth of knowing he wanted her.

"Emma, you know I want to be here for you," he said. "You can tell me what you're thinking, what you're worried about."

She nodded.

He continued. "I think this year will be great. I want to be with you when all of it happens, and for what comes after."

He cupped her cheek in his hand and leaned in to kiss her. His heat still overwhelmed her new sensitivity, but she welcomed it, letting it ripen through her limbs into a heavy yearning for more.

Could she fully let go? In that moment, the scales seemed banished from her skin, no longer lurking beneath the surface. Maybe this would help bury them, pulverize the memory of that startling nightmare on Crete. She opened into his kiss, angling to take his tongue into her mouth as heat pulsed through her.

The binding restraint loosened. She wanted to fuse into him, prove she could be vulnerable and human. Maybe this was how to stay grounded. There was so much uncertainty in the world, but Jason had been there for a year already, and she trusted the look in his eyes. He wanted to be there for her, if she'd only let him.

She welcomed the delicious weight of him as he climbed on top of her, pressing into her body. A heat throbbed in her hips, and his hands gripped around the slope of her waist.

Their breaths grew heavier in sync, and she curled one leg around his lower back, pulling into him.

I need to let go. But a thought got stuck in her mind. *Is this really what I want?* Guilt jabbed her. Was she just using him to feel human? *This is a big deal. We've never done this before.*

His mouth moved to her chest, and he pulled the neckline of her shirt down. Heat radiated from where his lips pressed between her breasts. For a second, the thoughts evaporated with pleasure. He traced an arch with his tongue to her collarbones and then opened his mouth onto her neck. She whispered his name as the yearning bloomed.

But the thoughts flurried back. *Where did he learn to do that?*

He slid his hand around the curve of her waist then trailed down her skin. She throbbed beneath the touch, tingling with desire as he slipped a finger inside the rim of her jeans.

She wanted to fully give in to him, to release. But something pulled her back then.

The scales might break out. They're unpredictable. He was so close, there would be no way to hide them. She stiffened to his touch, maybe out of fear, or something else she couldn't pinpoint.

"Wait," Emma said, her voice strained. Jason paused, lingering in that position. "Jason." Fear that he might get annoyed or resentful hovered over her. But he soon dispelled that.

"Are you okay?" he asked, still a hint of hopefulness in his voice as he studied her face.

"I just ... can't," Emma said, breathless and grappling for words.

A flash of disappointment crossed his face, but he nodded, swallowing and lowering his head. There was a pause as he lingered awkwardly there, perhaps wondering if she would change her mind. Then he moved onto the couch, sitting beside her and sighing.

"I just," he said. "Let me go to the bathroom for a sec."

"Sure," she said, feeling tense still but comfortable with her choice.

When he returned, she stiffened with the inclination to explain herself, but he only put his arm around her and kissed her on the temple.

"Are you okay?" Emma asked.

"Are you?" he asked back.

Emma nodded. He smiled and rubbed her arm.

"I just want to make you happy," he said.

A sense of accomplishment swelled as she cuddled into him, his soft breath grazing her fingertips as their hands entwined against his chest. She was human, and safe. They had a bond, an understanding. She felt, for a glowing instant, maybe he would be the key to her recovery from all of it.

But is it fake? Doubt butted in. *He doesn't know the truth.* But maybe, she thought with hope, maybe the scales were gone for good now, and the only obstacle would be what to do after graduation.

"You'll be at my game tomorrow night, right?" he asked. "For homecoming?"

She didn't want to sour things by telling him she planned to go to the lab the following night. She would just have to hurry and finish early enough to make it.

She smiled a little. "Of course. I'll be there." *A soccer game under the lights might be a nice distraction.*

"It should be a good one," he said and beamed with pride. "I'm starting." It would be his first time starting a game on varsity. Emma realized how much that must mean to him. She would have to rush things at the lab.

7

Emma took the train to Manhattan's Upper West Side then walked several blocks. The whirl of lights, whizzing cars, and bustling commuters threatened to unnerve her, but the chaotic energy funneled into an intense, invigorating focus as she paced across the red and white bricks of Columbia University and approached her lab building. Her goal was clear. She would go through the motions of her project, but her true intent was to take a look at her own blood sample under a microscope.

"Dr. Belken?" Emma called as she knocked on his open office door.

"Yes?" he said, not looking away from his computer.

"Um, I'm here."

"Yes, I see that," he said.

She waited to see if he would ask her anything else. This was their first meeting after her near death experience on Crete. But he said nothing. Finally, she filled the silence.

"So I'll just continue my experiment from a few weeks ago. I have a few more assays to run," she said.

"Yes, very good," he said, still not looking at her.

She was about to turn, when something forced the polite, accommodating girl inside her to a halt, and she poised to challenge him about what happened on Crete. "I have to ask you something," she said, mustering her strength.

"How's your experiment going?" he asked suddenly, almost cutting her off.

"It's actually about me," she said. "I haven't been feeling so well since the hospital in Greece."

He turned to face her, suddenly giving her all his attention.

"What's going on?" he asked, putting his pen down. She faltered under his newly intense gaze. She was too scared to mention the scales, even saying "rash" felt too revealing.

"I just feel *off*," she said. "I was thinking about going to the doctor—"

"No," he said suddenly. "I think it's good you told me first. Why don't I take a sample of your blood? I can take a look for any changes."

"Oh," she said, surprised at first. But it made sense. He had been drawing blood for previous experiments and had reportedly studied his own after injecting venoms. He might be more qualified than her to notice a change … but would he tell her the truth if he found something?

"Don't you think it's weird?" she said, avoiding his offer. "What happened to me on Crete with the antivenom?"

He hesitated. "I do. That was … an atypical reaction," he said. "But I think I've seen similar things in some mice studies."

"Really? What did their samples show?" She was eager to hear about changes in gene expression or something that would explain her skin's transformation.

"Some increased inflammatory markers and such," he said, vaguely waving a hand to Emma's disappointment. "Why?" he asked. "Were you looking for something specific?"

Emma stiffened. He wanted to know her symptoms.

"No," she said, but there was tension in the air, as if they both knew more than they were saying. "But I'd like to take a look at my blood with you," she said. Dr. Belken nodded.

Emma clenched her teeth as he lowered the needle to her skin, trying not to think about the last time he'd injected her. This was different of course. This time he was drawing blood, not adding something unknown. She closed her eyes.

"That's weird," Dr. Belken said. She opened her eyes. She hadn't felt the prick and noticed that her skin hardened slightly at the site, like it wouldn't let the needle in. "Must be too dull," Dr. Belken said, and went to get a different needle.

When he returned, she took a deep breath, remembering what her sensei had told her. She could *choose* not to resist. He slid the needle in. She was proud to see the blood drip into the tube but was immediately stunned by the potent *smell* of it.

She'd had cuts before but never remembered the scent. She tried to conceal her surprise, waiting to see if Dr. Belken would react. But he didn't seem to notice anything. Yet the sudden smell swarmed her nostrils. It was hard to qualify: slightly metallic but also like sweet earth, a fruit ripened to the brink of fermentation, and mixed with salt.

"I'll take a look at these later," he said.

"What? I thought we could look at them now," she said in protest.

"My abstract deadline is in an hour." His terse tone made her cower inside. But that scent lingered in her nose, captivating her attention as he placed the two vials of her blood in the fridge.

Baffled, and suspicious of his excuse, Emma retreated from his office. At her lab bench, she started her titrations to equally distribute the disintegrin protein for injection into the different mice groups. When Dr. Belken didn't return to her with any results from her blood samples, she went back to his office, only to find him already gone. She needed to be going too, especially if she was going to make it to the soccer game.

But she didn't want to wait any longer. She needed answers. She tore open the plastic package of a new needle and stuck her own fingertip, placing a droplet on a slide and smearing it before putting it under the microscope. She tried to ignore the scent. Maybe her new senses distorted the normal scent of blood, maybe it didn't mean her blood itself had changed. Still, she held her breath.

She zoomed in until she could make out spherical red blood cells. She found nothing structurally abnormal about them, and the cells were the right red color. Perhaps she should sequence the proteins in her cells to check for any changes?

Or maybe this was a sign that her blood was in fact *normal*, and she was working herself up for nothing. She took a breath. She should be relieved. But before she shut off the microscope, another cell floated into the field. She squinted.

Her mouth dropped open.

There, among her normal, round, and nucleated red blood cells, was something else—an *oval* shaped blood cell, with a dark, unmistakable nucleus in its core.

Human red blood cells didn't have nuclei. She knew that for certain. No, humans did not have this. Mammals did not have this.

This was the red blood cell of a *snake*.

She frantically turned the dial, scanning. She couldn't believe her eyes as she counted at least seven more. There was no chance of contamination. She had placed her blood directly onto a clean slide. Her heart began to race, and she sat back, a bit dizzy. This couldn't be real.

Has Dr. Belken seen this? He couldn't have, she thought. Maybe he hadn't looked at her sample yet. *If he had, there was no way he would leave without saying something.*

She cleaned off the slide, sweating. As she passed Dr. Belken's closed door, she smelled that singular scent emanating from her samples. Panic gripped her. She wasn't ready for anyone else to know what her blood contained. She tried to turn the knob, but it didn't budge. She thought about breaking in and taking the vials back, but no, that would reveal her desperation. Besides, even if he did discover this finding, he would help her, maybe explain it, right? Now that she knew what her blood showed, she could even test him, see if he would admit it to her, or lie.

Still, she felt anxious enough to vomit. An itch crept up her spine, and she was afraid to touch the skin she knew must be hardening there.

She took a few deep breaths, calming herself, coaxing her skin to relax. She remembered Jason's gentle touch. *Jason.* It was time to leave for his game.

She was lost in thought as she walked by a convenience store on the way to the subway station and realized the gnawing in her stomach was hunger as well as nerves. It would take about another hour to get to the soccer game. She should probably grab a snack. *Quickly,* she was already running late.

The store was empty, and the cashier looked annoyed when she entered, probably eager to close up. She grabbed a bag of chips. But as she approached the counter, an uneasy sense of dread rattled inside her, worse than what she had felt at the lab.

She shuddered at the vibrations coming from the street outside, her skin prickling with the approaching steps. They were too *aggressive.* It was strange, the way they seemed to shake her chest, telling her it wasn't the average pedestrian passing by.

A man burst through the door, a black ski mask over his head. Emma dropped her bag of chips, her pulse surging. The man pulled out a gun.

He did a quick scan of the ceiling, aimed, and shot a security camera with one bullet. Then he pointed his gun at the cashier, who screamed.

"Give me the money," the thief said, his voice deep and muffled.

The cashier pursed her lips and didn't move.

"You should give it to him, it's not worth your—" Emma began.

"Shut up!" he shouted at her.

The cashier had tears in her eyes and nodded quickly, reaching her stiff, trembling hands toward the cash register.

Emma was scared, but the fear was second to her mounting anger. Her skin itched with heat. Her awareness heightened. She had never felt this alert, sensing every small movement and sound. The woman threw handfuls of cash onto the counter, and the man grabbed it with a gloved hand.

Emma sensed a faint rustling near the back of the store. Her eyes narrowed. Then a gunshot ripped through the air. She ducked to the ground and turned toward the back of the store, where a man had appeared, holding a gun aimed at the intruder.

"Get out of my store," he yelled. But the shot had missed its mark, and the thief fired back.

Emma watched in horror as the bullet struck the shop owner and he slid down, blood spilling over the dirty floor tiles. His face was anguished, but she saw him clutch his arm. The bullet hadn't hit anywhere vital. He could survive.

Only now, the thief was storming over to finish him.

Emma didn't think. She sprang forward instinctively, moving so quickly the world seemed to slow.

"Stop!" she yelled, but the thief's focus was on the shop owner.

Emma swiped across the ground and knocked him off his feet in a sliding tackle. The money flew from his hand, and bills floated to the floor like dried leaves.

She knew that wouldn't stop him. She needed to get the gun away, only she didn't see it now. She had hoped he would drop it while falling.

But no. Her eyes darted, frantic to find it as he lay on his belly. It was somewhere hidden beneath him.

But before she could find it, a bullet ripped through the cloth of his jacket.

The world seemed to move so slowly she could actually see the bullet, a solitary bead of death. But she hadn't expected it, hadn't realized he was holding the trigger beneath his coat, and she didn't move away in time.

It struck. Right into her abdomen.

It didn't hurt the way she thought a bullet would hurt, but then again she hadn't spent that much time wondering what it would feel like to be shot. Maybe she was in shock. The sound had been so potent it seemed to crack the air around her. But the bullet didn't feel like a sting. She didn't feel it rip through her. It felt more like a punch. She stumbled back a step. The heat was heavy on her skin now, and she clutched the spot where the bullet had hit, expecting to feel blood seep over her hand.

But there was none. Holding her breath, she reached down and pulled up her shirt, her shock morphing into awe.

Instead of a wound, she found gray scales erupting on her skin, encasing her abdomen, as if some primal part of her brain had anticipated the bullet before her cortex could.

For a second, the thief looked confused. She straightened and felt the hardening spread over the rest of her skin, encasing her entire body, bolstering her. Her hair seemed to rustle from its tie despite a lack of wind, and she knew she must look like a monster, yet she welcomed it.

Although his face was mostly covered, the mask revealed his widened eyes, and his hands shook. She *tasted* his fear, rancid and acidic. He brought his arm up from beneath his jacket, clutching the trigger again, but she was too quick for him.

She knocked it from his hand with a blow from her foot. He tried to stand, but she kicked him in the mouth and sent him falling into a nearby display, knocking over boxes of cereal. Emma leaped onto him, bracing his shoulders with her knees, and rotated into a choke hold with his neck between her thighs. He was bigger than her, but it didn't matter. He tried to struggle, but her hold was too tight. It was a variation of one she had learned as a brown belt but had never been flexible enough to get into. She squeezed, taming her strength enough to avoid breaking the bones.

She was aware of the cashier on the phone behind her, calling the police. The thief struggled, managing to croak the word "wait" before his consciousness left him.

Footsteps reverberated outside. An accomplice. Another masked man entered, scanning the scene until he saw his friend. He raised his gun at Emma in what seemed to her to be a laughably slow gesture. By now, this felt like an easy exercise. She released her hold and propelled herself across the floor, alternating the use of her knees and arms, as if slithering. Her legs leaped apart into a split and she slid, poised in front of him. Then she opened her mouth and hissed.

Only it wasn't *just* a hiss. A stream of clear fluid shot from somewhere behind her teeth, powerful, fast, and precise, hitting her opponent in the eyes.

Venom.

It was automatic, like an instinct rather than a choice, and that scared her. It wasn't human. *Where did it come from?* The man yelled in agony and dropped his gun to grasp his eyes. Emma stood among the pile of cash. She glanced at the woman behind the counter. She was pale and backed away, as if more afraid of Emma than the guns. Maybe she was right to be.

Emma heard sirens outside. She saw the faint flashes of red and blue illuminating the streets.

She couldn't let them see her like this.

She bolted out the door and down the street, not caring what direction she took. She just needed to get away.

Around the block she dodged into an alcove between two buildings, hiding in the shadows beside a dumpster. She could hear the police officers' voices, even from several blocks away, as they made their arrests. She was relieved to hear no more gunshots.

For a moment, she swelled with pride for what she had done. But her relief froze.

Terror crept into her heart. What had she become? Her tongue traced the roof of her mouth and grazed over two small ridges on either side of her palate. She had shot *venom* from them, like a spitting cobra. *How could that be?*

She was human, she told herself, but she was feeling less and less like it. The sounds from the street were so loud she covered her ears, but the vibrations still shook her core. She shouldn't be scared of the world. She had just survived a gunshot after all. Her hand slid back over her abdomen. She unzipped her phone from her pocket and shined the flashlight on the spot the bullet had struck. The bright electric glow illuminated the scales that covered her skin. They had turned a greenish black to match the shadows around her. The spot felt tender, like a bruise, and when she looked closer, she saw a chip in one of the scales. She moved the light up her arm and saw scales lining not just her abdomen, but her arms, chest, legs, and—she looked into the dark screen of her phone and, in the dim reflective light of a nearby street lamp, saw her face veiled in scales. She turned off the phone's light, breathing heavily, scared to see any more. Trembling, she wondered if they would return to skin this time. Or was her nightmare coming true?

I'm a snake.

8

"I was about to call the police!" Emma's mom exclaimed, jumping up from the kitchen stool as Emma walked through the door. "What were you doing this late?" She looked distraught, her hair springing messily from a ponytail and her cotton pajama pants clashing with the work blouse she was still wearing.

Emma froze. She had waited in the lonely darkness behind that dumpster for nearly an hour, increasingly anxious that her skin would never return. Panic mounted like a tidal wave inside her with each noise from the street. She had gripped her bracelet, hoping by some magic it could transport her back to human form, but its reminder of Jason only hardened the scales. She had started to consider explanations in case they remained, thought of who she should show first and what she might say. Would Jason freak out? How could she go to school? It was only when she thought of Michelle and her calm demeanor as she agreed to train her that Emma was able to take a breath. Warmth tingled as it spread from her fingertips, and when she reached for her phone, the scales had gone.

"I was at the lab," Emma said, wondering if she looked unsettled enough to raise her mom's suspicion.

"The lab! No high school student needs to be staying at a lab until midnight. What on earth is he having you do? You know what, it doesn't matter. There's no way it could be anything useful enough to justify *this*." She snorted, pointing at the digital clock above the oven where the red numbers read *12:31*. "You're not going to win a Nobel Prize for sorting snake venom samples."

Her mom's rant gave her no chance to explain, which was good actually, because she didn't know how to. It still hurt though, how she discounted her project. *Why aren't you sleeping or at the hospital*, she thought, annoyed to have to deal with an argument after her stressful night.

"You were on the train this late?" Her mom folded her arms.

"No, I called an Uber." Emma eyed the stairs, eager for the solace of her room. "I was just going slow at the lab, that's all. My titrations took longer than I expected."

Her mom sighed, shaking her head and pressing a knuckle into her brow. "I don't ask much from you in terms of keeping in touch, but Jason actually called me tonight." Emma's heart sank. *Jason.* "He said you never showed up to his game and weren't answering your phone. I started to worry."

The game. She had wanted to make it. Told him she would. But the scales had taken time to disappear.

"Then I turned on the news and saw there was an armed robbery tonight not too far from your lab," her mom said quietly. Emma tensed, not expecting her to know anything about that. She tried to detach herself from the memory, but the skin of her abdomen stung, and she feared she might break out in scales again.

"Really?" she said, feigning surprise, afraid her mom would see through it. Even as she breathed, the motion hurt where the bullet had struck.

"We have to talk about your safety," her mom continued. "As a teenager you think you're invincible. But there's plenty that can happen to you."

An urge to protest flared inside her. *I deflected a bullet,* she wanted to say. But she stopped. She hadn't feared death during her fight, but the chipped scale and pain in her abdomen reminded her she was *not* invincible. "I know that," Emma said. Her mom seemed poised for an argument, but Emma was too tired for one. "I won't go that late again," she said.

"*If* you go at all," her mom warned. "We'll discuss it. Good night."

As Emma walked upstairs, the impact of her steps sent sharp pains through her stomach. In her bedroom, she pulled up her shirt to reveal the bruise. It was dark purple with a blue outline. *I deflected a bullet.* The memory of its impact sent shivers over her skin. What if the scales hadn't come? *I would be dead.* She traced the rim of the bruise and inhaled sharply. It was sensitive to even the lightest touch.

She lay in bed staring at the ceiling as she replayed the scene, too alert to sleep. *Did that man go blind?* She touched the roof of her mouth with a finger. It had flattened, but she still felt groves she wasn't sure were there before … not that she felt for fangs on the roof of her mouth very often. *What's happening to me?*

She had an urge to call someone, maybe Jason or Pria, but what would she say? She had dozens of texts from them, a lot of explaining to do, and no idea how to do it. School was scheduled to start tomorrow, but she couldn't imagine facing anyone. She messaged her sensei instead, asking to meet the next day. Her mind raced with uncertainties until exhaustion overcame her.

Any hope that sleep might offer peace was dashed as her dreams transported her back to an ancient world. In the damp shadows of Medusa's cave, a snake slithered over her scaled collarbone. Her scales didn't cover her entire body, as Emma's did, but rather spanned like armor over certain parts—her breasts and hips, her hands and feet and up over her knees. They speckled her cheekbones like jewels and traced her forehead almost like a crown. Emma wondered if they too could change colors, but she wouldn't know in that dark cave. She couldn't tell if the serpents were a threat or a protection, only that Medusa resented them bitterly, a curse from the goddess who scorned her, the goddess she had loved enough to serve and trusted to protect her.

Emma sensed the rage and loneliness roaring inside Medusa like a violent sea. She had loved the sea, born in its waters. She knew its swells, its waves and currents, its duality of gentleness and harshness, of life and death. Medusa too was haunted by questions. What had she done to deserve this cruelty? A wisp of memory for her family arose, a family of sea gods and goddesses, nymphs, and monsters, a family she had left behind, as its only human member. Why had none of them helped her?

Medusa's mind wandered to the darkness of the ocean's most forgotten depths, where her father ruled, if she could even call him that. There were rumors and doubts whirling with the sea sands. But he was her only hope, the most powerful of the family, wading with hard, prickled skin and claws, through the sea's cold blackness most would never dare enter, and if they did, would never return from. Why didn't he intervene? She knew to challenge Poseidon, a brother of almighty Zeus, might risk war in the oceans. Even if he wanted to save her, he would lose that war, or risk losing something he held more dear than his mortal daughter, in the bargain for her protection. She wasn't worth it. Maybe he even wanted her gone, to rid his legacy of her lowly birth.

The others were less powerful. Even if they wanted to help, how could they? Medusa thought of her two closest sisters, Stheno and Euryale, with whom she had shared a womb. They were born immortal, sisters who were kind and generous, with strong, wing-like fins and scaly flesh perfect for swimming. But their powers couldn't rival Poseidon's. There were still other family members she had never met—a *half* sister with a snaking fish tail and beautifully dark eyes, said to control the ocean's most dangerous currents. But what was an ocean current to Poseidon, ruler of the sea, who had the final say over its waters?

Then there was her mother, goddess of sea monsters, beautiful, timeless, last seen with her tear-streaked cheeks as she left Medusa on land … to keep her safe. Medusa choked on a bitter laugh at the irony. Her mother, too, played by Poseidon's rules. She had always warned her the gods could be cruel, unjust and proud, but maybe Medusa hadn't fully believed it. Until it all went wrong. *But how?*

She had loved Athena, purely, and secured for the first time in that temple a sense of belonging somewhere. Excitement had glinted with hope for her future, one that might even allow her to meet this beautiful and wise goddess. She knew temples were sacred places, that any defilement of one was a deep offense to the god it served. But Medusa resided there for that very reason, thinking Poseidon wouldn't dare harm her there. Until he did, and it turned out Athena would not punish her father's brother, an Olympian, but rather his mortal victim.

Is it my fault, Medusa pondered. *Is Athena right?* The empty cave echoed her uncertainties back to her, amplifying them, driving her to the edge of madness. "*No,*" she screamed, and her serpents coiled in unison, prepared to strike at some invisible foe. *I did nothing wrong.* But then why had everyone turned their backs on her? If her sister or mother still lived, why hadn't they found her there? Maybe they feared opposing Athena, Zeus's favorite daughter. Or maybe… Had Athena cursed them too? She shuddered, hatred burning for the gods. A thought spurred her to leave that cave, but she feared what part of Athena's curse might await her if she did.

Bright light overtook the cave, surging Emma away from the memory, away from Medusa. Then the image of a blood-stained man flashed again. His smile spread, and he seemed to speak directly to her, though his mouth was transfixed in a menacing grin. "I see you... I'm coming." His gray eyes pierced her like the point of a spear, bolting Emma awake.

9

Emma skipped her first period study hall to go to her jiu jitsu gym. She knew she might get in trouble, but this was urgent, and study hall would be a waste of time anyway. She messaged Jason, apologizing that she had felt sick at the lab last night and had fallen asleep as soon as she went home. She hoped it would suffice for now. After all, she *had* awoken from the nightmare feeling sick.

She knocked on the door of the back room at the gym, where Michelle went in between classes.

"Come in," Michelle called.

The room's floors and walls were padded in blue mats for practicing. Michelle sat on a folding chair behind the portable plastic table in the corner.

"What's going on?" she asked. "I thought you would come after school?"

"I was shot," Emma blurted.

Michelle furrowed her brow and stood. "What?"

"A thief shot me in the stomach. But it only left a bruise."

Her sensei stared in disbelief, her open-mouthed expression frozen. "What do you mean?"

"Remember I said something was happening? That I was changing because of that snake antivenom?"

"Yes, but what does that—"

"My skin turned into scales, when I was in danger. I'm not sure how. But the scales deflected the bullet." Emma recounted the entire incident, aware of how bizarre she sounded, but her sensei's face was solemn as she listened.

"Have you told anybody else?" she asked.

"No. I can't. I didn't even know if I could tell you."

"Why did you?" she asked, stepping forward.

Emma clenched her jaw, studying Michelle's face, her smooth skin and chestnut colored eyes. There was something comforting there. "I thought you'd be … understanding and that I could trust you with it. Can I?"

"Of course. I don't want to see you harmed."

"Do you believe me though?" Emma asked.

Michelle's unwavering expression gave no indication, its ethereal stillness always masking her next move. How did she get so good at that? Emma both envied and admired it, the way this woman beat any opponent she faced in the gym with a calm, near grin on her face. But right now, after Emma's story, she worried Michelle could be considering sending her for psychiatric evaluation.

"I know it sounds crazy, this story," Michelle said. "But I saw that something was changing with you. And who am I to say what's possible or not? I've known you for a long time and you've always been serious. I don't think you would make this up. Unless there are drugs involved that you're not telling me about."

Emma shook her head. "It'd be more straightforward if this was all from a drug, right?"

"Not necessarily," her sensei responded. Her eyes narrowed. "Can you show me?"

Emma lifted her shirt to uncover the bruise. Her sensei's eyes widened, and she blew air out her lips.

"Well that's a hell of a bruise," she said. "But I meant the scales. Can you show me them?"

Emma sighed. "I don't know how to make them come."

"Let's go," her sensei said, and paced to the back of the room where she kept an assortment of Bojutsu training staffs. "I'll attack and you defend," she said, and before Emma could think, her sensei grabbed the wooden staff and swung it. Emma ducked and slid out of the way.

Michelle swung again, back and forth in a routine that grew quicker and more relentless with each strike. She was pushing Emma past what she had done before, gauging whether or not she could take it. But while her sensei began to pant and her movements slowed, Emma dodged each strike with effortless speed.

At last, she couldn't help but go on the offensive. When her sensei swung, Emma's hand shot out and snatched the stick away faster than she could blink. Where her hand met the wood, scales appeared and began to spread, blue to match the mats of the room.

Her sensei froze in awe, her raging heartbeat vibrating into Emma's chest. Emma stood tall and dropped the piece of wood. She wasn't even winded.

"It's magnificent," Michelle said, her face awestruck. "Did that hurt your hand?" she asked.

Emma had felt the impact, but no, her scales had absorbed the force. She shook her head. "They're not impenetrable. The bullet still chipped them. But they seem to block most things."

"It's incredible," her sensei said.

Emma flushed at the compliment. "You're not afraid of me?" she asked. She felt naked, exposed standing in front of her sensei like this. She had feared a shudder, but Michelle didn't flinch.

"No," she said. "You're still Emma."

"I feel like … a monster."

"No," Michelle said. "Look at this." She gestured at Emma like she was uncovering a masterpiece. "*This* is a gift."

"Or a curse," Emma said, remembering the vivid dream from Crete. It was a *curse* by Athena that transformed the priestess. But Emma wasn't sure what she owed her own transformation to. What had caused her cells to change? "I'm still trying to figure out how this happened."

"Maybe that's not as important as what you do with it now," her sensei answered. Her eyes sparkled.

Maybe she was right. Emma couldn't control what had already happened, and while she wanted to know *how* it happened, she had choices to make *now*. Perhaps that was why she came—to decide what to do with this new thing, curse or gift.

"I need to train," Emma said. "I want to learn to control it."

Her sensei nodded. "I'll need to take a water break first." She laughed, and it sounded unexpectedly playful. When she returned her face grew solemn.

"I need to ensure you can control it too," she said. "Before we can get back to jiu jitsu."

"What do you mean?" Emma asked.

"Other martial arts focus on kicks, strikes. We can do that. But jiu jitsu is the *gentle* art. It's about contact. Close contact." Michelle took a step toward her, and Emma found herself breathless. "This is about what happens once you've collided. Once you pass the projectile weapons—pepper spray, guns," she said. *Or venom*, Emma thought.

She swallowed, baffled by how Michelle's words seemed to carry heat. There was a kind of intimidation in them, how they referenced danger, but also an unspoken tension Emma couldn't specify. Or was it something about her presence, the slightly sweet, earthen scent of her sweat that made

Emma's body flush with its newly stimulated senses? She wasn't used to standing so close to her.

Michelle took a step back, as if in response. "That's when the use of leverage, timing, angles, and an intimate understanding of anatomy come into play, to force an opponent into submission. Before we get back to that, I need you to control these abilities." She squinted at Emma. "I can't afford any broken limbs at the moment." Her calm expression broke into a smile, and Emma felt some of the tension release.

They worked into the afternoon, Emma evading Michelle's strikes as she swung the staff from different angles with impressive endurance. At first, Emma's scales appeared and disappeared, seeming to have a mind of their own.

"Good," Michelle said, her words breathy with effort. She lowered the staff. "Now change them back to skin."

"How?" Emma asked, her frustration only hardening the scales.

"Don't think about *scales* or *no scales*. It's never about the result. It's about the process. Think of *why*."

Emma nodded. It made sense in an abstract way, but the execution eluded her.

"I have a class to teach in five minutes," Michelle said. "You need to focus."

"Focus on what?" Emma's voice rose with panic.

"When you feel the attack, the urgency, they appear to protect you. It's about what you choose to pay attention to. Think about the present," her sensei said, soothingly. "Breathe. I'm not a real threat. Do you believe that? There's no danger right now."

Emma listened, closing her eyes, letting the safety of their trust calm her. It humbled her, to be taught by Michelle. Despite her relatively young age, she was a true master. She showed Emma that the art of fighting was about more than the technicalities of defense and offense. It was about mental discipline.

"Good," her sensei said, smiling when she saw Emma's skin return. "Good, Emma."

Emma took a deep breath and realized the ache from the bullet's impact the previous night was gone. She lifted her shirt and, to her amazement, found that the bruise had completely disappeared. *Healed.*

"Amazing." Michelle breathed in awe.

As Emma left, a deep sense of calm sprouted in her chest, until she checked her phone and realized school would be letting out. *Crap.* She had lost track of time. She broke into a run toward school. Ten minutes later she reached the familiar entrance to Springbrook High, jostling through the swarm of excited students that rushed from the building. She squeezed through them, looking for Jason.

She paced through the crowded hallway inside, trying to quell her urgency. She couldn't afford to break into the scales now, even if the frenzied movement felt threatening. Suddenly she heard a voice from the hallway to her right.

"Where have you been?" She turned to see his distraught face.

"Jason," she called.

"Did you miss school today?" he asked in a flat voice, looking her up and down. *I must look like a sweaty mess,* she thought, and hoped smelling like a locker room wouldn't repel him.

"Yeah, I … wasn't feeling well this morning." She stepped toward him.

"Are you okay?" he asked, his voice still hard, the safe halo they had built together now vanished.

"I'm okay now," she said.

"You never answered my calls," he said. She wanted to reach for him, nuzzle into his embrace, but his jaw hardened.

"I'm so sorry," she said. *If only I could explain everything...* "How was your game?"

"How can you even ask me that?" His rising voice had a bitter edge, causing a few students nearby to glance in their direction.

Emma flushed, her pulse rising. She looked down and took a deep breath before turning back to his gaze. "I'm sorry. I was so out of it from the fever. I wanted to be there." Her voice sounded pathetic.

He took a step toward her. "Do you even like me still?" he asked in a hushed but pressured tone.

"Jason." She whispered his name, eager to connect. "I love you." She reached for his hand, and he reluctantly let her take it.

"I have to go," he said after a moment. "I have an essay on *Metamorphoses* to write."

"I'll help," she said. "Let's go to the library."

He hesitated. "I thought you weren't feeling well."

"I'll get through it," she said. "I have work too. I'll take some ibuprofen."

He rubbed his neck, visibly agitated, then muttered, "Fine, let's go," and turned away.

They found a table in the talking section of the library's main room. A TV played in subtitled silence behind the librarian's desk. Jason turned his laptop screen to her, showing the introduction for his essay, spotted with quotations from the text. *Metamorphoses* was written in a less than accessible English style, and Emma was impressed he'd gotten through it considering he didn't love reading.

"What do you think?" he asked, but the TV behind him stole her attention. Her stomach dropped. "Emma?" She barely heard him. His hand appeared, waving in front of her face, but her eyes remained transfixed.

There, on the TV, was a news segment showing footage from the robbery. The video was blurry and from the back of the store, but she recognized it at once. There she was, her gray scales peeking out from beneath her shirt. She watched herself on the screen, like it was a dream, fascinated by her own movements. *Did I really look like that?*

"Witnesses say a woman masked by *scales* helped fend off two thieves before disappearing. They describe her movements as *snakelike*," the reporter's subtitles said. The screen broke to the criminals' mug shots then back to the newscaster.

"Police are now searching for the woman some are calling 'Serpentina' or anyone who has information about her."

Emma broke her gaze, suddenly terrified. *Police are searching.* She glanced around, but no one seemed to pay much attention to the TV segment. She looked at Jason, waiting for him to ask her to explain. It seemed obvious who the footage showed. *He must see it.*

"What's wrong?" Jason asked, his eyes wide and confused. A moment of relief passed. He didn't recognize her.

"What do you think about that?" she asked.

"About what? The news story?"

"Yea, about the woman?"

He shrugged and shook his head in annoyance. "The serpent lady? I don't know, probably someone in a costume. There are weirdos out there."

She thought at least he might recognize her clothes from the video. But maybe no one would suspect it to be her. It was too outlandish. Even she had trouble accepting the truth. But what if the video had been clearer or the other camera at the front of the store hadn't been shot by the thief … then everyone might know. The blood drained from her face. What if they checked the bag of chips she'd touched and found her fingerprints?

"You don't look so good," Jason said.

"You think she's a weirdo?" Emma asked, tensing. She pretended to be detached. She didn't even want to ask it, but she felt sensitive to his words, more vulnerable to them than to anyone else's.

He shrugged again. "She was probably in on the robbery. That's how stuff happens now."

"She was obviously trying to help," Emma jumped in defense, furrowing her brow.

"Why do you care so much?" he asked flatly.

She swallowed, not wanting to say more. She shouldn't be defending a supposed stranger. That would raise suspicion.

"I guess I think it's cool," she muttered.

She felt Jason fading away from her. She had wanted to tell him the truth, but she was testing the safety of it, and this exchange only made her recoil. Her own boyfriend didn't recognize her. How could he not?

"Your essay intro is very good," she said stiffly.

Jason reached a hand to her. Maybe he sensed the exhaustion in her voice, maybe he remembered her sick brother and felt sympathetic. Or maybe he had just missed her. He had every right to be angry. She had blown off his game, and it was important to him.

"Hey," he said, "thanks for coming with me today." The touch of his hand radiated warmth, and she smiled.

Maybe things would work out somehow. Maybe, if she could fully control the scales, she could let him close to her again.

But something pulled her emotions away, chilling his warmth. Those words, so mundane to everyone watching at the library, struck fear inside her. *The police are searching.*

10

At home, Emma pressed the blinking red light on the kitchen's landline. Between the voicemails selling auto insurance and claiming she had won a cruise to Bermuda, Emma found a message from her school counselor asking about her absence. She deleted it and went upstairs, starting to doubt how much she could get away with. But as long as she remained in her fully human form she hoped to elude her pursuers. Her pulse surged at the possibility of her fingerprints being left in that store, but she reminded herself of her unsuspecting boyfriend and her oblivious peers in the library to try to calm it.

Emma attended school the following day, grasping for a sense of routine and normality. But her body was tense as she sat through classes, nervous to face Jason or Pria. Thankfully, she didn't see them. But then she began to worry something was wrong. Were they being questioned about her? No, she decided, the stress of her situation was making her paranoid. Seniors cut class regularly, and Pria said she wanted to have fun this year. Emma kept replaying her exchange with Jason at the library, wondering if she should've said anything differently. She would normally ask Pria for her perspective, but this time she was only relieved to avoid both of them.

The moment the final bell rang, she slipped out, rushing to her martial arts gym. Despite the possibility of being hunted by authorities, a tingling of anticipation blossomed in her stomach.

"You're distracted," Michelle said, as Emma lost her footing and stumbled away from the training staff. Michelle's face was stern, but her words were more concerned than accusatory. Emma was struggling, and her scales were sluggish to appear despite the intense sparring.

"If you're not alert, you won't sense the present moment, and your scales won't appear," she said, and Emma marveled at how quickly her sensei seemed to understand the mechanics of her new defense.

But as she moved to defend against another strike, Emma's bracelet caught on the finger of her other hand. The band snapped, and beads scattered across the mat. *No.* The flush of embarrassment at not having removed it mixed with a sinking remorse at ruining Jason's gift.

Michelle lowered her staff.

"Sorry," Emma said, avoiding eye contact as she scurried about the mats to collect the beads, swearing she would fix the bracelet as soon as she got home. After placing its remnants by her water bottle, Emma sat back on her knees, dropping her arms into her lap.

"You don't have to apologize," Michelle said.

Emma nodded, embarrassed by the tears gathering behind her eyelids.

"What's wrong Emma?" her sensei asked.

"I just…" Emma faltered. "I feel like everything's falling apart," she said.

"Sometimes, when people train, their lives *are* falling apart," Michelle said in a soft but firm tone. "But the focus needed for what we do here is an escape from that. Even through the pressure, you can enjoy the fight, the energy. That's what makes people good at it. That's what makes *you* good."

Emma bit her lip, her heart lifting at the compliment. "I always liked it," she said. "The focus, the precision, and how I used to not think about any other problems when I was training. But..." She paused. "I just don't know what all this is for. I feel like I'm just getting myself into trouble with everyone."

Michelle sat, a small smile on her face. "Maybe that's the problem."

"What do you mean?"

"Would a singer still sing if she knew no one would hear her?" she asked. "I think so. I think the fuel comes from *within*." She pressed a hand over Emma's chest, and heat radiated from the spot, stimulating her energy. "People assume they're doing something for some end goal—a performance, a match, a race. But really, what they're getting from it is in the process itself. "

Emma nodded.

"You're at a time in your life when you have to choose a direction—where to go to school, what your next step is. And now you have this thrown at you. That's a lot. But you don't need to know what to do now, only *who* you want to be. Have you thought about that?"

She didn't want to be a doctor. She saw how drained her mom always looked. She wanted to have her own lab. But she didn't see how that addressed her worries. "A scientist," Emma said. "A researcher."

"No," Michelle said, and Emma looked up in surprise. "I didn't ask you *what* you wanted to be, I asked you *who*."

"Is there a difference?" she asked.

"Yes. You need to know *who* you are before finding *what* aligns with it. And *who* you are depends on your values. So tell me, what do you value?"

Emma paused, considering the difference. It seemed so simple she might've missed it, but in the question was a depth that lent her clarity.

"Life," Emma said. "I value life … and justice." She thought about the injustices that fueled her, the kidnapping of her childhood friend, even the rape of the woman she had never met.

"So that's your answer," Michelle said. "You might not know what these new abilities will be used for yet. But if you act in accordance with who you are, then that will naturally follow. And one day you'll find the right way to use them. You're already doing that."

"How?" Emma asked.

"I don't know if you realize how deadly you are," she said, her tone rising in an almost playful way. "Emma, you're a *weapon*." Her face grew serious. "But you're not using this to hurt people or get ahead. You're being responsible, honing them, making sure they don't hurt the wrong person. You're living justly already."

Emma smiled. Michelle sighed, then paced toward the back of the room where she lowered the training staff against the wall. Emma shifted, thinking it was her cue for dismissal, but when Michelle turned she gestured for her to rise.

"Come on," she said. "I think it's time for our first roll."

"You mean," Emma started, surprised. "You and me? On the mat?"

"Yes," Michelle said, with a chuckle.

"Are you sure? I mean, it's contact. Aren't you worried—"

"No," Michelle said, cutting her off in that same firm, reassuring tone. "I trust you. And you should trust yourself."

That night, when Emma was back home and lying in bed, her stomach stirred with a kind of peaceful exhilaration as she recalled her training with Michelle. Finally, she was able to train jiu jitsu again, and her fear of losing control had been quelled. Emma had approached Michelle timidly at first, unsure exactly why she hesitated. Of course, there was the obvious reason, that she might harm her sensei. But Michelle's own calm confidence lent itself to Emma, and she felt secure. There was also intimidation at facing someone so advanced in skill, someone Emma regarded so highly. Emma recalled the feeling of Michelle's toned, solid body pressed into hers and the way her heat radiated through her as they rolled over the mats. She closed her eyes, immersed in the memory of Michelle's scent as sweat broke on her moving body. It wasn't the sour, musty odor Emma was used to from her opponents at the gym, but instead, a rich, earthy scent with traces of spice that allured her.

Emma realized her heart was beating fast. Her thoughts budded with a sudden curiosity. She wanted to know Michelle's secrets. How did she get so wise and skilled at such a young age? Though their talks had focused on Emma, she was eager to turn it on Michelle. She was deep in thought when her phone screen lit up, and she glanced at it to find a text from Jason.

"Goodnight <3," it read.

Emma smiled, but it didn't reach her eyes.

"Goodnight … see you tomorrow," she typed, unsure if she actually would.

Emma's eyes wandered to the disjointed pieces of the bracelet Jason had given her, the speckled green beads now clustered on her desk. She would have to find a string to rebead them tomorrow. Her jiu jitsu training had momentarily allowed her to escape the thought of the many problems that now flooded back. There was the mounting tension and distance between her and Jason and Pria. And beneath it all, the root cause. Her sensei seemed to fully accept Emma's changes without questioning how it all happened. But that question was never far from

Emma's mind. A return to the lab was inevitable, and this time, she would expect Dr. Belken to have seen her blood.

The next morning Emma was awake early, preparing for her next exchange with Dr. Belken. Bolstered by the training sessions with her sensei, she felt a sliver of comfort as she prepared for school, dressing in shorts and a fitted T-shirt, less afraid of showing skin. The scales didn't feel so random and threatening, and she decided things could at least appear normal, even if they weren't.

Emma was walking through the hallway to her first period class when an announcement called all students to the auditorium for an emergency assembly. Her sense of calm erupted to panic, and she began to sweat. *What if this is about me? Or the robbery?* Her heart pounded. *Maybe the shorts were a bad idea...* Emma pulled a sweatshirt out of her bag.

Just then, she heard a familiar laugh down the hallway. From around the corner, Pria emerged with two girls. One of them was Rachel, arguably the most popular girl in high school, who wore polished outfits and had perfectly straightened hair every day. Today she clutched a handbag that even Emma could recognize the Chanel logo on, and she knew it wasn't a knock off. Rachel giggled at something Pria said, her golden charm bracelets dangling as she flipped her hair, and Emma felt smaller, suddenly self-conscious of her dirty sneakers.

When Pria spotted Emma she rushed over.

"Emma!" she called. "I was looking for you at the game the other night." The soccer game already seemed such a long time ago, but the mention of it made Emma's stomach coil. "Jason said you were sick." Emma thought she sensed something artificial in Pria's voice, like she was performing. In the corner of her eye she watched Rachel whisper something to her other friend and they walked down the hallway.

"You're friends with Rachel?" Emma asked, hoping not to sound the way she felt—a mixture of envy and resentment. Didn't Pria remember how Rachel had been the head of a bullying squad freshman year, back when Pria wore thick glasses and didn't have her brows threaded into perfect arches? Emma never forgot the look on Pria's face when they overheard those girls in the next row of the locker room, giggling that they smelled curry. Maybe Rachel was pretending to forget that too or pretending Pria was a different person from that freshman who went by Priyanka and hadn't yet begun applying winged eyeliner like a daily mask.

"Not really, we were just talking about shoes … stupid." Pria waved a hand. "Aren't you hot?"

"What?"

"You're wearing long sleeves, and it's like eighty-five in here."

Emma *was* starting to sweat, but maybe more from anxiety than the heat. "I have to do laundry," she said, forcing a laugh.

"Hey, are you okay?" Pria asked. "You look tired. I'm not trying to be mean. Just, I know you have a lot going on. But school just started, you shouldn't be too overworked." The question felt invasive, but Pria wasn't done. "How are things with your brother?"

"He's … stable." Emma nearly faltered. "I just, I'm not feeling so good. I've had some fevers at night." She wasn't sure if that was exactly true, but she had woken up sweating.

"Do you think it's still from that antivenom?" Pria asked, lowering her voice and leaning toward her.

Emma's skin began to itch as panic simmered. Part of her wished to share the new developments with Pria. But it didn't feel right, especially not here, with all her peers around. There *was* an aspect she could talk about though. "No," she said. "But I got such a weird feeling at the lab the other day, from Dr. Belken."

She wanted to say more, but Pria was already scouting the hallway. She tossed her hair back, reminiscent of Rachel's movement. Emma cringed.

"It doesn't surprise me," Pria said quickly. "He's such a weirdo. Here, let's sit together at this assembly."

Pria wrapped her arm around Emma's as they walked. She had never done that before, and somehow the closeness felt shallow. Pria found the seat next to Rachel and her friend, and Emma stiffened as they sat, aware the girls disapproved of her, or was that just in her head? Was she just tense because she dreaded what the assembly might be? She scanned the room for Jason but couldn't find him.

When everyone was settled in their seats, the principal approached his microphone. Emma's heart pounded so violently she was certain others could hear it.

"Thank you all for joining me on such late notice. Thank you to all the teachers who rearranged their lessons around this meeting."

There was silence. Emma thought she might faint from the suspense, or was it from the effort it took to suppress her scales from erupting? She could barely breathe.

"A lot of you have been talking about something recently, and I think it would be best for us to address it here."

Emma tightened her grip on the armrest. It didn't matter what Rachel thought of her anymore. Soon everyone might be scrutinizing her.

"There's been some increase in crime in our area," he continued. The back of Emma's neck began to itch. *The robbery… What if the police want help finding me? They were looking…*

"Now the kidnappings have affected a student's family from this high school," he said. Emma blinked. *Kidnappings?* She vaguely recalled her mom mentioning increased crime, but Emma had been more consumed with hiding the reaction on her skin to look into it.

"Over the past month," he continued, "at least a half dozen young girls have been kidnapped. The FBI has become involved, as well as local police, but not one has been found. Most have been taken from a local shelter and group home. But now, a younger sibling of a classmate here at this high school is missing."

Emma was numb, her body motionless with shock. Then her fingertips and toes began to tingle as if blood was rushing back into them. She was suddenly embarrassed that she had been so worried about herself. This was more serious.

The principal went on to describe efforts being taken to find the girls and recover them. Emma barely heard them. A scene seemed to unfurl before her eyes, of the street she was walking home on with her childhood friend, Amy. Only Amy wasn't there. She had been taken, and Emma, after screaming and running for help, had returned to the scene with a neighbor, who stood in the background calling the police. She had hoped it was a nightmare, that she would return and Amy would be there. But there was nothing, just the pet cage she dropped on the ground. Emma frantically searched for the hermit crab, as if finding it would solve something, but it was gone.

Emma swallowed, and a pit swelled in her throat. She wondered what Amy would've looked like now and what they would have done together. Maybe Emma could've shared her secrets with her.

The principal finished by asking the students to remain alert and help the police in any investigation. The room was quiet as students filed out. Pria didn't reach for Emma's arm again. She looked pale, and Emma smelled her worry, damp and sulfuric. Pria had a younger sister. Only young girls were disappearing, not boys. Emma shuddered at what that might mean.

11

Emma jumped from her chair as the final class bell rang. There was a somber tone hanging about the school, and Emma pushed through the weight of it as she set on catching Dr. Belken before he left the lab. When she passed the soccer fields, she saw Jason warming up for practice and slowed, lingering there a moment. He was an alluring sight, his wavy hair jostling and his muscles rippling as he strode. She waved, tense at how conspicuous it made her, but when he paused to wink back it livened her steps.

The packed train ride seemed to last an eternity. When she finally arrived, Emma nearly burst into Dr. Belken's office. But she took a moment to calm her breath, wiping the sweat from her face. Then she knocked on the door.

"Dr. Belken?"

He was hunched over his desk behind a sloppy mound of papers.

"Have you had a chance to look at my samples?"

"What samples?" he asked.

She squinted, her eyes scanning his room. She didn't see her test tubes, but she knew he had them. That same, familiar scent of her blood filled the air.

As if registering her suspicion, he responded. "Oh, you mean your blood."

"Yes," she said, trying not to sound too impatient. "Did you find anything in them?" she asked. She stared at him, but his face remained flat and unrevealing.

"I haven't had a chance to look at them yet. I'm sorry." He motioned to the piles of papers on his desk. "Grant writing is killing me."

She hadn't expected an excuse and didn't believe him.

"Is there something I should be looking for in them?" His eyes glinted the way they had when she found the snake on Crete—like an owl's. He studied her closely, and she looked away, as if afraid he could see the truth behind her questions.

"It sounds like you've been looking into them quite a bit," he said.

"No, I haven't," Emma answered quickly. "I don't know the right techniques to."

He nodded, seemingly satisfied by that answer. She wondered if he suspected she had examined her blood already and that this exchange was merely to test his honesty. He so seamlessly slithered out of it. She had expected to feel more in control, with the upper hand. But he turned the questions on *her*.

"Is there anything new you'd like to tell me?" he asked. "Any new *symptoms?*"

She shook her head, thinking not only about the scales but how quickly her bruise had disappeared. The potential healing properties alone were worth investigating. She could only imagine what it might mean.

"Are there any specific symptoms you're looking for?" she asked, determined to beat his game. If he wouldn't offer any information, neither would she.

He shook his head.

He knows. The thought crept into her mind, but she wanted to believe otherwise. She wondered if he had seen her on the news. He had a radar for anything associated with snakes after all. Maybe she should tell him the full truth, to ensure he was on her side. But an uneasy sense told her no. She didn't feel safe with him.

"I'd like to take a look at the antivenom you injected me with on Crete," Emma said, emboldened. She had an impulse to say more but held back. She wanted to put the pressure on him.

"I can understand that," he said thoughtfully. "But I don't have it anymore. The last of the samples were left in the hospital on Crete."

How convenient, Emma thought, but instead she said, "I figured that as a scientist you'd be dying to assess the compounds that could've caused a reaction that almost killed me." She paused. "I mean, if you're not interested in that I'm sure *someone else* would be."

He raised his brows. She hadn't planned on threatening him, but as the words left her mouth, a fleeting sense of power swelled. She could've said the *police* would be interested in it. But she wasn't sure she wanted to entangle herself in that now.

"I thought we went over this," he said. "The doctors and I studied the antivenom and didn't find anything unusual. The reaction was more specific to your body, so I think that's where we need to look."

We. The word infuriated her. It was *her* body, and she didn't want him analyzing it.

She wanted to demand her samples back from him but wasn't ready to start an outright battle. It was simmering beneath the surface, and if she could let it stay there just a bit longer, she might make more progress. She needed this lab to run experiments of her own.

She nodded and retreated to her lab bench where she jotted an outline in her notebook. She had a cage of mice with lymphoma and several formulations of disintegrin venom proteins ready to be tested for their potential healing properties.

She was going to add a treatment. Her own blood. She didn't know which proteins to isolate. She had never worked with human blood. But she decided she could start more broadly, using all of it. Of course, there was a risk of serum sickness or a reaction due to the incompatibility of her own blood with the blood of the mouse. But she needed a place to start, and without knowing more advanced isolation techniques, this seemed worth a try. She pricked her finger with a needle. She was committed to finding answers now. And no one was going to give them to her.

Emma left the lab with the levity of hope. She had separated the mice into different treatment groups, with one mouse receiving her blood. She watched the creature for at least an hour after administering it, afraid to see signs of a reaction. The mouse grew still, sitting near the edge of the cage and not scurrying to lick water from the bottle or feed on pellets. But it appeared stable at least, and the signs of lethargy could be from the lymphoma menacing its tiny body.

Though drained, Emma didn't go directly home. She reread a text from her mom, saying her brother had needed a transfusion that day. Emma strode through the halls of the hospital to Danny's room. She found him sleeping in the sunlight from his window. She settled quietly next to him and watched his chest rise and fall with breath. He looked so … innocent. Hot tears formed in her eyes.

"We'll play outside again," she whispered. "When you're feeling better we can play catch if you want." Emma used to be annoyed when Danny insisted she play with him. Now, she would give anything to toss a ball back and forth. She studied his face, the sunlight glowing off his pale, nearly translucent skin. Though asleep, his lashless eyes still looked tired. "It's lonely without you." She looked into her lap as a tear dropped onto her hand. "Maybe you would understand … something's happening to me. Ever since I saw that snake."

She looked up and was surprised to find Danny's eyes flickering open. Emma quickly dabbed her tears with the back of her fingers.

"Is that why your skin was changing colors?" he asked.

She paused, awed by his question. He was as observant as ever, despite his illness. And he asked it so innocently, as if, even if it were true, it was nothing to be shocked over. To him, fairy tales still mixed with reality and more things were possible.

"Yes," Emma said. "I think so." She warmed with relief, lighter with the confession, even though she made it knowing he would grow up to no longer believe it. She stopped herself, and the breath grew heavy in her chest. He might never grow up.

"Are you here because you're afraid I'll get taken too?" Danny asked suddenly. His voice was weak but laced with worry.

"What do you mean?" Emma reached for his hand.

"I heard the nurses talking about some kids getting kidnapped." Emma's pulse rose with anger that the hospital staff wouldn't keep that news away from children.

She shook her head. "No one can steal you." She squeezed his hand. "I won't let them."

"Would you fight them with your karate?"

She smiled. He never could remember it was jiu jitsu.

"Yes, they know better than to come for you," she said, not really knowing who "they" were and feeling a sense of unease she wished to shelter him from.

"I wish I was like you," he said.

"Why?" she asked, but her heart sank. Of course, any child would wish to be someone else if he was tethered to a hospital bed to stay alive.

"Because, I want to fight the bad guys. I don't want to stay in bed all day."

Emma swallowed, trying to quell her tears from falling in front of him.

"They brought in a therapy dog today," he said, and she brightened at his change of subject. "During the Halloween parade."

"They had a parade?" she asked.

"The doctors wore costumes and marched around the hallways with the kids," he said. "Well, everyone who can get out of bed."

Emma felt a pang in her stomach. "Did the dog wear a costume too?" she asked, forcing a smile.

"He was a dinosaur. But he didn't look very fun. His tail wasn't wagging. Maybe next time they'll bring a snake."

Emma raised her brows. "A therapy snake?"

He nodded. "You can bring one from your lab."

She smiled. "We'll see."

"They asked me about you," Danny said quietly.

Emma furrowed her brows. "What? Who?"

"The therapy dog people. After the parade passed. They came into my room to bring candy. And they asked me about you." Emma furrowed her brows. "I showed them the pictures we drew together, the one you colored of that snake. And they showed me a picture from a store and asked if it was you."

Emma's heart jolted and chills spread over her body.

"What?" She bolted upright, eyes wide.

He nodded. "I told them that looks like my sister, and if she fought the bad guys, it's definitely her."

Emma was trembling now. "What else did you tell them?" She leaned across the bed toward him. "Who were they?"

She saw panic on her brother's face, then it scrunched up and he began to cry.

"Don't be mad," he said. "They seemed nice."

Emma took a breath, trying to let her panic defuse. She grabbed his hand. "Oh no … don't cry. I'm sorry I got upset. It's okay." She rubbed his arm until his sniffles subsided. "I'm sorry."

Danny nodded and took a quivering breath. Then he smiled again.

"Listen," Emma said, as gently as she could. "No strangers should be talking to you."

"I know, but they were the therapy people. They had badges."

Emma nodded. Her neck and back were itching, and she feared any moment she might explode into scales.

"I know, Danny. But grown-ups can only talk to you if Mommy or Daddy are here or one of the nurses. Have you ever seen these people before?"

Danny shook his head. "Are you worried they're bad people?"

Emma didn't want to scare him, but at the same time, she was terrified. Could these be undercover cops? Or part of the FBI investigation? Was it possible they were trying to connect her to the kidnappings? She couldn't be sure, but she had a sense they were dangerous, and her senses were especially accurate these days.

Her pulse throbbed in her neck. It was an unethical method, she thought, targeting a sick child in a hospital for information. Maybe they were only curious reporters, she thought, but no, they had to have done some research to target Danny specifically. Maybe she could leave a recording device in his room in case they came back...

"We have to be extra careful now," Emma said. "If anyone asks you about me again, you can't tell them anything about that snake. And if anyone asks you if that's me in the video, don't say that it's your sister. Okay?"

Danny nodded. "Is it a secret?"

"A secret," Emma repeated. "If anyone tries to talk to you again like that, call the nurse, then call Mommy or Daddy. Okay?"

He nodded. "You're scaring me though. They were nice, they gave me more candy, the same type you got me." He pointed.

Emma froze, afraid to look. Spattered across his wooden table glinted the familiar shiny wrappers of the candy, the same kind she'd brought from Greece. Her mouth went dry. They had taken the time to buy that exact flavor, a specialty of Crete. Emma swallowed. There was no other explanation. It's not like Danny had met them before and they cared about the candy he liked. *No.* This was a message. But how far back had they gone? *How long have they been tracking me?*

She shivered, and scales prickled over her lower back. She took a breath, trying to quell them from spreading visibly. Someone was watching her, tracing her steps back…

Emma grabbed the candies from the table.

"Hey!" Danny said.

"I'm going to get you different candy, okay? I don't think you can take any from strangers."

"Okay," he said, and the disappointment in his voice pained her. He shouldn't be worried about anything in the world. He was a little boy who should care about friends and getting into trouble. Now *she* was weighing on him too, maybe even endangering him.

The scales crept farther up her neck, and she had to avoid hugging him as she left. Anger and fear pulsed through her. She wanted to stop, to demand information about the visitors from the nurses, but if she lingered a minute longer she might not be able to contain the scales. She paced toward the stairwell, bumping into a nursing cart and knocking over a clipboard as she rushed.

Overhead, another code gray on the medical unit was called over the loudspeaker. The hospital wasn't feeling like the safe place it should. But as she stepped out onto the street, she realized it wasn't just the hospital that felt unsafe. It was her entire world. The sun beat bright and relentless on her back and the scales magnified the heat. She felt the eyes of a predator on her, hunting her, with each step.

12

"Since when do you fail things?" she heard as she entered the kitchen. She was surprised to find her mother standing by the kitchen table. Maybe she had a rare day off or had worked the night shift. Her mom did look exhausted, with dark circles lining her hazel eyes.

"Your guidance counselor called today to say you've been failing social studies and missing classes. She asked me what's going on. I'd like to know the same thing."

Emma sighed. This was the last thing she needed. School felt like an echo of the stressor it once was. Grades and college mattered, but there were more immediate problems to solve.

"Is there something you want to share?"

Emma looked at the floor. She had coaxed her scales away as she walked home, but her frustration was mounting since her visit to the hospital.

"It was embarrassing," her mom said. "I know it's your senior year, but your grades still matter. Don't throw away all your hard work. Do you not care?" Her mother took a step closer. "Is it this Jason guy? Are you getting distracted? Or do I have to worry about drugs—"

"No, Mom. It's not that," Emma interrupted. "Maybe you were embarrassed because you're never here to know what's going on." She felt the words gather like venom before they spurted out, then regretted them.

Her mom pursed her lips.

"Sorry," Emma said. "I was just visiting Danny."

Her mom nodded, her face softening a bit. "I know it's a lot to handle. But until now, you *were* handling it. So I'm only wondering if there's something else."

Of course there was something else, and that something was taking over everything. She tensed, wanting to evade the topic. "I've been working at the lab a lot," Emma said.

Her mom inhaled sharply. "Is that really worth your time?"

"Maybe it'll help me get into Columbia," Emma said.

"Not if you fail classes. If there's another failure, I'm going to tell *Dr.* Belken that you're not working there anymore."

There was no use in arguing. Emma had to go back to the lab. It was her only chance to understand what was happening. Her stress was at the point of bursting, and the swarm of uncertainties stifled her. Who had questioned Danny? Were there cops studying the video of the robbery at that very moment? Emma only nodded, appeasing her mom before going upstairs.

When Jason's text came a few minutes later, asking to come over, Emma felt relieved to use the excuse of her failed class to be alone. She was too on edge, unsure if she could contain the scales around him.

"I have to study or I'm grounded," she messaged.

"I can't believe it, you never fail anything," he answered. She didn't respond. A minute later she saw him typing. It stopped. Then it started again.

"We have to plan our costumes for the Halloween party this weekend," he texted.

Emma sighed. "I'll have to ask my mom," she texted back, with a frowning face, and immediately felt sorry. They had once gushed about dressing up as Lola and Bugs Bunny from *Space Jam*, but Emma now dreaded the idea. Her parents wouldn't be home to enforce it, but she could still use the punishment as an excuse. What else could she tell him? She was forming her own plan for the weekend and was somewhat relieved to have an excuse that wouldn't hurt him. Still, her heart sank at the idea of missing him, and for a moment she resented these changes for taking over her life.

Emma barely slept. Her energy buzzed like a frantic fly. The night air outside carried the slightest chill, and she turned the heat on, which only stimulated her further.

She stared into the darkness, sensing the world around her. She could pinpoint each sound and practiced distinguishing them—footsteps on the sidewalk, the creaking branches on the maple tree, even a moth flapping by the window. It was as if she were waiting for something, anticipating it every second.

She thought of the snake cells in her blood and wanted to check them again. Maybe they had multiplied. She closed her eyes, but sleep felt a world away. She recalled the dreams on Crete, how the beautiful woman's golden skin transformed into scales. Then it happened to Emma. What was next? She had read the myth, read how Medusa had been hunted as a monster. Was this her fate now too?

I'm not the myth. That was a tale of gods and goddesses. *Her* reaction was from antivenom. That's what she needed to focus on. Her mind went back to the assembly then, to the children who had been kidnapped. And she thought of Danny, who, in his own way, was being targeted because of her. She felt a duty then, to protect.

Could she help get the kidnapped girls back? Help in the same way she helped foil the robbery? She thought of what had happened after that night, about the news segment and the threat of being discovered, of being misunderstood as a monster and losing her freedom.

But she also remembered Amy, kidnapped when they were just children. Maybe this was the chance she was waiting for to strike back, but she didn't know how. She didn't even know how to protect herself or what was coming.

Emma was at the lab by seven a.m. that Saturday morning, more alert than ever after her sleepless night. She stared in disbelief at the cages above her bench. She had done these experiments multiple times. The mice *always* died as the end stages of lymphoma took hold. All of them. But this time, one mouse was very much alive.

Her mind raced. This was … a *miracle*. To blind herself from bias in the experiment, she had marked the mice with a paint only visible under a UV light to identify which treatment they had received. She couldn't tell which one this mouse had, but already, her mind was jumping to the answer. *It had to be…*

She tried to hold back. *No, maybe another treatment had worked at last.* But as she placed the UV light over the mouse, its fur illuminated to reveal the mark. She held her breath.

It was the mouse treated with her own blood.

Had she made an error in infecting the mouse? Or had it truly survived this cancer? She was deep in thought when the mouse flexed and bit her finger. It didn't break her skin, but it startled her into dropping him. The mouse scurried away. As she snatched it by the tail, he squeaked and thrashed at her hand before she plopped him in the cage.

Her heart was a flurry of excitement. She would need to take blood samples from that mouse, however cranky he was. If this had truly cured him, it was groundbreaking. Of course, she would need to go over her methods with a finer touch. She had used such basic techniques. She could purify, amplify the proteins in her blood, but she would need more equipment … and instruction.

"Dr. Belken?" She knocked on his door. When he didn't answer she peeked inside and saw him in the back room behind his office. She opened the door. He was so engrossed in work that when he saw her, he started.

"Emma?" he said. Then he darted about the room as if looking for something. "What are you doing here?" He hurriedly pushed a Styrofoam box aside.

What are you hiding? She smelled her blood around them, earthy and sweet, and furrowed her brow, realizing her silence pressured him. She liked that. "I think I found something important," she said slowly.

"Really? What is it?" His demeanor calmed, as if to match hers, and he sat down.

She paused, studying his face. Then she told him about the mouse.

"You mean you used your own sample?" he asked. His voice was unusually stern. "You didn't mention this to me once."

She had expected him to be at least a little enthusiastic, not immediately reprimanding. After all, this was the professor who had followed her into the woods at the mention of an unidentified snake, and the same one who had injected himself with snake venom multiple times.

"It was just an unofficial experiment," she said, her voice faltering now, wondering if it was a mistake to tell him. But she needed his help to continue this research. She didn't know the techniques on her own.

"That's not how things work around here," he said. "*I* run this lab. You need my approval for anything done here. To use human samples at all requires IRB approval, regardless if they're yours or not. We definitely can't publish anything like this."

She hadn't thought about publishing it yet. She was still trying to understand how it happened.

"Aren't you at least a little interested in the result?" she asked, baffled and angry. Of course, he was right, technically. She didn't own any part of this lab. But she did own her blood, and that's what she had been testing. Since when was he so set on following rules?

"Dr. Belken, this could be something huge. I need help isolating the molecule responsible. This could be what you've—"

"Emma, it was one mouse," he interrupted. "It would need to be replicated many times to prove anything, and I can't let you do that without approval."

"Well, maybe we need to pursue a bigger study then." As she said it, his eyes flickered to the side, as if there were something in that room her words made him think of. "Or are you afraid of something?" she asked, anger flaring her nostrils.

In a fleeting second his eyes were back on her. "Is there something I should be afraid of?" he asked, as if turning her words into a threat.

"Well," she said, her heat rising. "I find it funny how you seem so concerned about me using my own samples when you still have mine. Tell me, have you looked at them?"

He paused for a moment, and she sensed his conflicted mind, his suppressed panic. It smelled of sulfur and rot.

"No," he said, suddenly sounding too easy going. "I haven't. But you bring up a good point," he said. "Why don't we do everything right? I'll help get the process going for permission to use your samples for study. Why don't you start writing the proposal?"

Her eyes narrowed. It was a kind of compromise, but was it genuine? He had dismissed her discovery, and that wasn't like him. It was possible he didn't believe it. She could scarcely believe it herself. But there was something else that unsettled her. The foul stench of his anxiety still lingered, layered over the sweeter smell of her blood that hung over their exchange like an unfinished battle.

She waited a moment, compelled to remind him that he couldn't do anything with her samples without her consent, but that would show her suspicion. She walked away, wondering if it wasn't that he didn't believe her, but rather that he did, and resented her for discovering it. Of course, that was a leap. It was only one mouse. It could have been a variant. Or maybe it was cured for now but would die soon after. Yet something inside her told her not to give up on this. This was significant, even if her mentor wouldn't admit it.

The twenty-minute train ride was a blur as her mind raced through possibilities. Imagine if her blood could *cure*? She remembered her bruise healing in less than a day, the pain from the bullet fading. This was a molecule in *her blood.* If she shared this, it would grab attention. People would want to know everything. She thought about Dr. Belken, working to advance science and gain respect in that community. Would he protect her identity in this pursuit? There was still a chance, she thought, if she played this right, that he would be a needed ally.

She rushed toward her house from the train station, eager to plan her next step. But her legs slowed as she neared the final street corner. She sensed tension, like a pool of rancid, stagnant water blocking her path. The air condensed and her stomach coiled. She paused. If something dangerous was near her home, she needed to be there to protect against it.

Emma ran from around the corner then halted at the sight before her—two police cars parked outside her house.

13

Emma stared as an officer got out of the car, looking straight at her. It was too late to run. She tensed as he walked toward her, his steps rattling her bones, and she focused to coax her scales from erupting.

"My name's Officer Brian," the tall, slightly chubby brown-haired officer said. "You're going to have to come with us."

"Why?" Emma asked, trying to sound innocent, but she feared it made her sound anything but.

"We can discuss it more at the station," he said. He stood with his chest puffed out, a hand casually grazing the weapons of his belt. Emma's nervousness was fading into anger. She had done nothing wrong. She shouldn't be cowering, even if they were trying to intimidate her.

"I have to tell my parents," she said, looking for an excuse not to go with them. If this wasn't exactly an arrest, did she have to go with them at all?

"You can call them from our office," he said. "After we ask you some questions."

Was this even legal? She wasn't sure. But she knew a conflict with the police was the last thing she needed. She walked toward the car, the officer trailing her. Her skin bristled at the vibration of his steps, his position a threatening reminder that this did not feel voluntary. She eyed the vacant periphery, sensing the heat of neighbors witnessing the scene from their windows. She crouched into the backseat of the car.

During the silent car ride, she sat rigidly, imagining ways to fight or escape. But would it be an escape if they hadn't cuffed or arrested her? They arrived at the station, and her mind churned with possible answers for what they might ask. They walked into the headquarters, with one officer in front of her and the other hovering behind, close enough for their heat to stifle her or for them to grab her if she ran. A man at the front desk nodded, glancing over Emma as they walked by. No photo, no body search. No fingerprints. At least not yet, she thought. They walked through an open space checkered with cubicles, where people were filing papers or engrossed in cases. They turned a corner and Emma held her breath, afraid of finding an interrogation room, but instead, Officer Brian opened the door to an office with a wooden desk, computer, and simple chairs.

He gestured to one of them, and she sat across from him. The second officer closed the door, and Emma tensed as he stood between her and the exit. Instinctively, Emma searched the walls, and her pulse sped as she noticed there were no windows.

"I don't think I can answer any questions without my parents present," Emma said.

"You're eighteen. We don't need them," Officer Brian said.

"But you can't hold me here. I haven't done anything."

"*That* I can't be sure of," he said, without arguing her word choice. Did that mean they *were* holding her? "But I thought you might want to help us."

"How?" she asked faintly.

"Tell me, where were you the night of September twenty-seventh?" he asked.

She shook her head, her insides shaking. "I don't know. Can I see a calendar?" She suspected what night they were asking about. She needed to stall to figure out a response. He showed her a calendar on his phone. She nodded, hoping to look casual.

"Oh," she said. "I think I was at the research lab in Columbia."

As much honesty as possible is probably— Without warning, he reached into a drawer and plopped several digital prints onto the desk in front of her. She tensed, afraid to look down. But she knew what they were. Snapshots from the convenience store. He pointed.

"Do these look familiar?" he asked.

She squinted at them, the skin on her back starting to itch.

"I think I saw this on the news," she offered. "But I'm not sure. These look like any robbery." Her voice sounded too stiff. He seemed to smirk, and she realized Officer Brian might not be that nice.

"It's interesting," he said, "that you would compare it to other robberies. Because there was something different about this one," he said. "Do you know what that is?"

Emma stared at him then shook her head.

"This man," he said and pointed to one of the thieves, "went blind afterward. The hospital determined it was venom that hit his eyes."

Dread seeped through her veins. *They must know.* She swallowed, grasping for the appropriate response of someone who didn't know the story. But she didn't just *know* the story, she'd *lived* it.

Emma raised her brows in feigned surprise. "Wow," she said. "Where did the venom come from?"

He studied her face, and a familiar sensation prickled the base of her neck as scales threatened to form. She took a deep breath, halting them. Scales were the precise evidence they were looking for.

"Is there a reason you're asking *me*?" she said. "Why would I know more about this than anyone else?"

He smirked. "Obviously, we have a reason."

Emma's heart thundered. Did someone report her or see her that night?

She sensed subtle vibrations through the floor, intensifying as she brought her attention there, until she flinched, recognizing gunshots.

"Is something wrong?" Officer Brian asked with mock concern. The shots came again, controlled, practiced. *A shooting range,* she realized. *In the precinct's basement.* But she knew she shouldn't be able to hear it. She needed to hide her powers, now more than ever. She brought her focus back to the room.

"I just don't know what this has to do with me," Emma said flatly, but her mind darkened at the memory of Jason's reaction to this crime on the news. *She was probably in on it,* he had said.

"The pictures from the back camera seem to show the venom shooting from this girl." Officer Brian tapped a thick finger on the image, leaving a greasy spot. "But we haven't been able to find her." His gaze was so intense she couldn't meet it. When he said *her,* he meant Emma.

Finally she faced him. "Why do you care so much about finding her? She's not the thief, is she? Didn't she save the people there from armed robbers?"

"Or maybe she's another criminal." The officer raised his brows. "Who knows." He leaned closer and lowered his voice. "Aren't you scared?" he whispered. "There are children being kidnapped. And now, some strange thing out there, spitting venom into people's eyes to blind them?"

Emma stared back, inclined to meet his threat. The tension in the air was palpable, metallic, like licking the edge of a battery. This was a test— she wasn't sure of what, but she knew she didn't want to appear weak. She gave a slight, slow nod and said, "If I were *you,* I'd be terrified."

She watched for her words to strike, waited for a rebuttal, but his face remained passive, reminiscent of her professor's. Then he smirked, and she knew he suspected who she was. Why else would they be interviewing her, here, when that crime happened in the city? She held her breath, bracing herself to be fingerprinted. That would prove everything, wouldn't it? But something seemed to hold them back from a formal accusation. She wasn't sure what they needed but was determined not to give it to them.

She reminded herself that if he was a police officer, he was meant to protect her, her family and community. They should be on the same side. But that wasn't the approach he was taking. He felt like an enemy. She considered telling them about the incident with her brother, if only to gauge their reaction and determine if they had orchestrated it or not. But they might also play it against her. Giving a child candy wasn't a real threat. What was she afraid of? An investigation into it might only reveal herself.

"As we try to find the source of this venom," he said, "we would appreciate full cooperation."

"Have I not been cooperative?" Emma asked. "My real concern is these kidnappings," she said. "Have any of the girls been found?"

He raised his brows. "I'm sorry, but that's classified. It's interesting you're so curious about the case though." His eyes gleamed.

"You find it unusual that I care about children disappearing?" If he wanted to argue that point, she could bring up her childhood friend or the fact that her current best friend, Pria, had a younger sister to worry about. But Emma stopped herself. She didn't need justification.

"Or maybe it's the thought of us discovering the truth that has you worried," he said.

She nearly laughed. "I don't need to defend myself for caring about innocent children, as a citizen, or as a human being. *Your* defensiveness might be the true cause of concern here." She clenched her jaw. He sat back in his chair as if amused by himself. His casual air surrounding such a horrific crime uneased her.

Did he have any real power to keep her there? He hadn't arrested her, she thought. It was time to test it.

She stood, and he only eyed her. She paused beside the officer standing near the doorway. His jaw was tight, as if braced to retaliate. But he didn't move. She walked to the door, sure to let her hair drape over her neck to block any surfaced scales. She turned the handle. Unlocked. She wasn't sure what she would've done if it wasn't.

She glanced back and nodded slightly.

"Thank you, Emma, for your help," Officer Brian said, then added, "I'll see you again soon."

She stiffened at yet another threat but tried to appear unbothered.

"I'd be happy to help more in the future," she said, and took one last look at him before walking out the door. He let her go. For now.

As she strode back through the office space, she noticed an open file atop an unmanned desk, with a large photo of a building on full display. She paused, angling to study it. It was vaguely familiar, but she couldn't place it. Footsteps approaching from the bathroom interrupted her and she turned, quickly pacing out of the station.

"The neighbors said they saw you get into a cop car," her mom said when she got home. She was standing near the doorway in blue scrubs, her lean arms folded over her chest.

Geez, Emma thought, maybe it was the neighbors she should be most worried about.

"Yeah, they wanted to ask me some questions." Emma tried to appear casual.

"About what!?" Her mom's forehead creased, and her cheeks reddened.

"They were nice," she lied. "They wanted to know if I had information about the robbery that happened near my lab." She forced a shrug. "You know, that one where the woman in snake skins stopped the robbers? They're calling her Serpentina." She inflected her tone in an attempt to make it sound outlandish.

Her mom shook her head. "I don't know about all that snake stuff. But they can't just take you. Unless you're under arrest— Wait, did they actually arrest you?"

"No," Emma said. "It was voluntary. They were looking for information."

"Still," her mom said, "what kind of tactics are these? Taking you off the street with them! Are they trying to scare us?"

Inside Emma felt a sense of relief. For once, her mom seemed to be standing up for her, but voicing her agreement would only fuel her mom's agitation. "I'm fine, really," Emma said, but her mom mumbled about filing a complaint. Emma barely heard as she walked upstairs, trying to make sense of it all. Maybe these cops were the ones who visited Danny, but something didn't make sense. The cops wouldn't have left Greek candies. That felt too ... psychological. Was it the FBI? She felt a bigger threat looming but couldn't pinpoint it.

Someone was watching her. She glanced out her window but saw only the leaves of the maple tree wafting outside, fiery red against an empty sidewalk. The streets would soon be full of kids in costumes, ready to trick-or-treat. She closed the blinds. Her mind went back to her conversation with Dr. Belken. If the police were investigating her and the snake venom, their search would likely end up in his lab. Her heart stopped.

Her blood samples.

If someone got hold of them, they would see what she was. *No.* What if they deemed her unhuman, took away her rights? They could dictate what happened to her.

Her pulse quickened and she felt the scales hardening around her chest. This time, she didn't fight them. In the privacy of her room, she let them spread as far as they wanted, basking in the feeling they created. *Safety.* They were smooth and cool, moving fluidly with her breath.

She needed to stay calm if she was going to figure this out. She sat at her desk, opening her laptop. The school principal had said the kidnapped girls were mostly from group homes and shelters. She searched residential facilities then scrolled through the images until one caught her attention. She stopped. It was the image splayed on the desk at the precinct.

She clicked on the description. Valley Cottage was a residential facility for children, about two miles away. She wondered why she hadn't seen it on the news. Her heart sank as she considered the possible explanations. Maybe they were accustomed to bad things happening there. Maybe there was no one to hold them accountable. It wasn't easy to find photos of the girls either, but finally, Emma found an article showing a girl with onyx eyes, bronze skin, and beautifully textured hair, another with freckles and a wide grin of spaced teeth, with hair so blonde it was nearly white. There were more missing whose pictures were not even posted. Rage and sorrow stirred inside her. To the world, they were nearly invisible now.

Emma sat back in her chair and called Jason. He answered on the first ring. She didn't make up an excuse or blame her parents for not letting her out. She told him she wasn't feeling up for a party. And though she was sure to minimize the day's events, she told him the police had asked her about the kidnappings and that the whole thing had riled her.

"I don't have to go to the party either," Jason said and offered to come over instead. But she encouraged him to go, knowing he had been excited for it. When she hung up, a soft calm enveloped her. She hadn't told the full truth, but she hadn't lied either, and his support gave her hope that soon she would be able to share everything with him. But not yet. Because tonight she wasn't going to stay home and mope. It was Halloween. Kids would be out in the open and vulnerable. And for once, she would have an excuse if anyone saw her in scales. She was going to that residential home.

14

As dusk fell, Emma sensed the rising heat of movement and peered out the window to find the streets spotted with a myriad of colored costumes, mostly donned by young children guided by their parents. Unfortunately for Emma, trick-or-treating had become less popular in recent years among anyone older than thirteen, and she realized she was likely to draw attention if she went outside in her scales, even if it was Halloween. Why would a teenager be walking alone in costume?

To calm her bounding pulse, she reminded herself that nothing she planned to do was illegal. She would only go to the facility and ask some questions. She would say she learned about what happened from her principal, express her care and concern, then offer some candy for the kids. Emma grabbed whatever stray sweets she could find in her kitchen cabinets, dressed in black workout leggings and a sweatshirt, then rummaged through her closet until she found a pair of fuzzy purple cat ears.

She stopped before stepping outside. What if someone from school saw her? What if Jason found out she skipped the party but went out somewhere else? Emma sighed in annoyance, returning to her closet where she found an old pink wig and winged sunglasses. She twisted her hair into an even tighter bun and tucked it under the wig, then placed the cat ears atop it. She couldn't help but laugh when she saw her reflection in the mirror, unsure if the ridiculous getup made her any less likely to be noticed. If anything, it might draw attention from people trying to figure out what the hell she was. Last, she slipped on a pair of faux leather gloves. She wouldn't be leaving fingerprints anywhere tonight.

The sun slipped below the horizon, its pale remnants casting a ghostly glow over the cool streets. Emma paced quickly toward Valley Cottage, remembering the map she had studied before leaving, and taking a route that avoided the house party, as well as both Jason's and Pria's homes.

Emma smiled as she passed trick-or-treaters, careful to walk slower than she'd like to avoid rousing suspicion. After walking for nearly fifteen minutes, the streets grew sparse, with fewer houses and no children, and shadowy without the copious street lamps. She peered to her right and saw that the path she had mapped led into a dark thicket of trees. She stiffened. Any hint of sunlight had vanished, and the sky's pale gray glow barely revealed the path.

Oh stop, she told herself. *It's not like it's haunted.* She had nothing to fear. But she looked around, wondering if there was another way. Of course there was. There must be a route to drive up to the house. But she didn't know it and couldn't check. She had left her phone at home, afraid her movements could be tracked through it or its storage later used to prove her location by police.

She inhaled sharply and stepped into the forest, her awareness heightened as she strode swiftly through the shadows then broke into a jog. It was even darker amidst the trees, and Emma removed her sunglasses, tucking them into her sweatshirt pocket. Scales crept over her skin like winter's first frost, and she welcomed them. She could always coax them away once she arrived, but for now, she was grateful for the protection. The faster she ran, the more it reinforced her fear. She stopped a moment, listening to her quivering breaths. There was nothing to be afraid of, was there? A rustling from the forest floor made her bolt upright. Her vision darted through the trees, burrowing through darkness. Only a squirrel.

She trudged on, deciding if she didn't find the housing facility soon, she would turn back. Just then, a faint light penetrated the branches and she saw a clearing in the trees where a four-story brick building sat, its uniform windows dark, except for the ones on the bottom floor. She recognized it as the pictured building in the police precinct, the one she had seen online. Valley Cottage. As she approached, it looked even more dilapidated in real life, with missing chunks of bricks and a shattered window on the top floor. She paused at the tree line, waiting. For what, she wasn't sure. But it didn't feel right to walk up to the door. Not yet at least. She surveyed the scene, focusing on the lit room of the first floor, sensing movement through the window.

She heard the rumble of an approaching motor and retreated slightly, waiting until headlights appeared from the opposite side of the house and a van pulled up to the door. The driver came out and swung the side door open. Emma watched as a dozen kids filed out, carrying nearly empty candy bags.

Emma stood, waiting, still as death. Besides the overall creepy appearance of the building, nothing appeared awry. The air cooled amidst the trees, her joints starting to stiffen and her muscles tighten. Her scales had receded. Maybe she should just go home. It felt too strange for her to appear at the door, even if she did offer candy. But she had come all this way. She wanted some answers.

Emma slid off her cat ears to feel less ridiculous and stepped into the clearing. She sensed the rustling of leaves behind her, and her own footsteps in the grass seemed amplified. There was relatively little emanating from the building, which was strange considering how big it was.

Something felt wrong, but she couldn't tell what. Was she just afraid because she was alone, in the dark, with the prospect of facing a less-than-welcoming reception by strangers?

Or was there something else? As she neared the house, the unnerved feeling intensified. She tasted it, like black mold seeping into water.

She stepped onto the front walkway, preparing her greeting, when the downstairs light suddenly went out.

She could see in darkness, that didn't scare her, but the abruptness and the sudden chill from inside the house made her freeze. As she contemplated retreating, a shrill sound pierced the air.

A scream.

From the far side of the building.

Emma dropped the bag of candy, bolting toward the sound, her scales instinctively enveloping her to match the dark night. She rounded the corner to find a gray van with an empty driver's seat and engine running. She narrowed her eyes, sensing for bodies. There was heat from the van's engine, but she couldn't sense anyone inside. Maybe the walls were insulated? Or had the scream come from somewhere else?

It sounded again, high-pitched and female. This time, so close, there was no mistaking the location. Someone was trapped inside, screaming for help. Emma lurched toward the van, her limbs unusually sluggish in the cold air. "Help! Help me!" The terror in the girl's voice intensified, and Emma was prepared to find something disturbing. She only hoped she could stop it, that it wasn't too late. She swung the back door of the van open.

Empty.

The van was empty.

She paused. Could someone have escaped with the girl through another door that quickly? There was a strange quiet around her, and she sensed vague swells of heat near the house, maybe from the radiators? Or maybe someone inside heard the scream and was coming out.

Then, through the ambient chill, a burst of heat exploded behind her. She whirled around to meet two masked figures lunging her way. She dodged their grasp. Her movements, unexpectedly slow, as if through water, were still faster than theirs. The scream sounded again, and Emma paused. It came from inside the van, she was sure of it, trusting her keen senses. But she swore it had been empty. She peered into the open van, frantic and confused, until her eyes settled on the speakers in the front seat. "Help me!" the scream sounded again. *A recording.*

Emma's stomach dropped.

This was a trap.

The moment of stunning realization allowed her attackers enough time to grip her wrists, pulling them behind her and jabbing a taser into her neck. She barely felt the shock, her scales repelling it like grains of sand. But she felt a surge of anger and energy, intensified by the heat of their bodies so close. She could break their wrists to escape, but she wasn't sure who they were.

"You're coming with us," one said, and she sensed two more bodies behind him.

"Who are you?" she asked, pretending to struggle with all her might, but using just a fraction of it. "Who are you?" she asked again. "Police? FBI?"

No answer. They yanked her back, but before they took another step, she slipped seamlessly from their grip and swung around, kneeing one in the crotch and jabbing her elbow into the other's stomach. She noticed their glasses, thick plastic goggles. They knew about her venom. Two figures behind them jumped toward her, but she moved with lightning speed, crouching and tripping both as she slid between them and sprinted toward the trees.

What the hell, she thought, her wig flying off her head as she sped through the woods, not taking the path. *A trap!?* They had expected her to show up. *Who* had expected it? Someone at the precinct? The police must have left that photo of the building out on purpose then watched her notice it. It meant they knew who she was. If they needed evidence to make an arrest, this would give it to them. Would undercover cops go so far as to fake a kidnapping?

Her mind raced, and her legs grew numb in the cold, her pace slowing, just as the sound of barking dogs echoed through the trees behind her. *Shit.* They would be able to trace her scent. She couldn't go back home. And in case the police wanted to question her again, she would need an alibi. She would be going to the Halloween party after all.

She broke through the trees and sped down the street, bracing herself for sirens, but none came. Still, any of the unmarked cars lining the street could be part of the trap. Emma struggled to remember whose house was hosting the party, but once she arrived in the general area, she heightened her senses for heat and was able to locate a house radiating more than its neighbors'. She crept beside the cream-colored paneling of the house, lingering in the shadows.

Footsteps padded the walkway behind her, and she stiffened, ready to bolt away. But they approached slowly, and the person seemed to be alone. They rounded the corner, and Emma turned to find a perky, blonde-haired, middle-aged woman carrying a bag of trash. She dropped the bag when she saw Emma then held a hand to her chest. Emma's mind raced for words to explain her scales, when the woman laughed.

"Oh my god," she said. "That's an incredible costume!"

Emma smiled with relief.

"But what are you doing out here? The party's inside!"

"I just needed some fresh air," she said.

The woman smiled like she could relate then turned back toward the door.

Relief nearly flooded her but halted in her stomach. She had hoped no one would see her like this, that she could use the party as an alibi. But it had felt too soon to let her guard down if she was being chased, tracked. *Hopefully she doesn't watch the news,* she thought, wondering if her schoolmate's mom would link her to the mysterious Serpentina.

Just then a car skidded down the block. Emma blanched as she sensed the nearing heat from the friction of its wheels on the pavement. She shut her eyes, swallowing the fear, coaxing her mind to distance herself from the danger. Then she slid on the cat ears from her pocket, along with the sunglasses. I'm just getting ready for the party, she told herself, and slowly, reluctantly, the scales receded. A lingering, muted gray tinged her skin, but it was good enough for now.

Emma followed the woman's steps to the door, the beat of music resonating through the walls and into her chest. Then she slipped inside, just as a dark, unmarked car turned the corner. As the door closed behind her, she sensed it slowing before continuing down the block. She braced herself for sirens or for a knock at the door, but as she sifted through the people, their heat stifling her breath, nothing came.

The house was dimly lit and packed with her peers. There was no sign of the mom who had taken out the trash or any other parent. Emma removed her sunglasses and spotted Jason standing beside a bowl of punch on a fold-up table. He was wearing the basketball shorts and bunny ears they had once planned together, and seeing them made her heart pang with guilt. But she was happy for him, for still coming. He deserved to have fun. He was looking to his left through the crowd, as if watching someone, when she reached for his arm.

"Jason!" she cried, smiling. His eyes widened and he smiled back, but it didn't reach his eyes.

"Emma … I didn't think you were … you didn't answer—" he said.

"Surprise!" she said, holding up her hands and cringing at how forced the gesture felt. "I snuck out."

His face lit up then, more delayed than she expected, but with a familiar warmth that assured her. He pulled her in for a kiss. As she drew back, Emma remembered the missing bracelet and held her wrist back behind her hip. If he noticed, he didn't mention it.

"How's the punch?" Emma asked with a playful smile.

"I haven't had any. It's spiked," he whispered. Emma grinned. By high school standards he was considered a sexy jock, making the way he followed rules particularly cute to her. "I'm standing here to warn people." He winked.

"Hey," she said, dropping her voice down. "I'm sorry about the costume—"

No sooner had the words left her mouth, when a voice came from behind her.

"Emma?"

She turned to find Pria emerging from the crowd in basketball shorts much shorter than Jason's, a cropped white tank top … and bunny ears. In one of her white gloved hands she held an unsteady plastic cup of punch.

There was an awkward pause as Emma stared at her, then back at Jason, the air leaving her lungs. Then the two of them began to ramble at once.

"Oh my god, I thought you weren't coming!" she said, her words slurring slightly.

"We didn't want to waste the costume idea," Jason was explaining.

Emma waved a hand and they stopped.

"No, I'm so happy," she said, swallowing the hard lump forming in her throat. Of course, she *should* be happy. It had been Jason's idea, and a good one, and she had planned to skip the party altogether. "I mean I'm glad you were able to coordinate."

The pause reformed, swelling with tension. Pria stumbled forward into a hug, pulling Emma closer. "It's so good to see you," she said, and Emma stiffened at the unfamiliarity of the embrace. She knew Pria liked to have fun, but she had never actually seen her drunk before, and the scent, both sour and volatile, was enough to offset her. "You wanna swap costumes?" Pria blurted. Emma smiled, somewhat comforted by the offer.

"No, you look so cute," she said, forcing a smile.

Pria turned, and Emma watched the perky, white bunny tail on the back of her full hips bounce as she walked into the crowd, like it was taunting her. *It's just a costume*, Emma told herself, but her eyes stung. Jason put an arm around Emma.

"Hey," he said, "she offered last minute when I told her you weren't coming. I only reached out to see if she had heard from you. Since you didn't answer my last text."

Emma nodded, somewhat grateful he didn't sound spiteful, and her eyes teared slightly.

"I'll be better about that," she said. The music got louder, drowning any chance to talk, and Jason pulled her in to dance. She tried to enjoy the moment, bask in his presence, in his affection, but more than one thing nagged at her. Not only had she failed to solve the kidnappings, but someone had set a trap to ensnare her.

She might have escaped that night, but surely they wouldn't give up.

She stared into Jason's deep-set, trusting eyes, so intent as they gazed on her, she couldn't help but grin. But she couldn't tell him the truth, even if the music softened. What if they questioned him about her? He would have to lie to the police… She couldn't put him in that position.

But she worried he would be involved, inevitably, if whoever was searching was truly persistent. She stiffened suddenly. *The stupid wig.* It had fallen in the trees. They'd analyze it for evidence. Surely a trace of her own hair would be left behind on it. She stopped, thoughtful.

"You okay?" Jason asked.

"Yeah, I just need a quick bathroom break," she said.

As she stood in front of the mirror in her classmate's white-tiled bathroom, she took out her tight bun and ran her fingers through her hair. They came back clean, no strands. She thought back to her hairbrush at home and realized she hadn't needed to clean it either recently. It wasn't something she often tracked, but now that she considered it, she realized there was a change. She wasn't shedding. What did that mean? Were her cells not turning over? Her bruise had healed, but was it new cells replacing old, or was it possible that the same cells were repaired? Her mind raced at the implications. She supposed, if someone was set on tracking her, seeking evidence with her cells, there was still one place they might look to collect them. The lab.

She left the bathroom to find Jason leaning against the wall, waiting for her, and with some relief, welcomed his offer to drive them home. But when he suggested she sleep over, she hesitated. There was an easy excuse—she could claim her parents would come home and she'd get in trouble, while the root of her hesitation was the need to keep her secret and a desire to protect him from an investigation. But Emma agreed. The truth was, she also wanted him, to be with him, close and safe.

She feared what questions he might ask or having to lie to hide truths, but in the darkness of his room, she realized he was more eager for her body, and she didn't have to worry about what she did or didn't say. When he fell into a satisfied sleep, she stared at the ceiling, her mind racing with the urgency to return to her lab and reclaim her blood samples.

Amidst the stress, her exhausted mind drifted into reluctant sleep, where the now familiar image of a grinning man with blood-stained cheeks flashed through her dreams. She jolted awake, a pervasive, chilling dread creeping over her. She thought of waking Jason, but one look at his face, peacefully surrendered in sleep, stopped her. She waited until dawn, then whispered that she had to leave. He scrunched his brows and squinted, whispering back "already?" then "okay" before returning to sleep. She slipped outside into the morning chill, her feet crunching over dried leaves covered in frozen dew.

15

"I'm not doing the proposal," Emma said.

It was Sunday, but she had counted on finding Dr. Belken at the lab. It was his life. He, however, hadn't expected her. He dropped the paper he was reading and looked at her from his desk, clearing his throat as if to obscure his surprise.

"Why the sudden decision?"

"I don't want to do the experiment with my blood anymore," she said. "At least not here. And I don't give you permission to store the blood samples. I want them back."

He blinked, and she thought she saw a flash of irritation, or maybe worry, in his eyes, but it was partly veiled by the glare of his lenses.

"You seem upset about something," he said. "What's going on?"

"I just want them back," she said simply. "They're mine anyway. I didn't sign them over to you." The assertiveness in her voice wasn't her typical tone, but she was done playing his games, dancing around what she felt. She had rehearsed what to say while on the train. She needed to be direct now and was convinced she had the right to make these demands.

"It sounds like you're worried," he said, adjusting his glasses. Or was he fidgeting? "Do you have a new symptom?"

"No. And I think if I did, I should get it checked by a *medical* doctor, not you."

He stood, and for a second she felt intimidated beneath his height. He still had more authority than her, and she was unsure of his intent. Their eyes met, and she struggled to discern his gaze. She paused, trying to sense his emotion, but it was bland and as nondescript as unsalted bread.

"I don't have them," he said finally.

And there it was. Emma took a long, slow inhale. To him, it might appear she was calming herself. But Emma was smelling deeply, that familiar, poignant scent of her blood. *He was lying.*

"Oh?" she said. "Where are they?"

He sighed, his owl-like eyes glancing at the floor. "One of my interns thought they were from an old experiment and disposed of them. It's my fault for not labeling them correctly."

Emma's eyes narrowed. *Why are you lying?*

"Both vials are gone?" she asked. "Why didn't you tell me instead of suggesting I write a proposal to study them?" She wanted to see how far he would take this.

"It just happened yesterday afternoon," he said. "Of course I planned to tell you as soon as I saw you."

Emma swallowed. She wasn't sure what the next step was, but something told her she shouldn't reveal she knew the truth, not yet at least. It wasn't so much that she needed him for her career, for a letter of recommendation. That used to be a priority, but not anymore. *No.* It gave her the upper hand—knowing something he didn't. She needed to use that power to her advantage and figure out why he was lying.

"You have an excuse for everything," Emma said quietly, the starkest accusation she had ever made to him. "First, the antivenom was contaminated. Now, my blood is conveniently missing."

"I understand," he said, his words reeking of condescension. "Even I, after so many years, make mistakes in the lab. This intern is new, and I'll also be discussing with her the proper storage of samples."

Emma stepped deeper into his office. She was silent, sensing the room's vibrations and breathing the scent that laced the air. The scent of her blood. She would recognize it anywhere, even through a box in the refrigerator. She let her eyes wander there, testing him. He tensed.

"Are you interested in more blood samples from me then?" Emma asked, her eyes flickering back to him.

"Of course," he said. "If you want to consider it still." His eagerness to accept was the proof she needed. *He wants my samples. There's something he's doing with them.*

"Well," Emma said, narrowing her eyes, "before I give more, I should have a chat with this intern. To make sure my blood isn't going to waste."

She wanted him to know he couldn't lie anymore. She had so much she could condemn him for, starting with what happened on Crete. Finally, she was regaining control. Unless … did he know something he wasn't saying? Had the previous night's encounter been reported as another Serpentina sighting? Stories like that were bound to catch his attention eventually.

"Sure," he said slowly, as if in question. It only confirmed his dishonesty. There was no intern to talk to.

Emma left his office and checked her lab station. The single mouse still scurried about the cage, alive and energetic, though his bedding looked more shredded than she'd ever seen. She paced down the stairs in thought. Was it time to report him? Who could she report him to? As she passed the front desk, she overheard the secretary's voice.

"Dr. Belken is speaking at five o'clock," she said into the phone. "Will you be attending?"

Emma stopped. She turned to see the secretary jotting a note and hanging up the phone, her blond hair in its usual stiff style.

"Excuse me," Emma said, approaching the glass window. "Did you say Dr. Belken is giving a talk?"

She nodded, still scribbling on her notepad. "Yes, at the symposium in Javits tomorrow."

Emma's cheeks heated. *What symposium?* He always told her in advance about his talks.

"Am I on the list?" Emma asked, her voice sounding faint as she tried to steady herself.

The woman sighed, as if the question were an enormous burden, and turned to scroll on her computer. Emma hadn't seen much of Dr. Belken's secretary since she'd chaperoned them on their trip and was flustered by the seemingly cold treatment the woman was giving her now. If anything, shouldn't she be sympathetic after what happened?

"I don't see your name, no," she said.

Emma thought quickly. "That's weird, he always has me go to these. Will you add me?"

"It's booked already," she said sharply, then picked up the phone again.

Emma left the building and, though perplexed by the exchange, knew what she needed to do.

Emma didn't have a ticket for the event, but she wore her white lab coat and waited by the main entrance of the Javits Center. She glanced over her shoulder, a practice she caught herself doing more and more, especially since Halloween. So far, no one seemed to be tracking her. During school that day she had compulsively scanned her phone for news stories on Serpentina or coverage from the residential home. There was nothing. In some ways that was reassuring. But it was as if nothing happened, and she knew it had. That unsettled her, and she felt even more isolated.

Emma watched as people arrived for the various events in Javits, which today included an international food show, until she saw a Mazda pull up with Mt Sinai stickers and figured it was for the science symposium. A middle-aged woman wearing a black pantsuit got out. Several college-aged people approached from the building to begin unloading posters and banners from her car. Emma swiftly joined them as if she had been assigned to. They greeted one another briefly, and though Emma had prepared various answers in case she was questioned, one girl only thanked her for her help. If they had suspected anything unusual, Emma squelched it with her confidence, a demeanor that was starting to come more easily to her. She carried a file of presentation notes as the group made their way to the entrance.

She smiled as she walked past the entrance security. One officer glanced at her ID badge, but it didn't rattle her. She had a volunteer badge from Columbia after all, and Dr. Belken was the keynote speaker. This guise depended on her believing she belonged there. And it seemed, by his casual response, he believed it too.

She followed the group and tried to conceal her surprise when they entered the River Pavilion of Javits. *This is where the symposium is?* She had never seen the large, glass-enclosed room often reserved for corporate events, and with its grand view of the river, it felt almost too elegant for the type of science symposium she was used to. The enormous glass windows shimmered like crystals in the afternoon sun.

She helped arrange the woman's poster, with its sprawling title detailing research on the immortal jellyfish. Emma might have been interested in reading more but she was on the lookout for Dr. Belken and quietly slipped into the crowd, immersing herself in the posters displays. She passed projects on aging, genetic mutations, stem cells, and several stands offering samples of anti-aging supplements and creams for marketing. *Weird.* Was the conference a hybrid between science and the beauty industry? She paused to inspect a display, formulating a question about how this particular supplement might produce "joint longevity," when an announcement called for attendees to take their seats. On the far side of the room, chairs were filed into seemingly endless rows before a stage with a podium in front of a giant projection screen.

There were more people in the audience than she'd ever seen for a conference, with an unusual mix of businessmen and scientists, the distinction mostly obvious by the varying degrees of suit tailoring and hairstyles, but also by their attitudes. The scientists were vying for grant money and the businessmen reveling in their elite position to endow it. How had Dr. Belken become the keynote speaker at such an event? Emma straightened in her chair as the speaker introduced Dr. Belken. He appeared, striding across the stage toward the microphone, his gait unusually fluid. She almost didn't believe it was him. But beneath the suit and tie, she recognized the subtle hunch of his shoulders and the slightly disheveled hair.

"Thank you for this introduction. And welcome," he said, scanning the crowd. He looked innocent enough, but the sharpness in his eyes did not escape her. He looked eager. Predatory. Only a slight tremble at the end of his words gave away his nervousness. He clicked his pointer, and a slide presentation appeared in vibrant colors behind him.

"As you may know, we are here to talk about *immortality*," he said.

The words stunned her. She had expected his opening to be catchy. He always had exciting ways to attract interest at presentations—a photo of a ferociously poised snake or a punny title about venom. *But this?* This was too big to fathom, and it wasn't even what their lab researched, was it? *He must be crazy,* she thought. How could he follow that introduction?

But he did follow it.

He dove into the various aging processes, the shortening of telomeres, the accumulation of mutations, the slowing and errors in DNA replications, and finally, an overview of cancer.

"But," he said. "What if I told you that my lab has identified a molecule, a complex protein never before isolated or purified, that creates immortal cells?"

The blood drained from Emma's face.

"I know what you're probably thinking," he said.

No, I bet you don't.

"The only immortal cells are cancer cells," he continued, his voice booming with pride. "And you would be right, until now. *These* somatic cells have been given the ability to replicate without shortening their telomeres, but while still correcting potentially harmful mutations that might otherwise lead to cancer."

Emma's pulse rose. This couldn't be… He could not have hidden something this immense. Surely there wasn't substantive evidence to back his claims.

But he went on to explain the molecule's entry into cells, through a ligand-gated channel that bound it, leading to a conformational change downstream.

And then she knew—an even scarier truth lurked beneath the surface of her fear. He had done crazy things, but he had never misrepresented research. That would cost him his degree and his chance for scientific acclaim. No, this molecule was real. And she knew, then, it was *hers. These* were the answers, of what her blood could do, the answers she was searching for.

He had been researching them all along. He had been holding onto them, hiding them from her. Why else would he have gotten so mad about her trying an experiment of her own? He was controlling her, marketing her. It was only a matter of time before people vied hungrily for the source of this molecule, for *her*... She shuddered. It had to stop.

"Of course, these findings hold immense implications for all of us," Dr. Belken said. Emma fumed, clenching her fists as she watched him. "One interesting finding thus far is that the molecule has only been tested in male mice, and the studies need to include female mice as well. Potential side effects are also an area of focus for our lab at this time."

Our lab. There was no *our*, she thought. This was *his* secret project. She wanted to shout at him, boo him from the stage. Control, she thought. Now was not the time to burst into scales.

When he finished his talk and opened the floor to questioning, the room seemed to explode. At first, there was a rising murmur as excited voices chatted together. The facilitator had to quiet the room several times, and asked for those with questions to raise their hands. Virtually everyone did.

"For those of you who do not have their questions answered tonight, we will share Dr. Belken's contact information with you." He proceeded to assign numbers to order the questions, and the audience fired away. Emma watched Dr. Belken grow more enthusiastic, as if feeding off the energy of the crowd and his own success at drawing it.

Emma scowled. How could he expect to get away with this? These were her samples, she was certain.

It wasn't worth raising her hand. He would never see her. Emma stood suddenly, and several heads turned in her direction. She didn't need the microphone.

"Where did you isolate this molecule from?" she shouted, interrupting the man in the front row just beginning his question. There was a shocked pause, before murmurs arose. The security guards in the corner jostled into motion.

Dr. Belken appeared flustered for a moment, then forced a smile that didn't reach his eyes.

"Everyone, this is an excellent volunteer from my lab," he said, gesturing at Emma. "Pardon the interruption, she brings up a good point." The tension in the air calmed. The guards paused their approach. "This molecule is from a never-before-discovered snake species. We are still attempting to identify it."

At that, the room exploded once more. Heat pulsated through Emma's veins. She couldn't shout over this crowd. But he was lying. They had never caught that snake. What an outlandish claim to make. The samples were from *her*.

But she had given herself away and perhaps lost her lead. He knew she was there now. What had she expected? To expose him in front of so many?

She wondered if she had enough evidence to stand on, to make a claim against him. What power did she have? She was a high school student with no credibility in the world. She couldn't make such a stark accusation against him, a renowned scientist, without coming across as crazy. And who would accept her into a research program if she accused her former mentor of sabotaging her in such a drastic way? Everyone would think it was a lie. *She* would be the problem.

But he couldn't get away with this. Maybe, if she only waited, he would discredit himself. After all, this was an immense claim—a molecule for immortality. And on top of that, he had also claimed to have discovered a new species. But Emma's heart sank because she knew he did have the evidence to support it. The evidence was right there, in her cells.

Emma pushed her way through the aisle as a round of applause erupted. She glanced back as the facilitator announced they would be taking a break. The stage was far away, but her vision was clear. In her periphery, Dr. Belken exited the podium and shook hands with a man in a gray suit, a pin adorning his jacket with a logo of two intersecting tridents above the words *Poseidon Co.*

He would be busy mingling, she thought, attempting to get his precious grant money. In the meantime, she would make a move. As she turned, she felt his eyes on her back and knew she had to hurry.

16

The ash gray waters of the Hudson river were swallowing the last thread of rusty sunlight as Emma stepped out into the city. She texted her parents she was at a conference and would be back late, but it wouldn't matter. They didn't come home for dinner, and they'd be in the hospital until ten at least. She had to find what she needed before then anyway or risk being caught snooping. She got a text back a few minutes later, telling her they'd be at the hospital with Danny. Her heart sank at the thought of him. Sure, she had wanted to attend Columbia. But somehow, this project had been for him, to find a cure, however impossible that seemed. How did it become such a mess?

She made her way through the swarming streets, her stride half breaking into a run as she approached the 34th Street subway station. The moon's silver light was already intensifying in the darkening sky as she paced down the dingy concrete steps. Her phone rang. A call from Jason. She couldn't pick up. Not *now.*

She silenced it as she stepped onto the busy platform. She glanced anxiously down the tracks and, in her periphery, noticed a man standing near the platform bench in a black trench coat. She stiffened. Hadn't she seen him walking down the same street as her earlier? He turned in her direction before quickly looking away, his hands in his pockets. *Is he following me?*

She narrowed her senses, picking up on the scent of his sweat. It was the nervous kind—acrid and sour. *He could be nervous for many reasons,* she told herself. *Maybe he only looked at me because I looked at him first.* But her heightened senses refused to calm. She watched as he pulled a phone from his pocket and stared at the screen.

The A train arrived at last, screeching to a halt. She moved toward the doors and couldn't help but notice the man's steps lagged just a second behind hers. Was he waiting on her move? Her pulse sped as she stepped into the train, turning to see him follow into the neighboring car, one hand still in his pocket. Sweat gathered on her brow as her eyes darted between him and the platform. Just as the doors lurched to close, she bolted out from the train.

The man stared at Emma through the window as the train sped away. Maybe it was the oddity of her abrupt move that caught his attention … or maybe he had been following her. She took a deep breath as she waited for the C train.

Fifteen minutes later, Emma burst into her lab building and took the elevator upstairs. She grabbed the handle of the lab door entrance and shoved her body forward, but the handle didn't budge and she was blocked by an unyielding door. She scanned her badge several times, but instead of the green light, it only flashed red. *Did he deactivate me?*

She retreated to the bathroom of the floor to think, trying to discern if her logic was sound. She needed to get in, preferably without being seen.

Her phone chimed, interrupting her thoughts. "Just finished practice. When should I come over?" the text from Jason read.

She hesitated before hurriedly texting back.

"I'm stuck at the lab."

She saw the dots appear and disappear as he typed, then nothing.

She wanted to tell him that it was too much to explain through text, and she couldn't risk a phone call now. But there would be a chance to talk to him about it, maybe later that night or tomorrow, once she had more answers and evidence on her side. There was more she needed to solve first. She muted her phone.

She could have waited to see if a janitor would open the door to clean, but that might take hours. Time was limited. If Dr. Belken returned, he would stop her from searching the lab. The situation was desperate now.

She marched back toward the lab door, her senses heightening as scales emerged over her skin. She took a sharp breath then smashed the glass window with her fist, the thick glass fragile against her armored hand. She had expected it to hurt a little, even with the scales sprouting to protect her. But her hand was unscathed.

Her adrenaline surged as the glass clattered around her. The empty frame was narrow, but she slipped her entire body through, her bones seeming to bend to accommodate the opening. Standing in the lab, alert and focused, she saw into the room behind Dr. Belken's office, guarded by another locked door. With a fluid motion, she broke that glass panel and slipped inside.

The scent of her blood tinged the air around her, fueling her. She opened the refrigerator and, amidst an array of tubes, saw a Styrofoam box in the back. Carefully, she removed specimens until she could reach it. As she brought the box out, the scent intensified. Inside, she found two vials of blood labeled *EM*, with the date from a few weeks ago.

She had known he was lying, but to see it with her own eyes flooded her with a sense of satisfaction, followed by rage at what he'd done. She needed to prove it to everyone else now.

She began searching the room for more evidence, her heart pounding. She opened his file cabinets, her movements bursting with speed. She tried to steady her pace, to stay calm. Why should she be afraid, after all? Even if he caught her, *he* was the one at fault. But her stomach clenched when she realized what she feared more than being caught was what she might discover there. What had he done with her cells?

From the back of the last filing cabinet, she retrieved a large envelope labeled "Project 25a." She slid the contents out and spread the papers over the messy desk.

One of them was a grant acceptance. The heading on the page read, *Poseidon Co. He already secured grant money weeks ago and hid the fact?* Her mind flashed to Dr. Belken shaking hands with the suited man after his presentation. She did a quick search on her phone. Poseidon Co. was … her eyes scanned the web pages … a private military contractor? *This can't be right.* She didn't understand why a military contractor would fund cancer research. She placed the grant acceptance aside, rummaging for the papers behind it. Her fingers met thicker sheets of paper and she paused.

Photos. Her heart began to pound as she flipped the images over. Then she gasped.

There, in her hands, were photos of *the snake.*

Five photos, to be exact, taken from different angles, outside, but also in a tank, a tank that she saw, when she squinted at the glass etching in the corner, was labeled with Dr. Belken's lab. She couldn't breathe.

He had caught the snake. He had taken it into the lab on Crete and not told anybody. Her hands went numb, trembling until the photos shook.

Her mind raced, but she tried to quell it. She needed to focus on the task at hand and not let the impact of each discovery disorient her from the goal.

She snapped her own photo of the pages then slid them aside. Behind them she found a log detailing activities on Crete. Her eyes could not read the words fast enough. She scanned the lines, first detailing the monotonous lab routine she was familiar with. Then the dates began to approach her hospitalization, and her eyes widened.

August 16th, the day before it all started, he wrote, "10 a.m.—Captured snake, attempted to identify; new species?" Then, "4 p.m.—extracted snake's venom."

"5:15 p.m.—Snake escaped."

She furrowed her brow. She had suppressed her suspicion, even doubting herself. But now she knew it had to be true.

That's what he had injected her with. *The snake's venom.*

She read his notes on the days she was in the hospital. On the second day it said, "went to village, see video."

She recalled Pria telling her he went out in search of help. Frantically, she searched the envelope again, shaking it upside down until a small flash drive dislodged from the envelope's crease and tumbled onto the desk. She snatched it, leaping to a computer.

She fidgeted, her legs shaking as she waited for it to load, then selected the video. Her heart threatened to burst.

She wasn't sure she was ready. What if the truth was more horrible than she could ever imagine? But there was no going back. This was her truth, and she deserved to know it.

She held her breath and pressed play.

An old, wrinkled woman with sun-browned skin appeared on the screen. She sat on a wooden stool. Behind her hung various strings of dried leaves and glass jars of colored concoctions. On her table sat a mortar and pestle, piles of herbs and bowls of oils Emma couldn't identify.

"She was bitten by this snake." Emma recognized Dr. Belken's voice from behind the camera. Her mind pounced on his words. She wasn't *bitten*. He wouldn't say she had been unless he knew she had the venom in her blood, and he only knew that because he had injected it himself. *This* was a confession.

The urgency to run and tell authorities made Emma nearly bolt from the chair. She would need to text Pria too. Her friend was right all along about Dr. Belken and could be a reliable witness. But Emma clenched her jaw and sat. She needed to see all of this.

Dr. Belken handed the old woman a photo, and she squinted at it. Then a hand went to her mouth. She looked just above the camera, at Dr. Belken.

"Are you sure? It was this snake?" The woman's raspy English was thickly accented, and Emma needed to focus to decipher it. "Where is she now?" the woman asked.

"She's hanging on for life in the hospital. They told me you might know a cure?"

The old woman straightened her hunched back, lifting a bit to inhale.

"I do," she said. "But it will come at a cost."

"I'll pay anything," he said.

At least, Emma thought, he had cared to save her? Probably to avoid consequences for *himself* though.

"It's not a payment you will make." The old woman chuckled. "It will cost *her.*" She paused. "The treatment will transform her."

"What do you mean, *transform*?" he asked. "What is it?"

"The antidote to the venom is contained in a rare flower," she said. "I have only one here. But it should be enough. If not, they grow deep in the forest but are rarely found. It could take months of searching to find one."

"Please," he said. "She might not live a month."

"She won't," the woman answered with certainty. "Without it, she will die."

"How do you know that?" Dr. Belken asked, his pitch rising. "Do you know this snake?"

The woman nodded solemnly. The camera wavered a bit, and Emma sensed Dr. Belken's urgency.

"I'll give you this flower," the woman said, her face solemn. "But only after you understand the consequences. This is a tale that's been passed down to me for more generations than you can imagine. This snake is not just any serpent."

"Listen," the professor interrupted. "I know that. I'm an expert, and I've never identified anything like it. But I'm in a very big rush now."

The woman held up her hand, and there was a majesty to her slow, deliberate gesture. "Do you want the cure or not?"

He sighed, seemingly frustrated, and Emma wished she could tell him to shut up and let the old woman speak.

"There was a creature of legend and myth," she began. "She was once strong and beautiful, but she was betrayed by the one she was most loyal to, cursed, and turned into a serpent creature, with scales as skin and snakes for hair. She was banished to the caves on a nearby island, and the world turned its back on her, made her into a monster."

"You're talking about the Medusa?" Dr. Belken asked.

Again, the woman held up her hand, closing her eyes as if reliving the story.

"She was mortal," the woman's voice croaked. "When the time came, her body went lifeless. But a part of her lived on. The snakes were a curse from an immortal god, never to be killed. A snake severed from her head, once a strand of her own hair, escaped into the forest, trailing blood from its tail. It slithered deeper into the trees, and where its blood fell on the soil, red flowers blossomed."

"That's the flower you have? A flower grown from mythical snake blood?" Dr. Belken sounded unenthused, clearly not believing the story.

"Yes," she said. "The snake remains secluded, only seen every few hundreds of years. And the flowers have mostly been picked by those unaware of their power, or they withered when the forests were chopped down. You're lucky I have one."

"What about the consequences you mentioned?" he asked hurriedly.

The woman paused before speaking. "If she has the venom inside her body, she will die. *But,* if she eats the flower, the blood of the snake, it will combine with the venom inside her, and she will be reborn."

"What does that mean?" Dr. Belken asked. "Nausea? Cramps?"

"She will take the form of the original source," the woman said, and her words gave Emma chills. "She will become the legendary creature— part human and part serpent. "

Emma couldn't breathe. She stared at the screen.

Again, the professor sighed from behind the camera. "Okay," he said. "Thank you for telling me the backstory of your herbs. Now, we are running out of time."

Slowly, the old woman rose. She took the stool to the cabinets behind her, brushing aside strands of dried leaves. She hoisted her body on top of it and appeared more solid than before as she reached into the shadows of the top shelf, scattering dust into the air.

Then her hand reappeared, clasping something.

"Do you need help?" Dr. Belken's voice came, but she shushed it with a shake of her head as she lowered herself, huffing.

When she returned to sit before him, she opened her hand to reveal a crinkled red flower, no larger than half her palm. She traced its dried petals with her finger, as if nostalgic. And although her face was angled down from the camera, Emma thought she saw tears glisten in her eyes.

"You're sure she's female?" she asked softly.

"What?" Dr. Belken asked.

"If the same thing happened to a male he would not become part serpent. He would remain human, but be sterile and grossly aggressive. It's happened before…"

Emma's mind exploded with questions, but Dr. Belken hadn't been interested in the woman's tales then. Instead, he answered quickly.

"She's female."

The old woman nodded, holding in her posture and eyes all the gravity of what Dr. Belken was about to do—transform a human.

"Be sure to think," the woman said, "if this is what she would want or not." Then she gave the flower to Dr. Belken, refusing any form of payment.

"I'm sure she doesn't want to die," he said quickly.

"No," the woman said. "Maybe not now. But if she takes this, her blood will hold immortality."

The screen went black.

17

Emma fell back into her chair, dizzy. The swarming emotions hardened the scales enveloping her skin.

Like a puzzle, the pieces of information began to fit together—her transformation, the dreams, her professor's actions. She wasn't just the result of a scientific reaction. Her new abilities had a mythical source. But who would believe it? The tale sounded crazy. *She* was the only real evidence. *She* would need to reveal herself to prove anything.

She wanted to watch it again, but there was no time. She needed to get out of there before anyone came and found the shattered glass door. She would take all the evidence home, maybe consult with Pria or her sensei about the best course of action.

She was about to turn and gather her things when she felt footsteps down the hall. The vibrations reverberated in her bones even at a distance. She had time to hide. She could blend in among the boxes in the corner. Her scales would change color. But no. She recognized those footsteps. It was Dr. Belken. She needed to confront him. The steps paused outside the door. Surely he was taking in the sight of the broken glass, weighing whether to enter. She hoped he was afraid. Finally, there was a beeping noise as he swiped a badge and the lab door clicked unlocked.

In her scales, Emma turned to glare straight into Dr. Belken's eyes. It was the first time he had seen her in this form, and she knew she was a fearsome sight. He dropped his badge, his hand visibly shaking as he gasped. The scales had spread over her face, and the only part left human was her hair, and even that seemed to bristle and coil as if alive. She stared at him with a confidence she once only wished to possess. Now she owned it.

"Hello," she said, and her normally polite voice had a hypnotic hiss to it. "There's something you've been hiding from me," she said. She took a step forward, and he cowered back. She grinned in satisfaction. She was going to make him confess everything.

"Listen," he said, holding up his hands as if he were innocent. Why had she ever feared him? He was despicable, pathetic. "You're in danger," he said, looking behind him.

She scoffed. "I know that now. And you're the one endangering me."

"No," he said. "I didn't know what was going to happen. I couldn't have predicted it."

"I was your experiment," she hissed.

"I can explain," he said, frantic. "I want to explain, but later. Right now there are people after you. They're coming."

Before he could finish, she felt vibrations in the hallway. Someone *was* coming.

"Hide," he said, his eyes wide and his face shining with sweat. Despite all he'd done, she sensed his fear, its iron musty scent. It was real, and not only directed at her. She realized exposing herself to whatever threat was coming might be unwise. She leaped into the corner, her scales changing color in the shadows as she peered out to watch.

"Who were you talking to, Dr. Belken?" a deep voice came a minute later.

He gulped. Emma sensed the heat of the man as he entered, his broad back to her. He was tall, with square shoulders and a balding head that reflected the fluorescent lab lights as he stepped into the room.

"Nobody, just trying to make sense of this," Dr. Belken said, and gestured to his desk.

"Your window's broken," the man said, his voice reverberating in Emma's chest.

"Yes, I was in a rush to get in," he said, his voice wavering. "I couldn't find my badge." Emma realized in surprise that Dr. Belken was covering for her. Or did he only want her for himself?

The man glanced down then slowly picked up the badge from the floor beside the entrance.

"It's right here," he said flatly.

"Oh," Dr. Belken said, his voice thready as he struggled to feign surprise. "Thank you. I must have—"

"Do you have the samples?" The man's voice was menacing.

Emma stared at her samples left on the lab bench. *Shit.* Why didn't she dispose of them immediately? Everyone would be after them. She saw Dr. Belken's eyes dart to the Styrofoam box. *Idiot,* she thought, as he gave them away.

"No," he tried to lie, but it was too obvious. His face went pale, sweat gathering at his temples. The man stepped forward, his solid weight sending vibrations through the floor.

"We've played your stupid game long enough. We've given you the money, paid for the rights. Now give us the blood. Or," he said, "tell us where to find her."

Emma froze. They knew about her. Her scales seemed to thicken. Ridges formed on the roof of her mouth, pressing into her tongue, poised to spit.

"I don't have them anymore," he said. Why was he lying? Did he want to keep the samples to himself?

"Are you refusing me, then, after we paid you so much?"

"Get out of my lab," he said, his voice stern but faltering. There was a tense silence. "Or I'll—" Dr. Belken began, reaching for his phone, but he couldn't finish his sentence.

Bullets pierced the air.

There were two shots, so loud Emma's ears recoiled. She had been so fixed on Dr. Belken's face, she hadn't followed the man's movement as he pulled a gun from his blazer. For all her expert senses, she hadn't expected this. She stifled her gasp. She knew the man was threatening, his energy hot and volatile, but *murder*?

The suited man walked past Dr. Belken's body, now crumpled in a pool of blood on the lab floor. Emma's heart thundered, her scales thickening. He picked up the Styrofoam box holding Emma's blood. *No.* She had to stop him. But she wasn't sure it was time to reveal herself. What if it was a trap? And despite her scales, she still feared being shot, unsure how much she could repel. Emma waited until his vibrations receded down the hallway, then leaped to Dr. Belken's side. He was still breathing in gasps, but his face was ghostly white.

"Emma," he said. "I'm sorry."

Maybe, if she hadn't hid, she could've stopped this. But could she blame herself? She hadn't been sure if he was an enemy or not. She still wasn't sure but hoped he would live long enough to show her. He had at least tried in some way to protect her. She grabbed her phone and called the police.

"Hello?" she said. "Someone just broke into our lab and shot my mentor." She gave the woman on the other line her location then hung up.

"They're sending an ambulance now," she said.

"Listen." He grabbed her hand. He suddenly seemed so small. "I was wrong. They're bad people. You can't let them have those samples." His eyes fluttered shut. She wasn't sure if he would make it, but there was no time to wait with him. If the police arrived, she'd be forced to stay for countless questions, and this time she'd be a suspect.

She peered out the window into the night and saw a black van parked down the street. The man was exiting the building, approaching it with a suave gait that would never hint at the violence he'd just committed. She turned to rush after him, but paused. This room was about to become a crime scene investigation. She grabbed the envelope and plucked the flash drive from the computer. She wasn't about to take her origin story with her to whatever villain she was chasing.

She took the photos of the snake and Dr. Belken's logs and threw them into the shredder, then tossed the flash drive into the microwave and turned it on. She wanted to keep it, but there was no place she could guarantee would be safe from a search.

She sprinted to the window and climbed onto the fire exit, her scales morphing jet black in the night. She could stop that man now, kill him, she thought, but no. It was too public and she was determined to not be the villain, or she'd have more people working against her. And if Dr. Belken died, the answers she sought might be lost too. She needed to know who was looking for her blood and why. *Immortality*, she thought, remembering the woman's words, repeated in Dr. Belken's presentation. Who wouldn't be searching for that, even killing for it? But why Poseidon Co.?

Her eyes locked on the van and she rushed down the fire escape. The man opened the back and disappeared for a moment. She crouched, weaving around the cars parked along the sidewalk, then retreating behind one as he reemerged, casually straightening his jacket before walking to the passenger side and leaning into the opened window to say something to the driver. Emma saw her chance. She held her breath and leaped toward the van, slipping inside just seconds before his footsteps returned toward the open door. She retreated into the shadows, concealing herself behind a metal rack stacked with boxes. *Please don't see me.* But the man barely surveyed the interior before slamming the door shut.

Only the van didn't move. Did they sense her? She reminded herself, as she sensed the heat of their breath from the front of the vehicle, that they didn't have the same keen awareness as her. She stood motionless, barely breathing until, finally, the boxes and bottles jostled as the van lurched onto the street.

Her vision was clear in the darkness, and Emma pinpointed a metal box, its lid shut and fastened with a combination lock. When she focused, she could detect that faint scent, even through the metal. *Her blood.* She fumbled with the lock, twisting through the numbers, trying to hear the clicks, but her efforts were futile. She considered using something to break the box, but the metal felt thick and hard like steel. If she tried anything more forceful, she risked alerting them.

The van increased its speed, and she retreated to the corner, holding onto a metal bar. The drive was much longer than expected, so long that they must have left the city. Her mind jostled as she tried to create a plan, uncertain what she would face when the doors opened. Maybe she would wait for them to unload the van, then attack and steal the keys? As if preparing, the scales remained on her skin and she decided to remove her clothes. They were identifiers after all. And she didn't need them. She would be the snake this time, take back control from anyone looking to use her. Her mind replayed the video then, still reeling at the new discovery. Her power came from *Medusa.* Could that truly be possible? It had to be. Those dreams, those memories of the myth were too real.

Her heart raced. Did that also mean the threat in those dreams was real? That same image of a man with blood-stained hands and face flashed before her. She shuddered, remembering Dr. Belken's blood as it pooled over the floor.

It must have been over an hour later when the van began to slow. Emma held her breath as it bounced up a rocky path, halting at several checkpoints. She listened through the metal as the driver obtained security clearance. At last, the ground smoothed and the air cooled as the van tilted down a slope and slowly stopped. The two men got out, and she traced their movements through heat. She retreated as far back behind two tanks as she could, her scales black as the ocean's depths.

The door jerked open. She froze, braced for them to see her, but they were too busy unloading. The men hoisted the metal box onto a cart and began rolling it away. She thought to strike, but another idea came. She could follow them, find out who exactly wanted her blood and for what purpose. She wouldn't let them know she was there, not yet.

In the dim light, she watched them recede and heard a door slide open, then closed. Minutes passed and nothing moved. The back door of the van was left open, and she figured they would be coming back. But she was alone for now.

Slowly, she crept out into the shadows and took in her surroundings. It was a warehouse, dimly lit with LED floor lights, reflecting off large crates and the other vans in rows around her. It smelled faintly of rubber and gasoline. The ceiling was almost four stories high, and the walls stacked with boxes and canisters. At the far corner to her left, dim light spilled through glass doors where the men had exited. She crept toward it.

Maybe it was a mistake to remain in snake form, she thought, as she peered through the glass at workers walking the hallways. Some wore business attire, others lab coats, and others khaki-colored uniforms. Her serpentine appearance would be easily recognizable, a target. But she wasn't sure she had a choice. Her nerves were so heightened she doubted she could change her scales back to skin if she wanted to. But she *did* have a choice, she realized. She was choosing to fight.

Just then, a man walked down the hall toward the door. He was coming her way. She recoiled into the shadows, poised, as the door slid open and he stepped into the warehouse. When it closed, she let him take two steps before she struck from the darkness, her legs scissoring his neck and pinning him to the floor, stifling the cry before it left his mouth. She squeezed, holding her true strength back to give him enough air to speak.

"Please," he cried, grabbing at her legs. His muscled arms bulged with exertion, but even his most dire attempt couldn't match her strength. It was like an insect fighting a lion. "Where are they taking the blood samples?" Emma hissed.

"I don't know what you're—"

She squeezed tighter, letting him know what she could do, then released a bit. He choked out a cough.

"Where are we?" Emma asked. "Answer or I'll make sure I'm the last thing you ever see." Only, in the darkness, he probably couldn't see her. She nearly chuckled. She didn't plan to kill him after all, but he didn't know that. Her muscles rippled with her grip as it neared his face, her black scales flickering with the faint light from the hallway. He stared at them, likely fearing whatever nightmarish creature they belonged to. His terror tasted like ash, a fire extinguishing.

"The basement," he said.

She rolled her eyes. "The basement of what?" she hissed.

"Poseidon ... headquarters," he said.

He started furiously tapping on her leg. *Is he actually trying to tap out, as if this is a wrestling match?* Amused, she squeezed tighter.

"Where's your lab?" she asked.

He struggled, straining against her grip.

"Second floor," he whispered, before slipping into unconsciousness. *Shit*, she had hoped to get a little more out of him. She turned him over on the floor, still breathing. He was so vulnerable, she could do anything to him. But who was she to decide his fate? She couldn't know for sure what role he played in all of this, how guilty he was, or not.

She flipped his jacket open until she found his badge and unclipped it from the lapel. The second floor, she thought. The ID badge gained her access to enter, but how could she get there without being noticed?

She had an idea. If this was the basement, it likely had the building's electrical center. She scanned the warehouse, unsure how to find it amidst the metallic jumble. *Electricity gives off heat.* She sensed only coldness beyond the man in front of her, but stepped over him, weaving through the crates and vehicles until she stood near the room's center. She shut her eyes, heightening her thermal senses until she detected a faint heat emanating from the far corner. As she stepped closer, she heard the faint buzz from the service room. The metal door was bolted, but when she scanned the badge, it clicked open.

She imagined the wires might be neatly labeled, that she would be able to intuit which one she needed to find. But no, the wires appeared like a tangled nest inside their metal boxes. She hesitated. *He'll wake up soon...* She needed to hurry.

She figured the central control panel for the building was likely the biggest one and slid her hands around that box. At the top, her fingers grazed the circuit breaker. The switch was thick and heavy, but she flicked it with ease.

Nothing. There was no response.

Or was there? She became aware of the faintest drop in temperature around her, so subtle she could barely detect anything. She crept out of the closet-like room. The dim guiding floor lights were out, and on the far side of the warehouse, where the glass door stood, the fluorescent hallway lights had been shrouded in darkness. She sped toward the door, leaping over boxes with stealth, her eyesight piercing through shadows with precision.

She stepped lithely over the man.

"Thanks," she whispered.

He just began to stir as she swiped his badge and stepped through the sliding door, locking him behind her. She paced through the plaster-tiled hallways lined with cement. Small emergency lights speckled the floors, not bright enough to reveal her to an ordinary human. At first, the halls were surprisingly empty, but soon she encountered workers, mostly flustered as they reached for their phones to illuminate their path. Emma broke into a run, her steps lithe and quiet, inaudible to those she passed. With her scales matching the ambience she was nearly invisible, and her speed ensured she was gone far before anyone could tell what she was.

A thought crept in her mind as she ran, locating a stairwell to the second floor. Any moment the lights might return. What was her plan if they suddenly blared bright, revealing her? She would have to escape. But she needed to find her blood first.

As she exited the stairwell on the second floor, the familiar scent wafted past her nostrils. *The samples.* She trailed it, turning a corner to discover the two men from the van, flashlights in hand as they delivered the metal box outside a door. Emma's eyes burrowed through the darkness to read the sign labeled *laboratory.*

Her anger solidified. This was the man who had shot Dr. Belken and stolen part of her. She watched him intently, a predator in the night. Then, as he turned, she hissed and the venom shot from her mouth with deadly precision, hitting him in the eyes. He cried out and fell to his knees, the beam of light from his flashlight chaotic as it clattered to the ground. His partner was quick to don a pair of goggles then turned to search the darkness. The terror in his eyes satisfied her. Then he reached for his belt and pulled out a gun.

"Would you shoot when you can't see what you're firing at?" she hissed. She crouched and slid to the other side of the hall before he could locate her.

He fired once, but she smiled at the distance he missed by. She rose, walking somewhat languidly toward him, reveling in his fear. *She* was not the one afraid this time, even with his bullets. She struck, knocking him to the ground, then straddled him before spinning to her side and leaning backward, her legs gripping his arm as it clung uselessly to his gun. As she thrust her hips upward, she felt his bones snap, the way her opponent's had in training, but this time it was no accident. His gun clanked to the floor. With lightning speed, she triangled her legs around his neck, stifling his agonized breath.

"What's the code?" she hissed, then squeezed tighter. "Tell me the code for the lock."

"One, nine, six, two," he squeaked, and she twisted the metallic lock with the fingers of her free hand, all the while squeezing tighter until she felt his consciousness slip.

The metal box sprang open, and Emma found the Styrofoam one inside. She let the man's limp body slide from her legs' grip. Then she snatched the box and opened the lid to reveal the two vials of her blood.

"Finally," she muttered, and plucked the samples from the box, turning toward the stairwell.

Just

as the lights

turned back on.

She froze, the empty, windowless hallway illuminated. In an instant, her scales changed from jet black to a creamy silver that matched the fluorescently lit tiles.

The man she had blinded with venom crawled away while the one whose arm she'd broken awoke with a moan. She stepped toward the stairwell nearest her, routing her escape, but a torrent of footsteps flooded her senses. The vibrations rose in crescendo, nearing her. She needed to get out. But they seemed to come from every direction. The doors lining the hallway burst open, and out stepped dozens of men in black armor, with masks and helmets to block their faces, and guns pointing at her.

18

Emma froze, surrounded. There were dozens of them, filling the corridor and blocking any escape. They inched closer, weapons poised.

"Stay away," she shouted, fearing she couldn't protect the blood samples she had finally reclaimed. Even if she managed to fight through them, there could be more waiting in the stairwell.

She clamped down on the vials, shattering them. The blood dripped crimson over her ivory scales, splattering onto the floor.

She took a step, envisioning herself ricocheting off the walls to escape them. She could try— The slightest movement flickered from a man beside her. His trigger finger. Emma prepared to dodge, but instead of a bullet, ribbons of wire shot out into a net around her, snagging ever tighter against her body as she twisted and pulled, hissing.

She was trapped. The men parted and from behind them, a taller, unarmored man emerged, his steps slow as they approached, like those of an ancient beast awakening from sleep. When Emma's eyes fell on his unmasked face, she stopped struggling.

The blood drained from her limbs. His brown hair was cut shorter, but she recognized that face, that squared jaw, those gleaming eyes, and that wicked smile.

The man from her nightmares.

"Welcome," he said, his deep voice rattling her ribs. "We've been meaning to invite you for some time."

Her mind flashed back to her dreams, visions of that same grinning face smeared in blood. Her mouth went dry.

"You," she said, her breath shaking.

"Have we met?" he asked with feigned confusion. Or was it real? He couldn't know she had dreamed of him, could he? "I didn't think so," he said. "Let me introduce myself. I go by Cain. And I've been waiting for you for a very long time."

He studied her like a spider watching the catch in its web. What did he mean, he was waiting for her? She was dizzy, almost unable to focus. *He* was the threat, and even closer than she feared. Her scales hardened and the hairs rose from her skin.

"Who do you work for?" she asked. "And what do you want?"

"Look who's asking questions," he said, raising his brows in amusement. He smiled at the men around him, and they chuckled.

"I work for myself," he boasted. "I'm the CEO of Poseidon Corporation, the most prominent private defense contractor in the US."

"So why were you funding Dr. Belken's research?"

"You saw the talk, didn't you? The possibility of immortality. Anyone should be interested in that, right?"

You saw the talk. The words rang in her ears, words that meant one thing—they knew her identity.

"You sent someone to kill him," she said.

He puckered his lips into a circle. "Kill him? No. There must be a misunderstanding," he said with taunting sarcasm. "Why don't we talk about this somewhere a bit more private."

Before Emma could respond, the steel net was jerked backward, knocking her off her feet.

"Stop," she cried, pulling on the net as they dragged her through the hallway. But a second later, she fell silent. She wouldn't fight them, not yet. She wanted answers. After that, surely she could fight her way out, couldn't she? A nagging fear threatened. Maybe she was afraid to fight and prove her powers inadequate. What if she tried with all her might to break free and it didn't work? It would show she was at their mercy. That she was truly trapped.

They dragged her through a doorway, and the air cooled. The ground was covered in thick dirt with pine trees scattered around them, and at first, Emma thought they had brought her outside. But steel-colored walls enclosed the space, and a glass domed ceiling covered them.

"This seems like a more suitable environment for you, no?" Cain said, and gestured to the men who ensnared her. They yanked the metal tighter across her body, wrapping it around the nearest tree to pin her there.

Her hope of escape waned, and a surge of fear gripped her heart as she imagined what torture awaited. The men stepped away, still clutching their guns. She wondered what kind of bullets they fired, and if her scales could hold up to them.

"So, about Dr. Belken," Cain said, sneering. "What happened to him was unfortunate. But we had paid a lot of money for your samples, and he didn't deliver."

Emma's blood boiled, but somehow, her rage didn't bolster her like it had in the past. Instead, a chilling weakness crept into her limbs.

"They were not his to give, or yours to take," she said. "You don't have the rights to anything that belongs to me, that I didn't consent to give."

He took a step toward her, his warmth eclipsing her, so close his smoky, marine scent stifled her breath. Then he crouched to look directly into her eyes.

"Here, we can do a lot of things without your consent." He didn't smile in a taunting way. He said it flatly so she knew it was absolutely true. She shuddered but wasn't ready to yield.

"I wouldn't stand so close if I were you."

He grinned. "I'm immune to your venom."

He knows about my venom. She shook her head. "How?"

He smirked. "I thought you might know. But I see you're naive to most of what happens around you."

His insult might've hit her if she wasn't busy putting the pieces together. Her body began to tremble. Had he somehow been exposed to the snake's blood also? She didn't see how it was possible, but maybe he had been to Crete before her? Found those flowers or the snake? She recalled the tape of the old woman. *Are you sure she's female?* The woman had warned against the same thing happening to a male. *The cost … aggression.* Or maybe he had already received some of the molecules from Dr. Belken and used them on himself. But that was still experimental, and this man faced her, unmasked, with confidence he was immune.

"I see the questions in your eyes," he said. "Let me answer them. And maybe we can reach an understanding."

She clenched her teeth. "Release me if you want to talk."

He smiled again. "You remind me of her."

"Who?" she asked, her stomach coiling into a knot. Could he mean… After all, he *was* from her dreams—Medusa's memory. "You knew her?" she asked, aware she wouldn't believe him if he said yes. That was thousands of years ago.

"You could say that." He seemed to revel in knowing what she didn't, teasing her with veiled truth. She recalled his blood-stained skin.

"What did you do?" she asked.

"The things I've done would make her … your blood curdle. And I have her to thank for all of it. But I'm not here to talk about the past," he said. "I'm here to start a new relationship. I'm here to work with *you*."

Emma's breath heaved, her mind reeling at his words. *This can't be real.*

"If you're from her time, you must have used her blood to live this long," Emma said, "then you must have the compound in your body. Why do you need me?"

"Males can only be carriers," he said, not discounting her claim of using Medusa's blood. *Was he really that old?* "We don't have the compound Dr. Belken isolated from you. We can't pass anything on. Only a female can."

"Well, it's too bad I destroyed your samples then."

He scoffed. "It doesn't matter. What is one or two vials lost, when we have you?" He mocked her with a sweeping gesture and smile. "The source."

She tensed her lips. "I won't give you my blood."

He sighed. "We knew you were our guest the moment you set foot in that van. So before you start thinking you have any control here, know that we were playing you all along."

She scowled, angry in her humiliation, and despite the heavy chill in the air, her limbs sparked with tension.

"What are you going to do with my blood?" she demanded. "Market a serum for immortality?"

He smiled again, as if aroused by a challenge. "Not a bad idea," he said. "But so basic. I already can't be killed by any illness. *Now* I'm more interested in military resources."

"You want to turn people into you then?" she asked.

"No one can be me." He stood taller. "Look, we'll offer you a multi-million-dollar deal. You won't need to worry about anything anymore …

and I know, you have a lot on your plate. College coming up." He eyed her intently. "Your brother's illness."

"Stop!" she shouted. *He* had sent the men to visit Danny, left him the candies, she was sure of it now.

"Oh," he said, faking sympathy with a hand to his chest. "Was that a sensitive topic?"

She would choke the grin off his face. She swore it.

"Don't worry about what we do with the blood," he said, sounding casual again. "You can tell yourself it's for the sake of national security, protection against terrorism, anything that will help you sleep at night."

"No," she said and could tell he was not used to hearing the word, and maybe even incapable of understanding it. The vein in his temple bulged, a muscle in his neck twitched, and his fists clenched. It was almost amusing. She grew calmer in the face of his volatility, as if it lent her more control than he realized. It seemed a struggle for him to stay composed.

"Money can buy you a lot of things," he said. "Sometimes, even, it means you don't have to follow the rules. It was only by breaking them that I started an empire, and I won't let you stand in my way."

He stepped toward her again. "I paid Dr. Belken. I've all but *bought* you." The way he said *you,* like she was *nothing,* ignited her rage.

"I was never for sale," she said.

He smirked. "There are plenty of ways to take what you won't willingly give."

"You can't get away with this," she said as he turned away.

He paused, the profile of his face cast in shadow.

"I can get away with quite a few things, it turns out," he said. "The police are the ones who gave me footage of you from the robbery. If there's anything I've learned how to manipulate in my long life, it's the law."

Still entangled in the wire net, Emma stared at the door Cain had disappeared through, shut and bolted. She had expected someone else to enter, dreaded what torture might be in store. But only stillness transpired, and she began to wonder if this was a kind of experiment. She sensed the body heat emanating from a wall of black glass behind her and knew they were watching. The expansive room, with its dirt and trees, resembled a life-sized terrarium.

A cage. That's what this was. She was like one of her mice now, a study subject. And they were taking their time with her. She needed to escape, but her chances seemed to recede with each passing minute.

She tensed, her hands itching to fight. She looked down and saw her nails had sharpened into points, glinting with a sheen of hammered bronze. *Claws.* Emma marveled, trying to conceal her shock so whoever was watching might not notice them. She knew, even before using them, they were razor sharp. If only she could use them on Cain, watch him flinch at the sight of them. Surely he wouldn't be immune to slicing. She would let him get close enough, and then…

She stopped the fantasy, almost recoiling at it. She had never remained this long in scales before, and her claws were proof she was transforming even further. Was she losing the part of herself that was human? Could her mind and heart turn serpentine also? She felt a shiver spread over her skin and realized it wasn't only from unease. The room was undoubtedly colder. She needed to move, break from her trap. That would help.

Her scaled skin undulated like waves along a water's surface, subtle yet strong, stretching and bending the wires that still ensnared her, inch by inch, until she created a gap in the net. It was tedious, but she took her time, contorting her body. Then she loosened, and in a fluid movement, compressed and stretched her way through the small gap until she was free. There was no sense of movement from beyond the dark glass, and she wondered if they were taking notes on her escape.

She spread her limbs over the ground, wondering why she felt more exhausted than she ever had from such small movements. Then she knew, as she took a breath and the air stole the heat from inside her lungs. *Snakes are ectotherms, which meant they derive energy from the heat made by the sun or their surroundings.* It made sense. She was part snake, and in the cold, she couldn't make the energy she needed. The ground beneath her felt almost like ice.

What an easy way to stop her. She felt almost embarrassed by it. Such a small, overlooked detail was incapacitating her. She couldn't fight anyone like *this*. Even her thoughts slowed like a boulder being pushed through sludge. She was vulnerable to whatever they might try. Then she reminded herself that part of her was still human. A small part that seemed to slip farther from grasp with each passing minute. Yet it was saving her. That human part shivered again, to keep her warm enough to stay awake.

She guessed a few more hours passed, but she couldn't be sure. She hadn't mustered the energy to move and lay lethargic and heavy in the freezing dirt. She still had no food or water, but at least her lowered metabolism meant she wasn't very hungry. She found herself fighting off sleep as the temperature dropped further.

As night fell, she watched the scales encasing her stiff body as they turned from pale green to black, coated in a silver sheen by the moon that hung high above the glass ceiling. Maybe she could scale up the walls to it, break it and escape. But the walls were so smooth. They had no ridges for her scales to grip onto. Finally, she drifted into a stony sleep.

As the sun lifted the sky into morning, Emma awoke, her lids like a heavy blanket of snow. She watched a ray of sun refracting through the glass ceiling, and her body was eager for even a thread of its heat.

Overnight, the temperature had turned the room's condensation into ice that now coated the tree branches around her.

An idea flickered in her mind, like a butterfly with fractured wings. Maybe it was a foolish one, emerging in her groggy mind. But it was worth a try. Slowly, she dragged her body up.

She studied the shimmering sheets of ice, searching through the branches and twigs until she found a disc-shaped piece between branches and broke it off into her hand. They were so cold the ice didn't melt.

She wondered if her observers would catch on. There was only an eerie stillness beyond the black window, like the void of a ceaseless universe. But she knew they were there. She might not be able to see them, but she sensed traces of their heat.

Maybe her movements were too slow to warrant their alarm. Maybe they would never think she was capable of what she was about to do. And maybe she wasn't, after all, but she would try anyway.

Slowly, she followed the beam of sunlight through the glass above her, gathering whatever dry leaves and kindling she could find as she moved, until she struck the proper angle. Then she held the ice disc between her clawed fingers, moving it until it caught the stream of sunlight. She wondered, as she beheld the glowing stream of air, if Medusa had ever left that cave to bathe in the sun's warmth or hope for mercy in the light of Helios's chariot.

Emma held her breath, remembering her physics teacher, Ms. Levine, mentioning this phenomena once during an ill-fated attempt to inspire the class. Emma might've been the only one paying attention, but she never thought that one day her life might depend on her teacher's words. At first, there was nothing. Then, in the brush beneath her, a wisp of smoke arose like a weightless serpent from the earth.

Surely, *now* they would come to stop her. Or maybe they didn't expect or understand this. They might have known what powers to watch for from the snake, but they had underestimated *Emma*. Her heart fluttered, and she tried not to smile, not before it had fully worked.

The twigs on the ground burst into flames under the magnified light of the sun. Then came the burst of frenzied movement beyond the wall. Even she was surprised by how fast it worked. She waved a hand to coax the flame, causing the heat to rise higher. Already she felt a wave of energy return to her.

She snatched more leaves and fed the flames, cracking branches and adding them. Another source of heart swelled from the bodies running toward the door. Now Emma smiled. The fire began to spread, and she backed away. It proved even faster growing than she'd expected, and she wondered if the floor beneath the dirt was coated in something flammable.

For a moment she feared they wouldn't unlock the door, that she'd actually sentenced herself to a fiery death. But no, she was an asset to him, Cain had proven it. They wouldn't let something he paid so much for burn to ashes before their eyes.

Just then, she felt rain droplets shooting from sprinklers along the walls.

No, she thought, *no*. Her *terrarium* seemed equipped with whatever weather her captors wanted, as if they were playing god to her. No, she thought, she wouldn't suffer at the hands of any god.

The droplets barely quenched the flames, and even as they simmered, the clouds of smoke stifled the room, threatening to burn her lungs. She coughed. Just then, the door flung open. Men stepped inside, hoisting a thick hose that spouted water across the room, while others in uniform rushed by, shouting and hoisting their guns. She recognized one device as the one that shot the steel net. But they would need to see her to ensnare her again, and the smoke clouded the scene, shrouding her as her scales blended stoney gray.

And there was another thing they weren't ready for. The heat had fed her, fueled her full power to return, making it vibrate more powerfully than ever before. Beneath the glass ceiling, now heated to the verge of melting, her scales ignited with slivers of fiery red, and she exploded through the narrow opening of the door.

There were shouts from every direction and men gathering in the corridors to stop her. She didn't slow. She charged through the halls, knocking some to the ground, leaving others with ribbons of blood in their soft skin as she slashed through armor with her new claws.

She turned the corner and saw a window at the end of a hallway. In the distance outside, a van was driving out of the headquarters. To her pursuers, it might have looked like she'd found a dead end. But her mind sharpened, and she gauged the van's speed and her own trajectory, clear and precise. Then she broke into a sprint, a second later shattering through the window and leaping into the air, a graceful bullet.

She flew, feeling suspended in time, before she landed with a crash atop the moving van, rolling to the side to diffuse the impact. Still, it shocked her limbs. The van swerved, and she pierced into its metal roof with her claws to hold on, her scales gripping at the knobbed panels. Then she swooped her body around the side, smashing the window with her foot and knocking the driver unconscious. She slid inside, gripping the wheel with one hand and tossing his body out the window with the other. She pressed the pedal down as far as it could go, barreling through the security checkpoint.

Her adrenaline pulsed, but a sense of serenity seeped into her core as she set her eyes on the road ahead. Only before taking a final turn away from the headquarters did she look back and see the stream of smoke rising in a gentle plume. The melting glass ceiling had caved.

She smiled as she sped onto a main road. She had taught this enemy something, something she had known a long time, from working in Dr. Belken's lab.

Snakes are very good at escaping their cages.

19

Emma sped down the highway, gripping the steering wheel so tightly its surface cracked beneath her palms. Despite her elaborately executed escape, she barely had her driver's permit, and *this* felt unnatural. Fortunately, the road was relatively straight and empty. But where was she? She studied the street signs for recognizable names. She had no clothes, no phone, and no idea how to get home. There was still plenty of gas in the tank. But if this was a Poseidon company vehicle, it was likely being tracked, and she wanted to get out as soon as possible.

She glanced in the rearview mirror. So far, no one seemed to be following her. Maybe they were waiting for something? To be more discreet? She stopped herself from pressing the gas pedal any harder, not wanting to attract police attention. She had already noticed the few drivers who glanced her way as she passed, their look of alarm and confusion as they spotted the woman in scales at the steering wheel.

After twenty minutes of tense driving, a rest station appeared alongside the highway and she swerved, a little more sharply than she intended, and pulled into the parking lot. She rummaged through the back of the van for something to cover herself with, and found a cloth, splotched with dirt and maybe mildew. Her nostrils flared as she wrapped it around her body.

But she couldn't step outside yet, not with her scales. She closed her eyes and tried to calm herself, to imagine herself as *human*, with soft skin and clear, round nails. Her body fought it, still tense and poised for a fight, replaying her capture and the adrenaline-fueled escape. If only she could have seen Cain's face as she fought his men, leaped from the window. Her knee twinged in pain from the landing, but she knew it would heal, the sooner the better. Her mind began to calm, until she reminded herself that time was limited. They might have sent someone to chase her. The scales hardened again.

Her thoughts scattered, searching frantically for any source of relief. As it seemed to recede from her grasp, Emma thought of her sensei, her calming words, and then of Jason, and the way he touched her skin when they lay beside each other. Slowly, the sharp nails receded and her hands looked human again. She took a breath, and as relief spread, the scales faded as well. She scavenged through the glove compartment, through gum wrappers, a cigarette box, and the van's user manuals, until she found loose change. She grabbed the coins and stepped out of the car.

She was hyper-aware of the eyes on her, naked beneath a dirty drape, smelling and disheveled. Her unruly hair sprang in every direction, and she couldn't recall at what point she had lost her hair tie. She spotted a pay phone on the far side of the building, across from a clothing donation bin and two garbage pails. *Please work,* she whispered, as she fed coins into the slot and pressed the rusted buttons. The phone looked like it hadn't been used in a decade. She glanced around, hoping no one eyeing her was disturbed enough to call the police. A moment later she was greeted by Jason's voice mail. Quickly, she dialed Pria's number, proud she knew it by heart, but it rang until reaching her voice mail. They must be in class, she thought, but it was strange for neither to answer. A flash of fear shook her. What if they were in danger too? Emma recalled the way Cain had mentioned her brother, so casually threatening, and her heart pounded.

But she took a breath. They probably were just ignoring an unknown number as spam. They likely had texted her cell, but she had no way to respond. She paused, straining to recall another number before dialing. She fidgeted as the ring tone sounded, noticing a child staring at her before his mom grabbed his hand and ushered him away.

"Hi, Michelle?" Emma said, trying to steady her voice, but the urgency cracked through. "This is—"

"What's wrong?" her sensei asked. A comforting pulse throbbed through Emma.

"I can't explain everything now," she said. "But can you come pick me up? It's an emergency. I'm at a rest station on the side of the highway." She squinted to read its name on the sign above the entrance.

"Wow, you're far away." Michelle paused. "Should we call the police?" she asked.

"No," Emma said. "At least, not yet."

Michelle paused again. "I'll leave now," she said. Emma exhaled in relief. She pulled the cloth closer to her neck then found a bench along the backside of the building to wait on.

She walked there quickly, hunching to make herself less visible, but it was no use. Her jarring appearance aroused suspicion, or maybe concern. As minutes passed, more than a few worried travelers seemed alarmed, whispering among themselves or looking around for some explanation for her appearance.

She needed to get out of there, the urgency mounting as she waited for forty-five minutes. Maybe she needed to find a less public place. She started to wonder if some of the visitors could be Cain's employees. Maybe they were preparing to take her again. Her eyes darted about, studying the man reading a newspaper on the bench in front of the entrance, then the woman holding french fries and glancing at her as she walked to her car. Through the window of the rest stop, she saw a woman clutching her toddler's hand and speaking to a security guard. She was pointing in Emma's direction. Emma tensed as the security guard rose and began walking toward her.

She would have to take the van again, escape while she had the chance. Or maybe she should talk her way out of this, ask for help. She was debating how to handle a confrontation, her pulse speeding, when she glanced toward the parking lot and saw her sensei drive in. Emma bolted toward the car and jumped inside, relief flooding her limbs.

"Thank you so much," Emma said. "You have no idea—"

"Pffu!" Michelle said, scrunching her nose. If she was at all shocked or disturbed by Emma's appearance, it was masked by her calm. She turned and rummaged in the backseat of her car. "I don't have any spare clothes but you can wear my gi." She took the training robe and tossed it on Emma's lap.

"Thanks, but can we start driving? I'll change on the way."

Michelle nodded, and Emma began twisting into the gi beneath her seatbelt. Her adrenaline had been surging, her survival instincts activated ever since Dr. Belken's shooting. Only now did a tangible sense of relief strike her, like a sun ray breaking a storm cloud. Her body felt weak and heavy on the seat.

"Okay, Emma, tell me what's going on." Michelle's voice was warm but firm.

Emma inhaled deeply, steadying herself. She started with her professor's presentation and the video she found in the lab detailing the mythical source of her transformation, aware of how bizarre it must sound. But Michelle kept her eyes calmly on the road, her face relaxed but pensive. Emma recounted how she had tried to confront Dr. Belken before he was shot. Then she described her capture by Cain and her escape. Michelle listened with a growing expression of awe, until Emma finally fell into an exhausted silence.

"So that's it then," Michelle said. "You're a Greek god?"

There was levity in the comment, and Emma smiled appreciatively, then shook her head. "Medusa wasn't a god." Emma paused in thought. "I think she's glad she wasn't, if you consider what it takes to become one. What it does to you." She shuddered at the thought of Cain. "Power, without consequence…"

Michelle nodded. "No soul. But, Emma, you fought them all? That's … *incredible*." She glanced over at her in the passenger seat. "You must be exhausted."

Emma nodded. "But it's not over." She took a slow breath. "Can you bring me to the hospital now? I need to find Dr. Belken if he's still alive. There's more he could answer."

"Of course," she said. "Why don't you rest now, it'll still be a while."

"Thank you," Emma said, basking in Michelle's peaceful essence. "I really don't know what I'd do without you," she whispered. Then, lulled by the steady engine and smooth road, she drifted into a deep sleep.

The darkness of slumber gave way to a familiar cave. It had been weeks since she had seen through Medusa's eyes, and she knew, even in her sleep, that there must be a reason for the return, her first since discovering the truth of her own transformation. Now, Emma's heart connected so strongly to hers, their fibers seemed to resonate at the same frequency.

Medusa's hair slithered, alive with serpents, but somehow, they appeared soft, their scales glowing with traces of gold from the sunlight at the cave's mouth. Memories of different men danced beneath her eyelids as she blinked, their bodies and faces turning to stone as they gazed upon her. The words echoed, more faint and distant now. *You are nothing.* Medusa had a sense of satisfaction then. Those men had come to kill her, only to cry out a second before turning to stone that would hold their horror forever.

Emma had a sense that many years had passed since the previous memory. Medusa gazed at her reflection in a puddle between rocks, wondering in her loneliness if she could turn herself into stone that way too.

"Goddess," a soft voice called from behind a pillar.

Medusa screeched and turned, her narrowed eyes full of fury. She would petrify him before he crept closer. How had he even entered the cave so stealthily? She poised herself to meet his attack, as she had met so many others.

"Goddess, I come in peace," his voice said. "I have no weapons, as I mean you no harm."

"Then why have you come?" she demanded, pinpointing his hiding spot by the sense of his heat and vibrations of his voice.

"To ask for your help," he answered.

She paused for a moment. A trick, she thought. But something held her there. No one had asked for her help before. Actually, since her time in the cave, no one had spoken to her unless to make a threat. A tattered hope glimmered.

"If you're not here to harm me, show yourself," she hissed.

"Yes, goddess."

I'm not a goddess, she thought to say, but she liked hearing him say it, admiration mixed with fear in his tone. He wasn't mocking her.

"Please, I know what you can do. I don't wish to be turned to stone."

"Then don't look me in the eye. Keep your head down and eyes closed."

"Yes," he said. "I will be at your mercy. Can I trust that you won't harm me?"

"If what you say is true and you don't attempt any malice, yes." Her voice resonated with power. "I will give you a chance. But if you so much as make one move against me, it will be your last."

She felt the vibrations of his pulsing heart as the visitor stepped from behind the rock. Through her sleep, Emma shuddered at the sight, for even with his eyes closed, she recognized him. He was younger, yes, and leaner, but the bold shape of his jaw and brow, his nose and mouth, were unmistakable.

Cain.

20

Kill him, Emma thought through her sleep. But no, this was not Emma's story. Medusa beheld him in amusement and intrigue as he groveled on the rocky ground, exposing his neck to her.

"You're very brave," she said. "I'm sure you've seen the stones lining the entrance to my cave, the men who came before you."

He nodded, still facing the ground. Medusa took pride in intimidating him, his supplication almost restoring something she had lost long ago.

"I would not have come if I was not desperate for your help," he said.

"Tell me, what do you ask?" she hissed.

"I know you've seen so much death," he began.

"Don't speak to me about what I've seen," she snapped, her body hardening. Perhaps his words struck too close to the truth in her hidden heart.

He nodded, bowing lower. "I only meant to say that I know there is life in you too. That your blood holds the power to heal any ailment, and I am wondering if you would give me the chance," he hesitated, "to use it."

No, Emma thought, *don't give him anything!* Medusa furrowed her brows. "Who told you this?"

"It is well known. Perhaps started by worshippers of the goddess Athena."

"Don't speak her name here," Medusa said, her eyes narrowing to slits. The snakes of her crown writhed and hissed with agitation, and her heart churned with bitterness. She wanted to strike at him in anguish, but she knew it would all end too easily. He would be turned to stone, and she would be left colder and harder for it. It had been so long since she had seen any facet of humanity other than hostility. Until this... She wasn't ready for it to end yet.

"I'm sorry," he said, bowing still lower. "I only meant to answer the question honestly. Did you not know your blood held such power?"

She pursed her lips. "What do you want with my blood?" she asked.

"I work as a healer," he said. "But my concoctions have not been able to heal my ailing father. I would beg from you to have just one drop of your healing blood. I will be your humble servant forever after, for whatever you might ask."

She considered his words. He was alone there. He had risked so much to come. Others might have been after her blood but had come with weapons to kill her and take it. He was *asking*.

"I will consider," she said. "But you must return here everyday so I can prove your loyalty."

And so he did, day after day, repeating his ritual of bowing with eyes closed in subservience. He started to bring her things—carnations, thyme and rosemary, figs or freshly cooked fish. Warmth seeped in her bones at these gestures, although once, when he brought a fragrant peony and olives, Medusa's mind flashed to Athena's temple, the type of floral offerings she would arrange from worshippers there and the olive groves she attended outside. But she simmered her revulsion, not wanting to punish her naive guest, not wanting his attention to stop. When he left, she drowned the peonies in the sea, holding her breath from their sickening stench.

To Medusa's surprise, her visitor proved observant, realizing which gifts she savored more. Or was it a coincidence? He didn't repeat his gifts of olives or peonies, and Medusa started to feel a strange, miraculous sense of being understood. He warned her if someone was coming outside the cave and praised her powers of protection when she used them to turn her attackers to stone. But he never fought, and Medusa thought him too gentle for it. Emma watched with unease, knowing what this man was capable of, as Medusa grew fond of his presence.

They sat one afternoon, back to back, swapping stories and memories.

"So, you're mortal?" he asked her, his deep voice gentle.

But she stiffened, guarding herself. *Why would he want to know that if he doesn't plan to kill me*, and her snakes hissed in agreement with her doubt. But beneath her hardened scales, she was human, yearning to tell someone the story of her loneliness.

"I am," she said. Slowly, the hissing of her snakes calmed, maybe assured by his unflinching support. "My mother gave birth to sea monsters by my father. He is one, after all, but she has a beautiful, human-like form, and so she wanted just one non-monstrous child, one who captured her essence. But the tradeoff was that I would have to be mortal. In the caverns of Mt. Olympus, she had triplets. Two are goddesses, immortal. And I, though we shared a womb, am no goddess."

A sinking note trailed the end of her sentence. He didn't attempt to console her, perhaps because he didn't catch it or perhaps his curiosity was stronger. She didn't blame him. She would ponder these same things too, on sleepless nights drifting on beds of seaweed, then on the cold temple stairs, and now, on the jagged rocks of her cave.

"But how was that achieved?" he asked.

Medusa sighed. "I'm still not sure. But I suspected, as in other such cases with the gods, that perhaps my mother lay with a mortal."

There was silence between them as droplets echoed in the far corners of the cave. She had never admitted this suspicion aloud, and as a child, the entire family had been forbidden from speaking about it. As she confessed it now, her heart lifted with new lightness, and she felt closer to this man who accepted it all, embracing her story as no one else had.

"So maybe my sea-god father is not my father at all," she said. "Or maybe it wasn't a mortal my mother involved but some potion that allowed this. Either way, the rumors abounded, and my father would barely look at me, resenting my existence. Maybe he knew my fate—a human in the ocean, too easily drowned or swallowed by a creature."

"But you survived," he said. Her cheeks warmed.

"I had help," she said. "My mother and sisters protected me, until they couldn't anymore. As friendly as the sea nymphs are, they do gossip, and tales of my strangeness and worldly looks spread through the waters. Poseidon's shadow always lurked. My mother told me he had once wanted her, but when she rejected his advances, he set his eyes on her daughter." Medusa's voice cracked. Though time had passed, speaking that monster's name still shook her insides. Maybe she had been doomed all along, even before she was born. No one born in the ocean escapes Poseidon, especially not beautiful women.

"You don't have to tell me such painful—" he began.

"I want to," she answered firmly. "Some said I should be grateful," she continued. "That as a lowly human, I caught the attention of such a great god. But he repulsed me. And my mother knew what I know now— when gods encounter humans, it never ends well for the human. So she tried to protect me. She brought me to live on land, and maybe he forgot about me for a time, found a beautiful sea nymph or higher goddess to entertain himself." The snakes of her crown writhed as if ready to spit.

"And what about…" He paused, and she tasted his reluctance.

"Athena?" she finished for him. She felt him nod against her back. "I thought she would protect me." Medusa didn't mention her intense longing, the love she had harbored for the goddess. No. For some reason, she didn't want to share that with him. Or maybe she knew the reason. Ruled by men, women were not made for each other, not in that way, not in that city. "I read all her stories," she said instead. "I knew that she had beat out Poseidon to claim the coastal city, so I thought, surely, she wouldn't let him find me there."

"But were you always sworn to her? I mean, or did you have any other … experience?"

Medusa chuckled, amused at the detail he chose to focus on. Virginity seemed so important to men, yet they were so eager to shed theirs. Still, his curiosity made her stomach flutter.

Her cheeks warmed with the memory of the sea nymph she had shared passionate kisses with, their bodies entwined amidst the waves. It felt so long ago now. Sometimes the sea nymph still visited her when she lived on land, but the visits became fewer and fewer, and then not at all, once Medusa pledged herself to Athena. But she couldn't mention this to him either. A female lover was not taken seriously, only dismissed as nothing. And a claim of more serious love would only be judged.

"I had many suitors," she said instead. "Many offers, some from quite handsome and reputable men." She recalled even fantasizing about being with some of them, but it meant sacrificing who she was, a creature of the sea. She felt him stiffen a little against her back, his breaths stifled.

"But maybe I was destined to be alone. I didn't quite fit in their world, just like I didn't quite fit in the sea. I was not a strong enough swimmer to match any sea god. I would too easily drown. Yet I could outswim any human and spent too much time in the water for them.

Offers of marriage meant moving into a house, leaving the sea behind. But Athena's temple was perfect."

She closed her eyes and, for a moment, recalled the serenity of those earlier days, lighting incense, cooking offerings or picking olives in the golden light of dusk, splashing through the waves as the sun rose, and swimming again as it sank with evening.

"So you've been alone most of your life," he said, cutting through her imagery. She opened her eyes.

"No," she said. "My sisters, Stheno and Euryale, were my best friends." She paused, contemplating her use of *were*. An aching feeling clawed through her chest as she thought how much she missed them, but the ache had spines of anger, piercing at the hollows of her heart, anger for the sisters who hadn't come.

She swallowed. "They would visit me even on the land, check on my life among mortals, bring me news from the ocean—what deadly monster was just born. Since I left, my parents had given birth to a dragon with a hundred serpent heads, who guards the golden orchard where apples glow that light the dusk. And they would tell me who had fallen in love—one of the most beautiful of my sea nymph cousins had apparently fallen in love with a shepherd, to the outrage of the gods. I didn't care much for this gossip, though it helped me retain a sense of my origins. Still, I liked it better when my sisters came to ask for my advice."

"What would you advise on?" He rushed the question, as if eager to fuel a more pleasant topic than her loneliness.

"Many things. Problems. Relationships. They always told me I was smart, when I fashioned rafts together or strung ropes to catch squid. I had to be. A mortal's mind needs to be smart to survive. Maybe that's also why I worshipped Athena, goddess of wisdom." A tightness gripped her throat.

"I'm sorry," he said gently, and his voice calmed her breathing enough to continue.

"As a mortal among the deathless, you need to be perceptive of how others feel, their motives and dislikes, so you can survive. They only care about those things to their own ends, which in some ways makes them shortsighted. But it doesn't matter because they have less at stake. The gods are quick to anger, and in that anger, impulsive. I tiptoed around them." She paused. "But I guess, in the end, my skills weren't enough to protect me."

A familiar dread clouded her vision, as if she now stared down into a dark abyss of sorrow and rage that threatened to swallow her. Just as she began to tremble, he spoke the words she had never heard before.

"It wasn't your fault."

She hadn't known how much she needed to hear them until that moment, how much they would mean, even coming from a man she barely knew. She bit her lip, nodding, and the darkness faded.

"I know," she whispered, and they sat in silence.

"It must be hard to be alone here," he said.

Again, a ping of defensiveness hardened her muscles and her snakes twitched. She reminded herself he wasn't the threat.

"Yes," she said. "I still hope my sisters will visit. If they can."

"They're probably jealous of your beauty," he said. She chuckled, thinking how men find the simplest explanations.

"I *was* more beautiful than them," she said, "but how could they be jealous of me? They swam along the ocean floor, watching starfish and catching clams, while I gasped at the water's surface. I suffered scrapes from corals, stings from jellyfish, and it took days to heal. On them, these things disappeared like they never happened. They watched my fingers prune and crack in the salt, and my skin burn in the sun. They remained smooth and supple, forever."

Another silence ensued, but it felt as if she could hear his mind churning.

"I will only disagree with one thing," he said. "You're still the most beautiful, I'm sure of it."

The hot salt of tears in her eyes surprised her. She wished, more than ever before, to turn, to take him in, all of him.

The scenes swirled forward as Emma slept, and she sank deeper into the ancient memory. At first, Medusa placed all responsibility on him to avoid her gaze. When he wasn't bowing and she allowed him to stand, he would blindfold himself so they could converse, working around her powers. But slowly it changed. Emma was aware, with each new memory and passage of time, something else was blossoming.

Trust. Their interactions began with her looking into the pool, waiting to see his reflection so as not to look him in the eye and petrify him. Then she began covering her own eyes in his presence, taming her own power for him, becoming vulnerable.

Then it became something more than trust. *Love.* Love that seemed to fade the scorned remnants of the kind she had given Athena. Emma marveled at the scene. Could this be possible? But yes, that's what Medusa felt, and it was a thing she had given up on ever knowing again in her life.

He would kiss her hand in greeting, and as time passed, linger near her lips, all the while avoiding her gaze. She had sworn off all lovers once, replacing any yearning with devotion to Athena, a love now crushed in shame. What had love ever gotten her but monstrosity? The only touch she had known was that of the spiny sea god. She shuddered, fearing she could not meet this new caress, that it would rekindle a pathetic longing and stolen hope. But when his warm lips touched hers, a wall inside her melted.

Medusa became consumed by the desire to look him in the eyes. It was all she wanted then, but she knew that would be his end. So she went on with this new torment, feeling rage at Athena all over again. But also, a swell of triumph. Athena had cursed her to become a monster, unable to receive or give affection, and yet, here she was, wading around those confines with *him*.

After a youth of being eyed by men for her beauty then punished for it, she found someone who loved her not for appearance, but for who she was. Even Emma began to believe that Cain might truly love Medusa. Shrouded in the darkness of the cave, their hands reached for one another, and the image of them clasping, scales against skin, struck something inside her. As Emma faded from the memory, she thought of her own hands, and Jason's. A rush of movement jostled her as the car bumped along the road. She awoke, disoriented.

"Oh my god," she whispered, squinting at the bright autumn day through the windshield.

"What?" Michelle asked.

"They were lovers," she whispered.

"Who?" Michelle asked.

"Cain ... and Medusa."

Michelle shook her head. "How is that possible?"

Emma recounted the memory, Michelle quietly listening as she drove.

"He must have used her," Michelle whispered, and her voice sounded softer than it ever had. There was pain in it. Michelle's throat bobbed as she swallowed hard.

The car slowed to a stop as they neared the hospital's entrance. Michelle turned her way, and though her eyes were clear, a trace of salt in the air hinted at the tears she was suppressing. Emma studied her, enthralled, wanting to know the unexplored crevices behind that wall of composure.

Without warning, Michelle reached over the center console and placed her hand on Emma's. They had touched before, locked in jiu jitsu holds, rolling over a mat so close they exchanged sweat and breath. But this touch was different. Soft. A tingling flurried up Emma's arm from the contact, settling low in her stomach. Her breath grew shallow. *What was this? Did she feel it too?* Emma waited for Michelle to speak, eager for her words to explain the feeling, but in the silence it only intensified.

"Let me know what happens," Michele whispered. Emma sensed she wanted to say more. But Michelle withdrew her hand, clearing her throat.

"Or if you need back up," she said, and winked, her swell of softness retreating. Emma could tell she was trying to stay lighthearted now, but she saw the hints of worry in Michelle's face and smelled a scent like alkaline mud pooling beneath that soft, earthen spice of her skin. *Fear.*

21

Emma paced through the hospital lobby and signed the visitor's log. Visiting Dr. Belken was a predictable move. But it was also in plain sight, and she had a feeling they wouldn't confront her here. The tall security guard gave her Dr. Belken's room number, looking her up and down a bit critically. She figured a martial arts outfit was only socially acceptable for a child taking karate, but he let her in without commenting.

Emma strode into the ICU, past rooms where patients lay in varying states of consciousness, some on ventilators, others with wires coming from every orifice. She tried not to look, already envisioning Danny as one of them. The smell of cleaning fluid and iodine mixed with putrid flesh. Her stomach coiled tightly, afraid of how she might find Dr. Belken. What if he couldn't even speak?

"Visiting hours are over," a nurse said as she walked up to the central desk. If Emma had hoped to sneak by, wearing her jiu jitsu gi was not helping.

"Oh, thank you," Emma said, sure sounding antagonistic might get her thrown out. "Is it okay if I just drop something off then?"

"Be quick," the nurse said, and turned to go into a patient's room.

When Emma walked into his gray, dimly lit room, Dr. Belken's eyes fluttered open. The irony struck her then, and she recalled that not so long ago, *she* was the one in a hospital bed, with him standing over her.

He looked too exhausted to be alarmed by her visit, his large eyes protruding from his sallow cheeks. "Emma," he muttered. He moved to sit up, but instead his face contracted in pain and he lay back like a fallen bird.

"You know why I'm here?" she asked, her lips tense.

"To finish me?" He exhaled, his breath like a dimming flame, and surrendered any attempt to move. She stepped closer and sat down on the plastic chair beside his bed.

"They tried to capture me, but I escaped," she said. A look of relief passed over his face. "I want you to tell me everything you know now," Emma said. "I deserve to know."

"I hoped you'd come." He nodded slowly. "Before they do. They'll be back to finish me." His face was pale as he spread his parched lips. " I thought they were my answer. My lab was going broke, my chance at prestige in research fading away. They were giving me funding like I've never had. But after my presentation, when I found out the truth, I tried to terminate the contract. That's when they came to the lab."

"What's the truth?" Emma asked. If the situation were different, she would be softer, more empathetic to a frail man in the hospital, but her voice had an edge.

"You weren't given antivenom. I injected you with *venom*. From the unidentified snake."

She nodded, anger congealed with relief at his confession. She had already discovered that much, but hearing him say it offered a sort of validation. He swallowed slowly, his breath wheezing when he opened his mouth to speak.

"I caught the snake in the forest. I couldn't identify it either. But I extracted the venom. I wanted to make an antivenom for it, and I needed to inject it into a human source for that. It was such a small amount, I didn't think it would harm you. If anything I thought it would help you form immunity in case you were bitten. It was even less than the doses I would typically use."

"Why not do it to yourself then?"

"I've injected too many, it was too messy," he said. "It would've been difficult to isolate the response in my own blood to study. But you, you were naive."

She scoffed at his choice of words. "You could've killed me."

"It was such a minuscule amount—"

"If you weren't a coward, you would've at least tried it on yourself first." The biting words were both painful and freeing.

He paused, then nodded ever so slightly. "I was scared, I'll admit."

"You didn't have my consent," she said, "to turn me into your experiment."

He nodded. "You're right."

"I found your *hidden* file."

"Emma," he said feebly. "I didn't believe that old woman on Crete. It sounded so crazy…"

"That's why you wanted my blood sample," she said. "And you told me you didn't look at it, but you had been studying it all along, while denying me the chance to do those experiments." Heat rose inside her. "The molecule in your *groundbreaking* presentation was from *my* blood."

He hung his head, his skin pale and lax. "Yes. What I found in your blood was truly remarkable," he said. "Imagine what it could mean, a molecule for immortality. I started to realize some part of that old woman's tale might be true."

"But you didn't tell me because you knew what you were doing was wrong," she said, her voice rising. It was more truth than accusation, and he knew it.

"It was wrong, unethical, I know. I'm sorry. I let the pursuit of my career in science take over. I wanted to cure illnesses."

"Did you? Or did you want something else? I thought you were trying to help me when you took my blood, but you were *selling* me."

"You know you need money to do good research, and my grants were running out. I thought I'd tell you eventually, that you might even be happy you contributed so much."

"When would I be happy? After you profited from what you stole?" She stood from the chair.

"When I knew more about it," he said. "The mice I tested it on were immune to everything … but the drawback was there. All the mice I used became aggressive. They ended up fighting each other to death in their cages if not separated. I didn't mention that in the presentation, but my sponsor knew."

His *sponsor*. Emma thought of Cain.

"The males become aggressive…" she said, remembering the old woman's words and the way that one surviving mouse had tried to bite her. "Is that why you haven't used it for yourself yet?" she asked. "You must have considered it."

"I always thought there would be a chance to, later, once I could confirm the effects. I could beg for that molecule now to save me from whatever damage has been done to my body. But I've realized something. This molecule should be hidden at all costs, your blood protected."

"Why?"

"Men were *not* meant to live forever. Especially not like that."

Emma folded her arms, bringing a hand up to her chin in thought.

"So you think it's true," she said. "This could really mean…" She took a breath. "I'm immortal?"

He hesitated. " I don't have all the answers, but you can review my experiments when I'm…" He trailed off. "From what I've seen, the regeneration of stem cells suggests that, yes. Although I suspect there are limits."

Emma nodded. "I'm not impenetrable. My scales chip. I bruise. And *Medusa,*" the name felt strange to say aloud to him, "was killed, wasn't she?"

"You would know better than me," he said.

Emma wondered if it were possible that the ending she had read of Medusa's myth, her beheading, wasn't the true end of her story. The revelation of Cain in those ancient memories was already outside of any poet's retelling.

"The snakes were immortal," Emma said, remembering the video and her awe as she viewed it in their later blood-smeared lab. "That's what the woman explained. Because they were a curse from the gods. And maybe, since the blood and flowers are from those snakes … so am I."

"If that myth is true," he said, seemingly opposed to the idea. "There must be a scientific explanation for it, if only I can get back to the lab." His voice strained. He shook his head. "An immortal snake. In all my years researching these species, I never could have imagined that."

A flash of empathy stung Emma as she thought of his long career, his aspirations slipping from his grasp.

"Emma," he whispered. "If you are…" He didn't say the word, but she knew he meant *immortal.* "You can't become like him," he said, his voice dropping. "A life of immortality without consequence creates a monster."

She thought of the dream, Medusa's memory of Cain. What if he hadn't been a sociopath to begin with but transformed? After all, he appeared so meek and tender at their first encounter in the cave.

"He told me he was waiting for me a long time," Emma said, her voice quivering as she recalled his sinister grin. "Do you know what he meant?"

Dr. Belken swallowed. "Not exactly. But I had no contact with him until after I returned from Crete. When I was looking for funding for this research, he was one of the first to reach out, persistent, and offering a lot. During my presentation, when you asked about the snake, that was the first time most people had heard about it. But not Cain. His interest in my research piqued when he knew it was performed on Crete, and he pressured me to admit that there was an unidentified snake species involved. It seemed his financial backing hinged on this fact, and he didn't want anyone else to know."

Emma nodded, wondering just how long Cain had been hunting her. "Tell me," she said, stepping closer. "What was it you found out about him? That made you want to break your contract and forfeit his funding?"

His breath quivered, and he peered to the door as if afraid someone was coming.

"Marketing immortality would be fraught with ethical challenges, but that's not what Poseidon wanted the blood for." Dr. Belken's voice croaked dryly. "He kept referring to test subjects. I thought he meant mice at first, or maybe rabbits or even cats, because he was asking for titrations of greater amounts. And specifically, he said they were all female." Emma tensed, her skin prickling.

"He's a private military contractor. He profits from new weapons, and what better weapon than someone fighting with the powers of a *snake*?" Emma's breath caught in her chest. "It doesn't transform males. It only makes them aggressive and difficult to train. But women, he's decided, will make perfect soldiers. They'll turn, like you, and still have enough control to be trained."

The blood drained from Emma's face. She felt heavy, dropping into the chair as her pulse throbbed through her limbs.

"Emma," he said. "His company has been kidnapping girls for this."

Her skin hardened into scales over her back. "It's been him all along," she whispered.

He nodded solemnly. "He's collecting them. I don't know how many, but mostly from group homes and shelters where they might not be missed and are young enough to mold."

"He can't do that. I destroyed my blood samples. They don't have the molecule," she said, her mind still reeling.

"Destroyed them how?" he asked.

"I shattered the vials and spilled the blood," she said, struggling to contain her scales as her fury swelled.

He shook his head. "The molecule is very stable. They will do all they can to retrieve it. There's a good chance their lab already has."

Emma jumped from the chair, dizzy with urgency. She needed to stop this. But Dr. Belken reached up a stiff arm, grimacing.

"Wait," he said. "I think he had plans to kill me from the beginning. Who knows what plan he has for you."

"I make my own plans," Emma said, resolved to make that true. He nodded, as if finally respecting her.

"Be careful," he whispered.

She studied him. "Thank you," she said, and in some ways she pitied him. He didn't know what he had gotten himself into. And she could tell, he did worry about her, in some distorted way he always had. He wasn't the real enemy.

She wondered how much damage Dr. Belken had done with that presentation. Even if she fought this one, enormous enemy, there would be others, rich and powerful and eager for her blood. That was, if she even survived this fight.

She paused outside her brother's hospital room. Through the window, she saw him asleep beneath a tiny bundle of blankets. She wouldn't bother him but wanted a glimpse, to ensure that one thing was stable in the world, even if it wasn't for long. He looked thinner, his bony shoulder faintly protruding from the sheets as if starting to disappear. She had read of the Fates in Greek mythology while searching for Medusa's story, the trio of shrouded women holding out the thread of each human life then severing it to send the soul to Hades's underworld. She thought of her brother's life, a wispy thread stretched to the brink of breaking. Emma bit back tears as she left the hospital.

Outside, she stared at the manicured bushes lining the fountain at the hospital's entrance, the tips of their leaves rimmed in crimson as autumn deepened. She knew she had to stop this plan, stop those girls from being transformed. It could already be too late. But she wasn't sure what to do first.

A chill spread over her neck. A sense of loneliness gripped her, echoing Medusa's isolation in the cave. Was Emma in a cave of her own? She wasn't the girl she used to be. In some ways it was for the better. She wouldn't let anyone take advantage of her again. But she had cast shadows on the things that once filled her life with meaning—school, Pria and Jason. She felt that life slipping from her and tried to grasp its strings before they vanished in the cold autumn wind. She needed to reclaim that warmth, that safety. She *had* to at least tell Jason what was happening, and Pria too. She needed allies.

She was ashamed to admit she had no idea what Pria was doing these days. She recalled how she seemed to click so well with Rachel at school, but surely that didn't mean much. Their friendship was stronger than any of that superficial bond. Pria had sat beside Emma for days in a foreign hospital. Just because she wasn't at the lab with her anymore didn't mean Emma should stop trying to be her friend.

And Jason. His last text to her felt like ages ago. But he had asked her something important, to spend time together. It had probably meant a lot to him... Maybe he had even been nervous to ask, since she had blown him off so many times before. She realized how she must have sounded— dismissive. She owed him an explanation.

She had to tell them everything, starting with Jason. It was the only way to make things right. She needed to swallow her fear of not being accepted and let him in like she once had. As she walked to his house, she convinced herself she could be that vulnerable, that it would bring them closer. But doubt clouded her resolve. She was changing into something less than human. How could that not drive them apart? And beneath it all, another possibility loomed. If she truly could be immortal, she would lose him, wouldn't she? Just the idea of attending different colleges had nearly divided them. How could they withstand *this*? Still, she had to try. Maybe he would see how crucial her role was in saving these girls, maybe he could respect her efforts, love her for her human heart, despite her changing appearance.

She played it out in her head. She would sit him down and say … *what?* The words froze inside her. Once she told him, there would be no going back. What if he was too shocked to understand? Or what if he was disgusted or afraid? A worse thought came to mind. What if he didn't believe her?

Then she recalled the time she had told him about the kidnapping of her friend when she was a kid. He had listened then. He understood, even praised her resilience. She needed to trust him now, again. He was someone she could lean on, even more so than Michelle.

Her phone was lost with her clothes in the van at Poseidon's headquarters. But she knew she didn't have to call. Jason always loved when she visited, planned or not.

But when she arrived, her heart pounded so fast she felt faint. She stared at the door of his house. Dim light glowed from his bedroom window upstairs, but no one came to the door when she knocked. He was probably listening to music on his headphones. Sometimes he didn't hear her. She knocked again, and when he didn't answer she opened the door.

His parents weren't home, so she walked to the stairs, her anxiety increasing with each step. Her heart was a flurry and sweat moistened her brow despite the cool air. Did she have the courage to tell him? What if she stared into his eyes and didn't have the strength to? *No, I need to make myself say it even if emotions try to stop me.* She needed him to know she valued him, that she cared and was sorry if she had hurt him.

She hesitated at the top of the stairs. She sensed an intense heat from his bedroom and knew he was there. Her mouth went dry. She decided the longer she waited, the harder this would be.

"Jason," she called and, with a deep breath, pushed open his door.

There, in the dim light of his room, she saw him leaning over on his bed, his muscles rippling with movement. For a second she didn't understand what he was doing, but at the sound of the door opening, he jolted from the mattress.

And Emma saw what had been beneath him, lying among the sheets. Her friend. *Pria.*

Emma's throat closed. Her eyes darted between the two of them. Pria scrambled to stand, grabbing the sheets to cover herself, but Emma had already seen she was only in her black-laced bra. The room swarmed around her.

"Emma," Jason said. He was sweating, and his voice wavered between heavy breaths. Heavy from… Again she sensed the intense heat of the room and thought she might vomit. Anguish and pain seeped into her numb shock.

"Look," Jason said. "I'm sorry."

Pria began to cry, holding her face in her hands, her shiny, beautiful hair rustling.

"We can talk about this," Jason said.

But Emma felt the scales sprouting from her skin. She bolted toward his bathroom and slammed the door, her chest heaving.

"I wanted to talk to you," Jason's voice came from outside. "I've had a lot happening and you haven't been there."

He was right about that. And she had been sorry, she had been set on making it up to him. But *he* hadn't. In just a few weeks he had replaced her. Or … who knows how long it had been going on. It felt like another bullet to her abdomen, but this was a kind she couldn't deflect. Her body quaked, her stomach burned, and prickles of heat rose to her cheeks as her scales spread.

"We didn't mean to," he continued. *Stop,* she thought. "We just started talking more, at first about how you kept disappearing. Then we were meeting up without realizing it." He rambled, his voice warped in her ears. "Neither of us wanted to hurt you."

Bitter tears stung hot in her eyes. From the bedroom she could hear Pria cursing between sobs.

"I know this … I know it's a mess. But can we try to talk about it?"

Talk. That's what she had wanted so desperately to do. But the chance was gone now. She could never tell him the truth. A storm swelled inside her. The tears spewed over her scales, but she silenced her sobs. She stopped hearing his words. They were only sounds. He rattled the door.

"Come on," he said. "Open this. Emma!"

He banged on it, sounding more urgent as he called her name. She leaped toward the window, catching a scaly glimpse of herself in the mirror. *A monster.* She opened the window and jumped into a nearby tree just as the door swung open.

"Emma?" She listened numbly to his call, and from the shadows of the tree branches, watched him peer out the window, his face distraught. She tracked his footsteps as he ran back through the house. Then he stepped outside, his silhouette outlined in dusky light. He turned, and she held her breath, her body pressed against the tree bark, until he went back inside … to the *human* that had been her friend.

22

Gripped by the torrent of bitterness, rage, and despair, Emma struggled to coax her scales into skin before making her way home. Just hours earlier, her biggest fear had been being tracked by Poseidon Co., but for a moment now, she nearly forgot about that. Her steps were slow and heavy. It was as if a knife had pierced her heart, sinking deeper with each beat.

She entered her house expecting her mom or dad to be there, waiting or worried that she had been gone, but it was empty, dark and cold. She didn't turn on the heat. She shuffled upstairs and stood in the doorway of her room. A tightness stifled her chest, and the tears felt trapped there. Her eyes wandered over to her desk, at the fractured bracelet she had never fixed. She stormed over, shoving the speckled beads onto the floor. As they clattered, she collapsed into her bed and the sobs released.

Finally, drained and numb, she fell into a defeated sleep. The dream came quickly, as if it had been waiting for her, and she was back in Medusa's memory. Cain was in the cave, whispering sweet words that Medusa eagerly embraced. She was leaning into him as he stroked her forearm. Seeing his skin brush against her scales made Emma shudder.

"My love," he whispered. "I hate to leave you. But I have to tend to my father. I think he only has a few days left. Unless … I don't want to pressure you, but your blood—"

"I would give you anything you ask," she told him, "for you've given me what I thought I would never have."

She had collected her blood into a small ceramic flask. She was sure he must have seen it, but not once had he reached for it. It only confirmed her trust in him. Now, at last, she reached beneath the rock and put the flask in his hand.

She watched him leave, jumping over puddles that shone with the golden embers of dusk. Then he turned, looking toward the ground to avoid her gaze, and bowed deeply in thanks, a hand pressed to his chest in what Emma thought was a gross exaggeration. But Medusa pressed a hand over her own heart.

"Return when your father is well again," she said, sure that if her blood worked, it would only be a few days. She was glad to give this gift, but Emma watched, her stomach contorted in horror, wishing she could stop him from leaving.

The cave was quiet and colder to Medusa as she sat in his absence. But her heart was warmed by the dream of his return. She yearned to hear how her blood healed his father and helped his house survive. The sun rose and fell, and nights passed away, the seas dark under a waning moon. She wondered if something went wrong, if her blood had not helped, and if he was angry with her or grieving.

She began to feel even colder than she had before. The snakes of her hair writhed in restless agitation. She began to worry. An inkling of doubt arose, but she chased it away. More than once she hovered at the mouth of the cave. But she couldn't leave. Athena had stolen that liberty. She was hunted. She couldn't walk among humans without risking her life or the lives of unsuspecting onlookers.

Long days passed, and her heart withered. What if he had never loved her, what if he had only wanted her blood? No, she thought, that couldn't be. Medusa wrestled with her doubts, and Emma bore witness with her own broken heart.

More than once, a rustling came from just beyond the cave, and Medusa's heart lifted with the hope of greeting him, only to find another attacker, vicious and eager to slay her. At the sight of the first one, she hesitated, gave him a chance to explain himself or offer another bridge to the world she used to be part of, but none of them did. They were hungry for one thing, and as they attacked, gripped with violence, she turned them to stone, one after another, her heart hardening each time.

Until one day, a man came and stood outside her cave.

"Great goddess," he cried. His voice trembled as he spoke, and at first Medusa wondered if it could be her lover's return. "I have come to deliver this message." Her heart sank again. His voice was too young and boyish. It could be a trap to summon her, she thought.

"Leave it there," she demanded, "or face my wrath." The echo of her hiss carried through the cave, and from the shadows she watched his tiny body retreat.

She waited until the cover of nightfall before creeping out to retrieve the scroll. The moonlight illuminated the page as she unwound it, but she didn't need its light to read. Her eyes were sharp in the dark.

"I am writing this to tell you that your blood has worked with marvelous power."

Her heart leaped with joy. It was from *him*. But already she was disappointed by the letter's length. How could he possibly account for all the time that had passed in his absence, tell her all that had happened to him, with only a page? She read on eagerly.

"My father was already dead before I met you," it said. She froze, then reread the line several times, sure she was mistaken. But there it was, inked onto the merciless page.

"I wanted the blood for myself," it read. The stark words pierced like knives in her heart. This couldn't be from him, she thought. She was desperate to believe that.

"It has made me strong, stronger than any man I've encountered. I've served in the war and killed countless men to the praise of kings. I've cheated death and been rewarded. Thanks to you. I only tell you this now so that you know. I never loved you. I was revolted by your touch, your smell, your taste, but contained it for my own end. I hope you learn from it, that you see what you are. And don't let anyone else trick you, as I don't want another to have your blood. I want to be the only one, unrivaled."

Her heart twisted inside her chest and her face contorted in pain. *It can't be true. It has to be a trick.* She cried out his name over the sea, into the jostled, empty air above the waves. Her tears dropped, swallowed up in the expanse of black sea, as if they were nothing.

Dizzy in her rage and sorrow, she retreated to her cave, withdrawn from the brutal world. As she splashed through a pool between rocks, she watched the water flicker gold for a moment, glowing in the darkness as if a ray of sun had fallen into it. She squinted and, with a sickening realization, recalled that this was the golden glow of Athena, from all those years ago when her curse was first born.

She stared into it, determined to meet the sight no matter how much it burned her already stinging eyes. The tide surged through the cave, washing over the puddle, warping its fiery light. As it receded, the ripples merged together into an image. She gasped. It was Cain, but with his body more muscular than she remembered, his face with a menacing grin, and his skin drenched with blood. Slain bodies defiled the sand around him as far as she could see.

"You fool," a voice came, rattling the ground beneath her feet. *Athena.*

Athena's invisible grip over her tightened then, so constricting Medusa thought she might cease to breathe. She almost wished for that. She could not escape her curse. This was proof of it. This was her destiny, her punishment for attempting any other fate. That solace she had found with him, the gift of understanding, was a farce. Now she only felt robbed, without knowing she had anything left to be robbed of.

Emma felt something slip away from Medusa then, a final, sacred essence of life. Memories swirled forward, and Emma felt her own heart's anger and fear grow. Then, at dusk on the final day of that memory, Medusa gazed into the pool of water, surrounded by stony corpses, and there was only emptiness in her eyes.

Emma didn't want it to be the end. She tried to sense Medusa's emotion but found only the dark pit in her core. She wished she could reach out, offer a word of kindness. But this was not her memory. She saw those cold, hardened eyes and knew how this beautiful woman's story ended.

But what about her own fate? Was Emma's transformation destined to reach this end? Would her own heart be lost, devoid of love? Maybe it had already begun...

Emma became aware of distant voices, tense and mounting. The image of the cave began to fade, and her eyes flickered open from sleep. She didn't recognize the noise at first. It was rare to hear both her parents home at once. They were arguing. The clock beside her read midnight. As she sat up, the image of Jason and Pria flashed in her mind and she thought she might vomit.

She rose and made her way to the kitchen to find her parents standing around the table. Their faces were strained when they turned to see her, suddenly falling silent.

"Emma," her mom said. There was tension in her neck and jaw, and her eyes were puffy. "Did you get my voicemail from earlier?"

Emma stared, thinking about her phone, and wondered what they would say if she told them it was in a van inside a military contracting headquarters' basement. Part of her wished they understood all that she'd been through.

"No, sorry … I lost my phone." She studied her parents, her pulse quickening. She felt the impending question. *Where had she been?* But it didn't come.

"We've been staying in the hospital the past two days with Danny," her mom said. "I'm sure you realized we weren't here."

No, Emma thought, and was partly relieved they didn't question her absence. But her stomach clenched at the mention of Danny, and she felt nauseous again. "Is he okay?" Emma asked. "Did something happen?" Her mother let out a heavy breath. "Is he okay?" she asked again. She panicked, thinking of the way Cain had mentioned her brother and wondered if he had done something. She began to sweat.

"Emma," her mother said. "There's no easy way to tell you this." From the tone in her voice, Emma knew what they were going to say. Cancer was a bigger threat than Cain. She wondered if this was how her mom broke bad news to patients, if it made her any better at doing it now.

"He's not going to make it … is he?" she asked.

Her father looked down with a hand over his eyes, his brow contorted, and her mother's face grimaced as she swallowed back emotion.

"The last chemo didn't work." Her mom's voice trembled as if it might shatter. "He may have only a few weeks. There's nothing left to try."

She imagined how hard this was for them, to work in a field that attempted to fight death yet be left helpless in the face of their own child's. Hot tears stung her eyes and her own worries seemed to fade in the presence of this. Danny… Emma couldn't imagine him gone. Her mom put a hand on Emma's shoulder. She was relieved they didn't hug her, because they'd feel the scales that had spread over her chest in a futile attempt to protect her heart.

Her mind was a torrent of chaos as she retreated to her room. How was everything unraveling at once? She thought of Cain and Poseidon, the trafficked girls Dr. Belken had told her about, and then Pria and Jason. She suddenly felt so cold. She wanted to call him, tell him the news, and allow herself to cry. But the thought only added to her pain. They had betrayed her, just as Medusa had been betrayed. She wanted to fight this destiny, to save the things dear to her. *Danny.*

She thought of the molecule in her blood, the one Dr. Belken proved imparted immortality through healing. For a second her heart lifted in hope. What if she could *cure* Danny? She thought of Cain, the villain from her nightmares. Could she save Danny if it meant cursing him? No, Emma thought, there must be a way to guide him, to prevent such an outcome. If she withheld a life-saving treatment and stood and watched as her brother died and her family fell apart, she would never forgive herself. She thought of the molecule created in her blood when the venom and flower were combined. Without the lab, she couldn't study or isolate it. But she remembered what the old woman had said.

Emma approached the cactus in the ceramic pot by her desk. She rummaged through her drawer for a safety pin, opened it, and pricked her finger quickly. The scales didn't come, as if they knew it was her intent to break skin. She squeezed a drop into the soil beside the cactus and watched. Nothing. Her heart sank as she stared at the dirt.

A few minutes later, there was a knock at her door and her mom entered slowly.

"Em?" she said. Her tone was soft, as if she feared breaking Emma, but it was flatter, less emotional than the one from earlier. Emma turned.

"What is it?" Emma asked, her voice hollow.

Her mom sighed as she sat at the edge of her bed. "I hate to give you more bad news, but I wanted to tell you before you found out some other way."

More bad news? What could be worse than what was already happening?

"Dr. Belken died," her mother said. "My colleagues at the hospital told me."

Emma's heart began to race. "What?"

"I didn't know he had gunshot wounds or was even admitted there. Did you?"

Emma gulped, shaking her head. She couldn't tell her mom that not only did she know but she had witnessed the shooting.

"Emma, I'm feeling less and less comfortable with you having anything to do with that lab," she said. "Dad agrees we should've never let you get involved with him."

Emma nodded. "I stopped going," she said. She was terrified to ask her next question, but she steadied herself. "How did he die?"

"I didn't see the reports, but there's buzz all around the hospital about it. Apparently it wasn't the wound that killed him. It was *venom.*" She said the word like a question, as if it was outlandish to even consider.

"What?" The blood drained from Emma's face.

"It happened after a visitor came," her mom continued. "They're thinking they may have slipped him something, raising the possibility of suicide or … homicide."

Emma stared. She knew who had done it. Dr. Belken had said they would come for him. But why venom? Of course, Dr. Belken had been known for injecting himself with it. Maybe they wanted his end to be ironic. But another thought crept inside her.

If the police were still after the girl who spit snake venom, she would be a suspect. And if they checked the visitor's log, they would see Emma's name that day. Emma shuddered. She was an easy villain. With scales and claws she looked the part.

"Listen, we want you here, until all of this settles down, until we know what he was involved in. You could be in danger," her mother said.

You have no idea…

"Your dad and I will take turns being here and being with Danny. We're taking a break from work this week."

Emma nodded, but there was an urgent, frantic energy inside her veins. She recalled Dr. Belken's final words to her. They were planning to use her blood on kidnapped girls. It could be happening any minute, and it would be *irreversible*. She needed to stop them but wished there was more time. She wasn't ready and wondered if she could crawl her way out from the heaviness that pummeled her.

23

Emma's parents argued downstairs, their tense voices amplified in her ears. They were trying to decide who should stay home when and who needed to go back to the hospital. *They'll probably get divorced after this,* she thought. *Parents divorce over things like this.* The front door shut. In the desolation of her mind, Emma realized, with a faint glimmer of hope, there might be one person in the world who could help her through this. She walked down to the kitchen and saw her dad leaning on the counter, rubbing his temples.

"Can my sensei come over?" she asked.

"You have a *sensei?*" her dad replied.

"Yeah, my trainer for jiu jitsu."

He squinted, as if still a bit confused.

"Wouldn't you rather invite that girl Pria over or something? Isn't she your friend?"

"No," Emma said bluntly. "She stole my boyfriend."

"Oh," he said, awkwardly straightening his posture, the pitch of his voice rising. "Yeah, then, your sensei can come over."

After Emma's call, Michelle arrived in less than an hour. Emma opened the door, graced by a familiar warmth at the sight of her. It was the first time Michelle had ever been to her house, but it felt natural, almost as if she'd been there before. Emma had confided in her more than anyone else, shared such intimate details. Now, to have Michelle in this physical place, this private sphere of her life, resonated with the depth of her vulnerability. She was raw.

They sat in Emma's room, and she shared Dr. Belken's revelation about the kidnapped girls and Jason's betrayal. But she didn't tell her about Danny, maybe because she feared her words would collapse into tears if she tried or because she couldn't find the words to capture the depth of her despair.

Michelle shook her head. "I only left you a few hours ago. It's like you've lived a lifetime since then."

Emma nodded, her throat constricting. "I'm not sure how to overcome this."

Michelle watched her intently, leaning forward with her elbows on her knees. "What are you most afraid of?" she asked.

Emma swallowed, the lump in her throat throbbing. "What they'll do if they catch me again. And what happens if I fail. "

"But you've already beaten them once," Michelle said. "Maybe you're really afraid of what your powers can do."

The insight jolted her with its truth. Maybe she feared who she was morphing into. Rage at those who had wronged her pulsed with a hunger for revenge. It wasn't just rage at Jason, but rage at Medusa's fate, at Poseidon and Athena, and at Cain. The pain of every girl who was and continued to be taken advantage of burned inside her like a match, one spark away from igniting. What if it all came unleashed and she lost control, became a monster instead of a heroine?

"Maybe I'm afraid of what I'm becoming," she whispered, and recalled that dark void in Medusa's eyes.

"You might not be able to stop the fear," Michelle said. "But you have to act in spite of it. The only way past fear is *through* it. And your powers?" Michelle's eyes twinkled. "Let them free. You can trust yourself enough to do that."

Emma took a long breath, nodding as she absorbed her words. It all seemed impossible.

"Can you turn them to stone?" Michelle asked, and though her tone was light, Emma wondered if any part of Michelle feared her. If so, Emma couldn't detect it. "That's the myth, isn't it?" Michelle asked.

Emma smiled and shook her head. *That* power seemed to be the distinction between her transformation and Medusa's. Maybe that step was reserved somehow, only for the myth and inaccessible to her. Though she wasn't sure why she was spared, Emma was thankful, as it seemed to be the part of Medusa's curse that barred her most from humanity.

"So far, no. I haven't turned anything to stone."

"Maybe," Michelle said, "that's waiting."

Emma shuddered, the idea only terrifying her further. How much more change could she handle? Would her heart become serpentine too? "I think then I'll truly be a monster," she said.

"No, you'll always be Emma," Michelle said, her eyes soft but intent. "Even if anything more happens to you. You still have those same values—life, justice. That's how they know you'll fight them. That you'll want to stop them."

"I know," Emma said. She sensed the movement of a car outside, slower than most that passed by. It could be a neighbor driving away, but no. This car came to a slow stop. She peeked out the window and saw a black limo pulled over on the side of the street, its engine still running. "They're already here."

"What?" Michelle asked, raising her brows. She crept beside Emma, her skin blanching.

"The limo?" Michelle asked. "But that could be—"

"I know it's them. I can sense it," she said. "They've already made their plan. They're waiting for me to step into it."

"I'm going to call the FBI," Michelle said.

Emma stiffened, alarmed at this abrupt shift. "No, you can't!" Bitterness rose inside her, piercing like thorns. Was she wrong to trust her sensei? She would betray her like the rest. "They'll hold me as a prisoner and won't reach the girls in time!"

"Look, maybe the police were paid off by this company, but the FBI won't stand for girls being kidnapped. If they're already investigating the case, they'll at least search the headquarters, won't they?"

"Maybe, but we can't be sure. It could ruin everything. And I don't need any more enemies right now." Her voice was rising.

"Emma, I'm not going to do it now," Michelle said quietly, calming her. "You have every reason not to trust them, but if I don't tell them what I know, their only evidence is from your enemies. Listen, I'll wait until you've gone. Then I'll make an anonymous call."

Emma tried to calm herself, unnerved that she had become so rattled, so easily paranoid at someone she trusted. "Okay," she said. There was fear like she had never known inside her, pooling like acid into every weak crevice, so potent her scales were already spreading over her skin.

"Now, let's practice a little. It'll help you focus," Michelle said.

Her sensei led her through a routine, teaching her a few holds she had never fully mastered before. At first, Emma felt slower than usual, her movements laden by her aching heart. If Michelle noticed, she didn't say so and instead only remarked on her speed and agility. Soon, the rhythm and movements eased Emma's nerves, or maybe it was the proximity to Michelle. It almost felt like Emma could absorb the calm of her essence through the warmth of her skin and breath. Her spiced-earth scent held a note of healing as she inhaled it, and Emma felt more alive, the thought of Jason more distant in her presence. When their bodies were warm, Michelle stood, wiping sweat from her brow, nodding with satisfaction.

"I have to tell you this," she said.

Emma became suddenly still, not sure what to expect. At first, she almost expected to be coddled. Maybe that's what she wanted, after all that had happened. But no, Michelle's focus was sharp.

"I did some research on Cain," she said, hesitating a moment. "I took his picture and used one of those apps that matches faces to historical paintings. He had a ton of matches. Of course, it could just be coincidence. I mean, if I put my own face in there it comes up with countless matches and some aren't even female. But his were *so* similar, and there were so many—a gladiator in the Colosseum, an adviser of kings, a war general, a prince."

"I believe it," Emma said, her body constricting like a snake's coiling around a branch.

"I didn't know if I should tell you or not. But I think there's an advantage in knowing your enemy. It can help you win."

Emma nodded, but inside she faltered. "What advantage?" she asked. "If his power is from the same blood as mine, he could have the strength, the speed, the agility to match my own, and he's had centuries to train them."

"But he doesn't have the scales," Michelle said, her eyes gleaming. "And you think differently than he does. Maybe you won't even need to fight," she said. "Maybe you can negotiate, convince him." Her voice sped, and Emma tasted the rusty dankness of her worry.

"I don't think snakes strike very good bargains," Emma said, thinking of Dr. Belken's death. "He *wants* to fight." She peered outside again at the limo's outline, black and menacing in the moonless night. She shivered, and her scales encased her fully.

"Then you'll hand him the fight of his life," Michelle said, grinning, her eyes flickering over her scales in admiration. She rummaged through her bag and handed Emma two bands for her ankles and wrists.

"They're heated," she said. "In case he tries to use the cold to weaken you again." She waved a hand. "I use them for skiing. They last about six hours."

Emma snapped them onto her limbs. Then Michelle handed her an earpiece and a smartwatch.

"You can get me on the phone with this. I can listen to what happens, record it for evidence."

"Thank you," Emma said, and stared at the earpiece.

"What is it?" Michelle asked.

Emma shook her head, wondering what state those kidnapped girls were in. "I just wish we lived in a world where women didn't need superpowers to be safe."

Michelle paused. "Me too," she said, a forlorn look in her eyes.

"Anyway, I'll pay you back for these—"

"Oh stop," Michelle said. "They're old anyway." She tried to chuckle, but Emma sensed the anxiety that stiffened her, sinking its putrid teeth into the air around them. Emma could be leaving to her death. Surely Michelle knew that.

Emma knew it too. But it was worth the risk. She would do it for Danny, and for the girls that were taken. And she would avenge Medusa in the only way she could. She would give this fight everything she had.

"Michelle," she said, as she gazed toward the window. "If I don't come back—"

"Stop it. You're coming back. For your black belt ceremony." She cut the last word short, her pitch rising, and clenched her jaw.

Emma swallowed, her eyes swelling with tears. "Well, in the meantime then, will you watch out for my family? I wouldn't put it past

Poseidon to send someone after my parents." Emma's pitch dropped with a shudder.

Michelle nodded solemnly. "Don't worry. I'll take care of any threat. I'm more worried about what excuse to give your dad if he realizes I'm up here alone." She smiled, and Emma joined in, despite herself.

"Thank you for training me," Emma said. Her voice wavered as she realized how final her words sounded.

"It's been an honor," Michelle said. "But we're not finished." And Emma realized, even if she failed, even if she lost Danny, her best friend, and Jason, she still had something to return to if she survived.

Her sensei stepped closer, as if to tell her a secret, then reached a hand up and pulled Emma's hair from its tight ponytail. "Let it free," she whispered.

Despite Emma's habit of tying it back, to stop it from being pulled by an opponent in jiu jitsu, or simply because it seemed an ugly, frizzy mess in need of confinement, this felt right.

As Michelle drew her hand away, it caressed Emma's cheek and grazed a lock of her hair. Emma's heart flurried and her skin tingled, but not in the way that triggered scales. Michelle's eyes searched hers, ripe with anticipation. *Was it for their plan?* Or something else? The space between them seemed alive with an inexplicable pull, intensifying with each heartbeat.

"I'll be here," Michelle whispered and gave the slightest nod.

Emma leaped out her window and into the night, carrying that heat with her as fuel, as black scales shrouded her. Her heart fluttered in her chest, vibrating her ear drums, as she approached the limo. When she stepped beside it, the driver rolled down his window, simultaneously placing goggles over his beady eyes. Beneath the frames, Emma saw them scan her, deeply set in his strong-boned face.

"I was wondering when you might come out," he said, devoid of emotion. She didn't recognize him, but he was wearing a suit with the logo of Poseidon labs pinned to his blue-checkered tie. In the passenger seat beside him, another man sat, this one facing forward and wearing a full face mask, with a large gun resting on his lap. Her heart sped at the sight of it, unsure what kind it was, how strong its bullets fired, or if it shot the wire net that had ensnared her before.

"There's an invitation for you to join us at our headquarters," the driver said. "For a negotiation."

"And if I decline?" Emma asked.

He grinned subtly. "If you don't choose to take the limo, there are a few other vehicles nearby, ready to assist. But this method seemed the most *chivalrous*, for a lady like yourself."

Her mind flashed with all the ways she could end him, but she held back. *Not yet.* She crouched into the back of the limo and shut the door.

24

The limo windows were tinted from the inside and a partition separated Emma's seat from the driver's, but if they were hoping to disorient her, it didn't work. She knew she could escape if she needed to, despite hearing the doors lock when she entered. But she was determined to see this through, to face Cain again, now that she knew who he was and what he'd done.

Throughout the drive, Emma played different scenarios in her head, concocting plans while trying not to let the uncertainty paralyze her. But her limbs tingled and her heart pounded against her tightened chest, her breaths shallow and quick. Cain had been hatching a plan for so long, probably since before she was born, and she wondered how she could expect to defeat him. But she caught her doubt, choking it from the neck. She had a power too, its source more ancient than Cain, and it was like a beast awakening inside her, hungry after centuries of sleep.

She gazed at the dim, scaled reflection of her face in the dark window, and alienation struck her. She was truly alone. Though she tried to compartmentalize, pushing her chaotic life aside, the thought of Jason and Pria swelled. She had struggled to muster even the smallest hope of being close to him again. A fleeting memory of their struggles, the hurdle they maneuvered past when it came to different colleges, not wanting to be apart, left a pang in her side. A cold, barren emptiness seeped over his place in her heart. That hope she had invested in their future, now lost. She swallowed hard, embracing the pain, letting it harden her. She could channel this anger.

The turning patterns of the road felt familiar, and Emma held her breath as the limo paused by the security checkpoints. When it stopped at last, and the door opened, Emma stepped out into a gray, windowless warehouse to face a crowd of men. They were armed, with faces covered, poised for her strike. She stood before them, covered only in her now slate gray scales, and watched more than a few of them meander over her body, the movements of their head giving their gaze away. There was a time when this might have threatened her. But not anymore. Even as their captive, they would not make her feel small.

"I thought I was here to negotiate," she said to her driver.

"Yes, but we won't let you any further without handcuffs and blindfold."

Emma considered. Fine, she thought. *Blindfold me. I don't need my eyes to tell what's around me.* She brought her hands forward to expose her wrists. When the cuffs clicked around them, she smiled to herself, assured she could slip out of them if needed.

They led her through the building, turning again and again until she couldn't be sure of the way back. But she would figure it out if she had to, she could trace their scent trail. Finally, they slowed. The air around them had grown cooler, and she smelled the presence of someone else in the room. She had only met him once in the flesh, but his scent was distinctive to her memory, like smoldering ash by the sea. Cain.

The metal door bolting shut vibrated behind her, and she felt a tingling, then pressure in her ear as the earpiece was plucked out.

"You won't be needing that," the man whispered, and it crunched as he ground his foot over it on the floor. Emma fought the prickles of panic.

It's fine, she told herself, there wasn't much Michelle could help her with anyway, locked in this room miles away from her.

The man beside her tore off her blindfold and her gaze fell on *him*. It didn't matter how much effort she had spent trying to prepare. Her heart burst into a flurry, like frenzied birds flapping from the water's surface to escape a shark. She swallowed, steadying herself.

He leaned casually back on his chair behind his mahogany desk. The man beside Emma motioned for her to sit across from him, but she held up her bound hands without budging. She could slip out of them herself, she thought, but would rather show her strength by making this demand. The man looked inquiringly at Cain.

"You can remove those," Cain said. "We don't need handcuffs to negotiate."

The man beside her clicked them off, and Emma sensed his fear at standing so close to her, unbound. *You should be afraid.*

But Cain remained relaxed. He paused for a moment, looking her up and down, languidly absorbing her presence. She tried not to let it fluster her. It felt like a cheap trick she wouldn't fall for. She sat finally, and he straightened on his chair. His was slightly more elevated than hers, the difference made even more dramatic by his towering height and broad shoulders. She met his gaze with her chin up, refusing to show her fear, despite how it gripped her stomach.

The room seemed ready to constrict her, its solid steel walls interrupted only by a small pane of black, opaque glass to her left. She assumed someone could be watching through it, but she didn't sense any heat from there.

"I have to say," he said, drawing her focus back to him. "Your stunt was impressive the other day. And it offered us important insight into your abilities." She was silent, not wanting to give away how pleased she was with her fiery escape. "I invited you here in hopes of continuing our negotiations, which were somewhat unproductive last time."

Emma nodded. She caught his eyes flickering over her gray scales again. She hoped he felt threatened.

"What do you propose?" Emma asked.

"By now I'm sure Dr. Belken told you about my plan," he said. "When you visited him. By the way, I'm sorry for his passing. It's a shame. I know you two were close."

He was a murderer, with no remorse. Emma writhed inside, fuming that he would taunt the dead with his sarcasm, but she kept her expression steady.

"Why did you target him, Dr. Belken? How long were you working with him?"

"I've been trying for a long time to recreate you, to recreate her. When I returned to the place where her blood was shed, I found red flowers and tried for years to use them to create the same formula that had empowered me, immortalized me. But I never could. I never realized I needed that venom, or even that the snake existed. But Dr. Belken's proposal caught my attention, and I pressed him on his source until he revealed it was an unidentified snake, one his expertise could not identify, and on *Crete*. That's when I provided funding, a lot of it. I had a feeling there was something else he wasn't sharing… He never admitted that you were even involved. But there were reports on the news. It wasn't hard to put things together. You, someone from his lab. *Changed.*"

"So you tracked me?"

He sighed. "We are a reputable contracting company. When we expressed interest in tracing down *Serpentina*, a monster terrorizing the city and quiet suburbs, the police thanked us. We've been in collaboration, negotiating the terms of your capture, and our need to experiment."

A chill crept over her at the word *experiment*. She wondered what other tests he had in store for her, before she escaped.

"So it was you at the residential home?" she asked. "The trap?" She clenched her jaw, her mind grappling for answers, putting the pieces together.

He sneered. "You have the FBI to thank for that botched capture. We gave them tips and allowed them to try their best, which isn't very good. Lucky for us, you came right here and offered yourself. And we know how to keep our … guests."

He meant *prey*, she thought. But she shook her head.

"All this, while kidnapping girls," she said, her tone accusatory. "The crime they were trying to solve, right under their noses."

"I would rather say *recruited* than kidnapped," he said. "I see Dr. Belken explained a lot before he died."

Before he was killed.

"Let them go," Emma hissed.

He raised his brow. "You state your demands very clearly," he said. "Good, then let's get right to it. I'm offering a different option, a chance to work with us, to train these girls once they're turned."

So they haven't been turned yet, she thought, her heart lifting.

"I can't train girls you no longer have. You're letting them go," she said.

He smiled as if delighted then stood. He stepped around his desk and she studied his movements—the twitches of muscle, the imbalances of weight he was unaware of. He approached her and lingered, half sitting on the front of his desk. He towered over her, heat radiating. She tried to fight it, but the intimidation he exuded hit her like a stifling cloud of smoke. The smile dropped from his face, and he reached forward, brushing a thick hand over her cheek. She stared, furrowing her brows in disgust, but didn't flinch away. She could grab his hand, snap his fingers, but that would be the end of negotiating.

"We are so alike in fundamental ways," he said softly. "I don't see why we need to be at odds."

"We're nothing alike," she spat. "You betrayed a woman who lost everything. You're out for power, and you profit from others' suffering." She recoiled from his hand, and he brought it back to the desk, his jaw clenching.

"Do you know what it's like to be a man?" he asked, his voice low and menacing. "The burden the world puts on you? Having to carry the weight of your entire family and country's livelihood? Protect them, feed them, fight their wars, risk your life, but have no say, no real power, only servitude. Subject to the whims of wealthy leaders who parade by, waving from golden thrones and throwing you scraps from their banquet floors." His voice quivered with a hint of anger, like the rumblings of an early volcano.

She considered all the worlds he had lived in, all he had done to climb atop the hierarchies and achieve his power.

"Can you imagine what it's like to be a woman in that world?" she asked.

He scoffed. "Women's responsibilities aren't the same."

Emma's pulse throbbed with heat. "No, they're not," she said darkly. "The responsibility of continuing the human race is entirely different for women."

He sneered, clenching his hands into fists, and she wondered if he was struggling not to strike her.

"You had a family?" she whispered, recalling in his bitter comeback, this detail that seemed so oddly misfit.

"A few," he said. "Those were always my weaker years."

A heavy silence unfurled as Emma imagined the scenario, this man resenting the pull of a family against his ambitions, his drive for ever more power. Did he ever love any of them? Did he cry when he lost them, and did that only harden his soul more? Or did he detach himself completely? *I've been trying to recreate you.* His words echoed, and she wondered in sudden horror if he had ever had a daughter, and if so, if he had used her to experiment or punished her when his own blood could not turn her into Medusa's form.

"But I have power now," he said. "Real power. And I can share some with you. You should want that for *her.*"

"Don't talk about what I should or shouldn't want," Emma said, baring her teeth at him. "You've had all these years to build an empire, but when it comes down to it, all your power, everything, you owe completely to a woman. You're nothing without her." Emma's voice quivered as she spoke, and her eyes heated with tears as she recalled his betrayal.

His mouth tightened into a grim line, and for a fleeting second her words seemed to disrupt him, before his smirk returned.

"Knowing how to wield power is more important than simply having it. She had something special, but I was the one who achieved something with it."

"You stole it. She was cursed to live in a cave, a victim that you took advantage of. And now you want to do it again, with me."

He sighed deeply. "No," he said, his voice suddenly soft. "I'd rather this be a partnership."

Emma shook her head. "Never."

"I would consider my terms a bit more seriously," Cain said. "I have a lot to offer, starting with protection. I can stop you from being held in jail, for example."

"Staying here sounds a lot like another form of jail," Emma said. "Ownership, not partnership."

"You'll stay with us, yes," he said. "Eventually, we'll tell authorities we have you, but that you're far too dangerous for them to hold. They can even come here to observe, if interested. But I'll be sure to explain you're not really human, and it's safer not to apply the laws of civilians to a monster."

"That's supposed to persuade me?" Emma asked.

"I'm sure it's a better plan than any you've come up with."

Emma scoffed. She hadn't come up with a plan of dealing with the authorities, but thus far she'd managed okay. He meant to rattle her with his condescension, but she enjoyed something about being underestimated.

"Or I'll leave and tell them the truth," she said. "And there'll be evidence, when they see these girls transformed."

"They don't suspect us," he said coolly. "After we allied ourselves, helped them find you. They'll never put together that our new weapons were the kidnapped girls."

"You can't get away with this," she said. "When you try to market *human* weapons, the government won't stand for it." Cain straightened, standing at his full height over her.

"They won't be recognized as human by the time they're sold."

Emma cringed at the word *sold*.

"People are so shortsighted," he continued, pacing back to his chair. "Their lives are just a blink in time. But I've been through centuries. I can wait, it makes no difference. By then they could be explained as a genetically engineered prototype, or even a robot. There are many ways to make it sound ethical."

"I won't let that happen. I'll tell them the truth," Emma said.

"I admire your conviction," he said, and she knew it wasn't true. "Your loyalty to truth and justice. But it's time to be more practical, Emma. Even if, by some wild chance, you did escape me, they wouldn't believe you. And I will make sure you're stopped long before any of that. You're not leaving here. Ever. The state of how you'll remain with us is your only choice." His words had a bite at the end, but he paused, seeming to retreat, trying another approach.

"You're such a beautiful thing," he said, his eyes leering the way Poseidon's had when he approached Medusa on those ancient shores. "Powerful, strong," he whispered. "These girls could use someone like you, once they've changed."

"I won't let you change them," she said, her tone rising.

"We're doing them a favor," he replied, his voice rising above hers. "What else did most of these girls have to look forward to, born into poverty, without families? We're giving them strength, power, a chance to be useful." He paused. "Makes me wonder if you want that power only for yourself."

"Don't pretend that I'm selfish, or that my powers have made my life any easier," Emma said, nearly shouting. "You know it's not about that. This is about consent. It's not for you to decide their futures."

His brow twitched, and she figured he wasn't used to being yelled at. He smirked, but even that looked forced, his muscles oscillating on the brim of agitation.

"You need a bargaining chip to make a demand, and you don't have one," he said. "You thought you got away and saved your blood. But we still have it."

She wasn't shaken. Clearly, he thought it was another point of leverage, but she had expected it. Dr. Belken had warned her. But what came next, she did not expect.

Cain pressed a button on his keyboard, and the black glass of the side wall illuminated to reveal a room behind it. Emma gasped. Inside were six girls, strapped to chairs. *How had she not sensed them?* There were Ivs in their arms, with lines hooked to bags strung over them. To their right, a digital clock ticked away in glowing red numbers on the wall.

"Their infusion starts in thirty minutes," Cain said, grinning.

Emma tried to conceal her panic, but her eyes widened and her heart pumped frantically as she looked at the girls. She thought to jump up, smash through the glass, but she told herself to *think* first. Only, the blood seemed to drain from her head and she felt dizzy.

"You're either with us or against us. And if against us, we have no choice," he said. "This is just the beginning. There will be more batches of them, and we'll need more blood. You can give it willingly, but if we have to, we'll take it."

They're going to kill me, she thought, her mind racing.

"And in case you still consider fighting us, we have one more card," he said, his tone merciless.

Emma lost her breath. In a sweeping motion, like the director of a theater, he pressed a button on his desk and a final light illuminated the room beyond the glass.

Another chair was revealed, and strapped to it was *Pria*.

25

Emma gaped. The sight of Pria was like a punch to her gut. Feelings she had tried to swallow now regurgitated, churning with fear and shock. Pria wasn't fighting her bindings but sat hunched over in defeat, the legs of her sweatpants lopsided and her gray, wrinkled T-shirt stained with sweat. Her normally lustrous hair was matted around her wide, panicked eyes and creased brow. Cain smiled menacingly.

"Why her?" Emma asked, her mouth dry. Bitterness and panic congealed in her stomach.

"What better bargaining chip than your best friend?"

He obviously didn't know everything, she thought, or maybe he did, and this was a cruel joke.

"She knows too much about your transformation," he said. "She could give us away if kept alive."

"She's not my friend," Emma said, her voice quaking as she tried to control the emotion. "And she doesn't know anything about my transformation or what really happened on Crete."

"Well, we'll see how much she means to you then. If you don't cooperate, we won't hesitate to kill her, preferably using snake venom. So when her body's found in some dark alley near, let's say Columbia, no one will hesitate to name the suspect."

Emma struggled to breathe. He was talking about *murder.*

"But if I cooperate, you'll free her?" she asked quietly.

He smiled wickedly, but before he could answer, his cell phone rang, its shrill tone rattling Emma's eardrums. Irritation flashed on his face at the interruption. He answered in a hushed voice, but Emma could hear the exchange clearly. There was a problem upstairs. Someone had arrived at the headquarters with a search warrant. Emma tried to hide her smile. Michelle must have called. It was the right move, and Emma felt bolstered by it. She wasn't totally alone, after all. Cain hung up and cleared his throat, straining to resume his casual arrogance.

"Why don't I leave you here for a minute to think about it," he said. *Oh, you might be gone more than a minute.* She glanced at the timer, now reading twenty-seven minutes. "Remember what your choices are," he said. "You'll sit here and watch these girls turn, and when they do, you'll either join us or die. We can use your blood either way. But I would hate to destroy such a beautiful creature."

The way he spoke, as if he *owned* her, made the fangs sharpen on the roof of her mouth. With that, she was left alone. As soon as the door bolted shut, she jumped up, her heart racing as her eyes darted between the timer and the girls' faces. She tried not to look at Pria, not wanting those feelings to seep in and cloud her judgment. But she glimpsed Pria's frantic gaze and pale face. Emma realized then it was her *human* heart tempted to let Pria suffer for what she'd done. It was the snake, the *monster,* that felt a duty to save her.

She approached the glass, tapping it for weaknesses until she found its thinnest point, and drove her claws into it, cracking a hole. She knew she had to act quickly, but after a moment passed, she wondered why no one was coming to stop her. She smashed her elbow into the crack she'd made, and the window shattered.

She leaped through, ready to grab the girls and sever the IV lines before finding an escape. But what she found instead, beyond the glass, left her breathless. There was *nothing*. The small, closet-like room was empty.

On the wall in front of her was a flat screen, projecting the girls' image. Her panicked mind scattered. *Of course.* Cain wouldn't have been foolish enough to lead her right to them, to leave her alone there. He had broadcast the girls from wherever they actually were. *They could be miles away*, she thought, her pulse pounding in her ears.

Emma's eyes darted about the space. She needed to get out, to find them. She saw the faint outline of a panel on the ceiling above her and jumped up, knocking it free to expose a dark space above her. She listened and sensed for any heat or motion. There was only a faint hum resonating through the building. Emma sprang into the vent.

She was still a moment, grasping for any sense of direction, taking in a deep breath. She smelled steel and dank mildew with dust. But buried deep beneath it, under layers of grime, rubber, and glass, she caught the faintest trace of something else, something she would recognize anywhere. *Her blood.* Wherever her blood was, the girls would be, and on the verge of transformation.

She slithered through the narrow vent, chasing the scent. But the passage didn't lead directly toward it, and with such a faint amount to guide her, she struggled to tell if she was moving closer. She envisioned the clock ticking down. Her pulse surged.

At last, there was an opening in the vent. Air rushed over her face, laced with her blood's scent. Emma slid forward, peering out onto a grated platform lit by orange lights. She slid out from the vent and landed, crouching onto the metal grid beneath her. Her eyes darted about the scene, desperate to pinpoint the source of her blood. The grated flooring was checkered with valves emitting plumes of steam around her, stacked metal boxes, and stairways leading from platform to platform. At the center, the grated floors ended in a drop spanning six stories. *Like the skeleton of a shopping mall*, Emma thought, *but without the railing.*

Her eyes locked on the sight of a large metal enclosure, like a shipment container, one flight above her. Heightening her focus, she sensed the heat from beyond its door and the scent emanating from inside—not just her blood, but the sour, ammonia-like smell of fear. *The girls were in there, terrified.*

She bolted into motion, sure the minutes were dwindling. But as she neared the stairs to the next platform, she froze, for beneath the smell of her blood, the putrid steam, and the girls' acrid fear, she caught a whiff of something else—coal and salt. Her stomach coiled. She knew that scent. She turned, pinpointing its source, and from behind a stack of boxes stepped Cain.

He wasn't wearing his gray suit anymore. Instead, slick red armor lined his body, with a belt that held an array of weapons. He was there to fight. To *kill.*

"Are you going somewhere, Emma?" he asked, his voice low and deep.

He stepped toward her, and without thinking, she stepped back, trembling.

"It's been a long time," he said, the bloodthirst in his voice reminding her of a wolf baring its teeth. "Since I've had a good fight. But I haven't had a worthy partner. You could be what I'm craving."

Emma's scales hardened, flickering orange with the room's light. But they didn't camouflage her. She could tell by the way his eyes tracked her every move. Inside, she cowered, wishing she could disappear through the floor. Her eyes darted around for an escape. But she stopped herself. *No*, she thought, escape was a victim's mentality. She had to face him. She had to save the girls. Her nails pointed into ever sharper claws, and her will burrowed through the fear.

But before she had a second to prepare, he lurched with startling speed. *Snake-like* speed. If he had been another human, she would have easily dodged him, but his speed matched her own, and the impact of his fist on her chest sent her spiraling over the floor.

She heaved for air and stood, shaking herself, as he lumbered toward her. She swung at him as he neared, her nails slicing into the side of his arm, leaving a trickle of red through his armor. She grinned, satisfied, before she caught the scent of his blood, its notes disturbingly similar to her own. Horrified, she had no time to hesitate. He was already striking back. She dodged him now, ready for his speed. She was smaller, but it didn't have to be a weakness. She was more agile and dodged him with precision, even setting him off balance as he struck air instead of her flesh.

She spit a stream of venom, more out of instinct than logic. As he wiped it away, unbothered, she formed a strategy. She could stay just out of reach. He might be stronger than she was, but it wouldn't matter if he never got a hold of her. And as he chased her down, she could guide him, maybe even toward that drop at the center of the platforms…

She leaped away, evading his relentless attack. Her training with Michelle surely helped, but her sensei's speed was never close to Cain's and a hint of fatigue slowed her step. He knew the space better than she did, and despite her attempt to guide their path, she soon found her own back nearing the platform's ledge. She dodged his thrust and rolled away to avoid a fall, stumbling into a stack of metal cartons.

He grabbed something from his belt as she rose. A multi-pronged knife, the weapon's shape reminding her of a trident, glinted in the orange light. She paused at the sight, telling herself her scales could block those sharp edges, a split second before he hurled it toward her. She contorted, stretching her muscles to avoid the prongs as they pierced into the metal behind her, pinning her there.

A sting shot through her body. She scrambled, pushing against the blades to free herself, horrified as she realized a line of scales along her abdomen had been sliced into. He had designed weapons specifically for this, for her. He lumbered toward her, and she pulled at the prongs, frantic, unable to shift her weight for leverage.

He was only three strides away when the blades loosened, screeching as she pulled them free. In the same motion, she hurled the weapon over the ledge before he could grab it back. He turned his head as the distant sound of it clanking to the floor six stories below. Then he grinned.

"So you'd prefer to finish this barehanded," he said.

He swung at her with lightning speed. She ducked. *Just like in training*, she thought, steadying herself, but knew she couldn't do this forever. This wasn't training. Here, there would be only one outcome, one winner. And she was running out of time.

Offense, he doesn't expect that. She slid beneath him, knocking him to the ground in a tackle. They rolled over the floor, locked in the battle she had wanted to avoid. Swift and powerful, she tightened her legs in a triangle around his neck, blocking his air.

But a second later, her grip slipped under his immense strength as he pried her legs apart.

All at once, he flipped her onto her back.

No.

It was a position she knew all too well from training, a position of defeat. But this time, it wasn't a match she would lose, it was her life. His knees pressed her wrists into the floor, and the weight of his body trapped her down, constricting her breath.

No. This was it. Her eyes darted chaotically, searching for a nonexistent escape.

"I see you've made your choice," he said, gritting his teeth. "I can use your blood, dead or alive. And we will, we'll make so many of you."

The scales encasing her chest hardened in an attempt to protect her. Her heart thumped violently against her compressed ribcage, pounding in her ears. She tried to thrust her hips upward to throw him off of her, but he only clamped down tighter, grinning.

This is the end. Will my scales remain when I die? Or will they find my body naked here? No, she thought. *I'll never be found. They'll drain my blood and burn my body.*

Cain snatched yet another knife from his belt. The pain in her abdomen seared as if anticipating its sting.

"It was a good fight," he said, his voice dropping, almost sounding gentle.

Then he thrust the blades toward her face.

She thought of the girls. A fire ignited inside her, burning the last embers of fear, eviscerating them into vapor. For a split second, it was as if her hand became liquid and it slipped from his hold. She clamped onto the weapon's handle as it surged toward her, arresting in her grip. Surprise flickered in his eyes, before reverting to determination. He pressed it down.

Slowly, it inched closer. She pushed against him, fighting his strength and leverage. The blade's point glinted as it crept ever closer. She clenched her teeth, grunting and pushing back with all her strength, but still, the knife advanced. For a second, she hoped her scales might block the blades, then realized from his leering eyes that he aimed for the one spot they didn't cover. Her mouth.

Slowly, the blade's tip grazed her lips and pried her mouth open. His thick hand clamped down on the sides of her jaw, locking it forward to face him as it slipped inside over her tongue. She couldn't shut her mouth now without slicing it open. One final shove would send the blade into the back of her throat, piercing her brainstem. Her breath would cease. He outpowered her. This was the end.

She shut her eyes, feeling his stifling weight on her like Poseidon's on Medusa.

Medusa.

Poseidon's low menacing words rumbled in her memory. *You are nothing.*

A cry bellowed from deep inside her, energy surging through her limbs like an explosion of flame. Her eyes burst open and locked onto his, the eyes from her nightmares.

His weight retreated as she shrieked, his hold receding as she jumped to her feet, one defensive hand on her throat. He stumbled back, his eyes wide with confusion and shock through his goggles. *Had she scared him?* Gone was that wicked, pompous grin, and he seemed to shrink, his movements slowing, stiffening, until he took one final step. He opened his mouth to scream, but no sound came. A flash of agony passed over his face, right before his flesh turned, gray and motionless, into *stone.*

The world stilled. Her panting slowed. There was friction on her neck, scales gliding over scales. A tongue flickered in her periphery. Then her hair lifted around her, floating in a fiery halo of serpents.

26

Emma stared in disbelief at the frozen figure that had been her enemy, her chest still heaving from the fight. She had once feared this final step of transformation, but instead of revulsion at the snakes' presence, they felt familiar, their weight and movement welcome as they slithered around her. In a way, she had expected them. She wasn't horrified as Medusa had been the first time they replaced her hair but felt strangely whole.

She stepped closer until her face was inches from his, then grazed his solid cheek with her fingertips, in awe that this powerful, murderous monster could now be nothing but stone. The cold, unyielding surface assured her.

But there was no time to let it sink in. The girls would be just minutes, maybe seconds, away from the inoculation, if she wasn't already too late. She left Cain's remains behind, ascending the stairs until she reached the highest platform.

The door to the metal contraption looked welded shut, with only a metal handle beneath a digital keypad to permit access. The scent of her blood deepened in her nostrils. Emma clutched the handle, the vibrations of small heartbeats inside intensifying her speed. The door didn't budge. She clawed at it, trying to pierce the metal. It barely made a scratch. Desperate, she threw herself against the door. It didn't even rattle.

Think. She studied the digital keypad above the bolted handle. How could she ever guess the code? There was an optional fingerprint authentication, but with Cain turned to stone, it was useless. Her heart sank. *No,* she thought. *I didn't come this far to fail.* But what else could she do?

"I'm sorry," she whispered, hanging her head.

She closed her eyes, and an idea glimmered to mind, as if whispered, or hissed, into her ear. She looked up, inhaling sharply, and heightened her senses, the stimuli magnified by the snakes orbiting her face. She sensed the frantic energy in the room but didn't let it overwhelm the smaller cues beneath it. She picked up faint, precise points of heat in front of her, on the keypad. Burrowing through the chaos, she grasped onto them.

She blocked out all else, her focused attention intensifying the pattern of heat on the keys, left by whoever had last accessed the lock, and she could distinguish the slight variations, indicating the order the numbers had been pressed. There were at least nine digits in the code. She wasn't sure her panicked mind deciphered the order accurately, but there was only one way to test it. This was the only solution.

She took a breath, trusting her senses completely, letting go of logic, and deliberately pressed each button, listening to the heat, feeling it beneath her fingertips. As she pushed the final one, a buzz sounded and the door bolted open.

But Emma froze. She was ready to rush in, but with snakes for hair, she risked turning the girls to stone, as she had turned Cain.

In this place of danger, where her life was threatened, she had to scale back her protection. But how? She needed *calm,* but the situation called for anything but. She took a breath, as if slowing time. *Thank you,* she told her serpents. *You can return. I don't need you right now.* She talked to them the way she talked to herself when she tried to coax her scales away, the way Michelle talked to her. At first, she wasn't sure they would listen. She might have come this far only to let her own powers get in the way. But then, slowly, she felt the coils relax and float down. She reached up to feel human tresses.

She pushed the door open, stepping over a solid metal floor and found, with a rush of relief, the girls. A few of them screamed at the sight of her.

"No one panic. I'm here to rescue you," she cried. Then Emma saw the digital clock ticking on the far corner of the wall, right above Pria's panic-stricken face.

Five seconds.

Emma lurched into motion.

Four seconds.

With her claws out, she swooped from girl to girl.

Three seconds.

Slicing through the IV lines.

Two seconds.

Stopping the flow of infusion.

One second.

She severed the final cord.

Zero seconds.

The fluids containing her blood spilled over the floors, leaving the girls untouched. She had done it.

"Pria," she said, untying her from the chair. "You need to help me carry these girls out of here."

"How do you know my name?" Her voice shrieked. Emma finished untying her, feeling the rigidity of terror that gripped Pria's body. "They said they'd kill me if I tried to escape," she cried.

"Cain is gone," Emma said, wondering if Pria recognized her voice. But no, it now sounded more like a hiss. Bitterness prickled Emma's skin as she stood so close to her, but the stakes of the situation ran deeper than their severed friendship.

"Even if no one's here," Pria said, her pitch high. "He said everything's flammable, that even if someone rescues us, we'll go up in flames."

Emma's eyes widened. Her mind went back to her first escape from the headquarters, when she started that fire and the ground had so easily ignited. Was that Cain's final fail-safe to conceal his plan, to burn everything?

"Then we'll just have to hurry," Emma said. It wasn't just flames she feared but other workers from Poseidon who might flood in at any moment, bolting the door closed and locking them in.

Emma began to untie the rest of the girls, finishing five before Pria's trembling hands fumbled through one. She recognized the dark-haired girl and the blonde one from the news article, but barely. There was no hint of that broad, toothy smile or the beautifully combed hair. It was her first encounter with the girls, and she wished she had more time to check they were not harmed or ease their worry. They were so small, so light in her arms as she scooped them up.

"Follow me," Emma shouted, and the rest of the girls clung to her as they ran out. Her eyes darted, desperate to find the closest exit.

A pipe ruptured on a platform above them, igniting a spark. A girl with straight, jet black hair screamed as she clung to Emma's neck. Emma panted, overwhelmed with heat. She needed to get them out. Seconds later, a pipe beside them burst and flames ignited, flying toward them.

The shrill scream from the girl on her shoulders pierced Emma's eardrum. Emma pulled her down, hoisting her and another girl into her arms. Then she turned to two others, their faces dirty and contorted in terror.

"It's going to be okay," she said, trying to convince herself of the same. Her scales morphed into fiery red. She knelt down, looking into their wide eyes. "It's time to be brave. Get onto my back," she said.

The girls listened. She instructed a fifth girl to cling to her chest, the girl's legs wrapped around Emma's waist. Laden with their weight, she turned to ask Pria to carry the other two girls. But Pria shook her head, tears streaming down her cheeks, and the image of her crying after leaving Jason's bed flashed in Emma's mind.

"I can't do this." Pria sobbed.

"You have to," Emma yelled, her voice thick with irritation and urgency. But she watched as Pria turned ghostly pale then fainted.

Another burst sounded and flames licked up the stairs from the platform below them, consuming their exit path. *Shit.* A wave of heat rose, the metal floor scalding Emma's feet, as the air thickened with smoke. The girls began to cough between cries. A few more minutes and the flames would consume them. But for now, the heat made Emma's strength explosive.

She eyed the gap at the center of the platforms, a drop spanning six stories. At the ground level, she saw a faint silver light emanating from one side. *There must be a window or a door there.* She had no time to hesitate. This was the only escape.

"Close your eyes and hold on like your life depends on it," she told the girls clasped to her body like magnets. Then Emma leaped over the ledge, dropping with mounting speed through the empty space. Screams surrounded her. Then, still clutching the girls, and with keen precision, she caught herself on the third platform, her legs coiling around the grated metal at its ledge.

But the impact sent a shooting pain up her right leg, and she was nearly certain a bone was broken. She took a single breath, afraid of the pain but knowing there was no other way out, and leaped again, this time onto the ground floor, tumbling sideways to soften the fall but not escaping another wave of searing pain. A girl cried out as she rolled away, but Emma scooped her up, just as a fiery shard of metal struck the ground beside them.

Dizzy with pain, Emma located the door and sprinted, limping with each stride as she carried the girls, exploding into the cold autumn night. She wished for even a second of reprieve, but there was no time. She dropped the girls down and disappeared back into the building.

She peered at the stacked platforms, crumbling in a flaming tower of smoke. The metal was beginning to melt. Soon the entire structure would collapse. This was her last chance to carry everyone out before the flames enveloped everything. She sprang into motion, biting her lip against the pain, telling herself she could recover after, but only if they all made it out. She jumped up the platform levels, shifting weight on her left leg as frenzied energy pulsed through her. The metal she gripped threatened to burn her. Smoke clouded her lungs and stung her eyes.

The platform of the sixth story was beginning to slant beneath her feet as the pillars caved, and the two remaining girls gripped for balance as Pria began to tumble, still unconscious. Emma hoisted Pria over her shoulders, then clutched one girl in each arm.

Her mind began to cloud as smoky air filled her lungs and pain throbbed through her. She hovered over the drop. What if she let one of them slip and fall?

But this was the only way. Above her, a pole crashed to the floor, sending a wave of flame spiraling toward them.

Maybe a human couldn't make this alone, she thought, but I can. She pinpointed the ledge three stories below, gritted her teeth, and jumped off her left leg, faltering slightly. The metal's impact sent shards through her skeleton as she landed, catching the grating between her legs.

She squeezed, hoisting the weight of two children and Pria, who hung precariously wedged between Emma's neck and shoulder.

Below her came shouts from people outside, faint beneath the roar of flame and crashing metal. She made a final leap, landing with a roll. Pria loosened from the grip near the end of the fall and tumbled beside her, landing a bit harder than the rest of them.

Oops, Emma thought, allowing herself a flicker of satisfaction. Then she plucked her back up, gripped the girls, and in a lopsided sprint, dodged the pieces of ceiling as they collapsed around her. Emma burst through the open door into the night.

Outside, a frenzy of cars gathered at the scene, their bright, intrusive lights flooding the night, glaring at her like predators. Emma staggered, her aching body seeming to shrivel in the cold. An ambulance was poised, its lights a flurry of color, and a fire truck rolled out its hoses to drench the flames. The silhouette of photographers, stretchers, and guns surrounded her, and for a moment the scene blurred. Her pulse surged with surreal terror at the thought that, with one look, she could turn all these people to stone. Even if she didn't want to, fear could make her lose control.

Though her body crumbled, exhilaration stole her breath, her own abilities mesmerizing. As people flocked toward her, she knew no one could touch her unless she allowed it. It was power and control like she had never known. She fought the staggering pain and stood, tall and still to meet the chaos as it crashed into her.

Paramedics and police officers shouted, grasping the girls away from her, strapping them onto stretchers, placing oxygen masks on their small faces. One hoisted Pria from the ground, just as her eyes were fluttering open. But no one offered oxygen, bandages, or casts to Emma.

An officer pointed a gun at her, demanding she put her hands up. She did it without flinching. She stared into his eyes, knowing it was he who should fear. Another officer approached, showing her his FBI badge and telling her to get into the car with him. She let them handcuff her. She obeyed, cameras flashing and sirens buzzing in a whirl around her, all the while swelling with pride at what she had done. She had defeated them, and even more importantly, she had saved those girls.

As they drove away, she took a final glance at the building, wondering if they would put out the flames in time to find the remains of Cain. She wondered what they would make of his stony corpse. Then she turned and left the billowing smoke behind her for the second time. The final time.

As they drove, the throbbing in her leg began to quell, the scales on her abdomen starting to weld back together. She knew it would take more time to heal, but it was good enough for now. When they began to drive through streets lined with trees she recognized, she slipped her hands from the cuffs, sliced the seatbelt with a claw, and smashed the window with a flick of her arm.

Before anyone had time to react, she jumped with lightning speed into the branches of nearby trees. The line of police cars screeched to a halt, but she was already too far away for them to pursue her, retreating into the night, refusing to be anyone's captive.

27

Emma moved swiftly through the shadows, blending with the night, until she slipped through the narrowly opened window of her bedroom. Her sensei was pacing about the room, more distraught than she'd ever seen her. Emma stood a moment, her body hardened beneath her blood-stained scales, as if gripped by a shiver that wouldn't end, and realized she had entered so quietly her sensei hadn't heard. Michelle looked up, and her eyes widened.

"Emma," she cried, rushing toward her. In a sudden wave of fatigue, Emma fell into Michelle's arms, her breath shuddering.

They lingered there, and Emma wondered if she could feel the pounding of her heart, the residual chaos from the hell she had endured. Finally, her sensei drew back, placing her hands on Emma's shoulders, studying her face. Emma broke the gaze, suddenly afraid she could turn her to stone without warning.

"My hair," she said. "It changed. The snakes came. I turned him to stone."

Michelle touched her hair, stroking it gently, and her lack of fear calmed Emma enough to meet her gaze again. "How'd you get it to go back?" she asked.

"I focused. Like you taught me."

"You did that all on your own," Michelle said, smiling softly. "You've mastered it."

Emma shook her head. "But I don't know if I'd be able to do it again, if they come back. I'm scared of what I might—"

Michelle silenced her, placing a finger to her lips. The gentle brush of warmth stole her breath. Slowly, Michelle lowered her hand again.

"The scales," Emma whispered, tears surging to her eyes. "I can't make them go away. I think…" She was trembling. "I'm stuck like this." The night's events reverberated deep in her bones, like a part of herself she would never escape. When she closed her eyes, the image of Cain flashed, his knife's tip disappearing into her mouth, its threat of death still so near.

Michelle gripped her shoulder. "You're okay," she whispered, then reached up with her other hand and held Emma's face, forcing her to meet her gaze. "Look at me," she said. "You're okay. It's done. You're safe. You're here now."

Emma's vision blurred with tears. Michelle pulled her into another embrace, and Emma felt the soft, earthy warmth envelope her. "You're safe now," she whispered again, and Emma softened.

A tingle of breath caressed her as Michelle turned her face toward the base of Emma's neck. Emma's own breath quieted, her trembling body falling still. She couldn't tell if it was on purpose or not, but Michelle's lips brushed over newly emerged skin.

The softness spread, emanating from the spot where Michelle's heat grazed her body. Slowly, the scales receded like a gentle tide rolling back over the sand. One by one, they faded to reveal human flesh, until she stood there naked, her skin blotted in soot and bruises but consumed by the radiating warmth between them.

The skin on Emma's body tingled with anticipation, so bare and open. Michelle inched closer, lingering, the air alive with electricity as she wiped a strand from Emma's face, where scales still covered her cheekbones, chin and brow, remnants of armor.

Then, Michelle's full, soft mouth was on hers.

A swell of heat rose within her, the pulse of adrenaline exploding into passion as Emma grabbed her waist, kissing her back with mounting force. The final sprinkling of scales melted as Michelle's lips moved against Emma's cheeks then down onto her neck. There were no thoughts, only bliss.

A knock at the door interrupted the torrent.

"Good night."

Emma's eyes widened at her dad's voice.

Michelle drew back, her face flushed and pupils dilated, a sheen of perspiration over her skin. Emma imagined she must look similar and hurried to cover herself.

"I locked your door," Michelle whispered in reassurance.

Emma's dad called through the door again. "I made some extra toast if you want some!"

Michelle let out a laugh then covered her mouth. "He's been like this all night," she whispered. "Insufferable."

"No thanks, Dad!" Emma called back quickly.

She noticed Michelle's breathing calming almost as quickly as it had risen. She wondered if Michelle's skin also still burned with lingering heat where they had touched.

When her dad's footsteps padded down the hallway, Michelle knelt in front of her and Emma inhaled, swelling with anticipation as the warmth from her movement traveled down her body.

"Let's get you cleaned," she whispered and picked up a towel from the ground.

Emma's first instinct was to protest, but she gave in to it. Michelle was right. Soot and blood covered her skin with a sickening smell. *Whose blood was it?* She shuddered at the thought.

Later, she allowed herself to collapse with exhaustion, surrendering all defenses as Michelle coaxed her into sleep. She didn't know what to make of it, this closeness, the kiss. Was it only to help the scales fade? She wasn't sure, but she craved more.

Emma drifted into a quiet sleep, fading from the danger of the day, and was surprised when that same ancient cave appeared. She had expected, from Medusa's desolation, that the memories would end. But now, something felt different there. In past memories, an air of rage like burnt blood and fear like sulfur had clung to the cave's clawing mist, but not this time. The air held a lighter sweetness, delicate as a spring meadow.

In the shadows of the cave's far-reaching crevice, Medusa huddled, arms wrapped around her knees, her snakes coiling restlessly.

"Medusa?" A voice called from the cave's mouth, so unexpected, Emma felt the surprise through the memory. Medusa's snakes shot upward, hissing at the sound, as she raised her head to peer into the light. *Has someone really just called my name? And a woman's voice?* It wasn't Athena's either, but strangely familiar. "Medusa, are you here?" she called again.

No, it can't be. This must be some trick of my mind, Medusa thought, poised to petrify yet another enemy. But her visitor spoke again.

"It's me," she said, and a graceful silhouette entered the cave, like a vision stepping out of the past.

"Sister?" Medusa asked, her voice cracking, afraid to do something wrong, something that might make the vision vanish. "Stheno?"

"Yes, yes, it's me," she cried. She stepped closer.

A sudden bolt of terror seized Medusa. "You can't look at me," she shouted. "Or you'll—"

"You can't turn me to stone," she said. "The gods assured me."

Medusa's chest heaved. This could all be another setup, another way to hurt her. "The gods are liars," she cried.

"All right," Stheno said softly, her voice like an incantation, echoes of the songs that had lulled Medusa to sleep as a child.

"How do I know this isn't another trap?" Medusa asked, her breaths quivering.

"I'm closing my eyes," Stheno said. "Now, you step into the light."

"You promise?" she asked. Her voice sounded smaller than she remembered it. When was the last time she had spoken a word?

"I promise."

Trembling, Medusa stretched her stiffened limbs, peering beyond her rocks, afraid to hope, afraid— She stopped. There, standing in her cave, was her sister. Her heart flooded with a kind of stinging warmth, like hot sun on salt-crusted skin. From where this intense joy sprang, she couldn't be sure, for her soul had felt cold and barren for so long.

But her sister's form was not the same as she remembered. She still had her chiseled cheeks like sloping reefs, blade-sharp collar bones and broad, muscled shoulders covered in pearlescent scales. But Medusa couldn't help but stare, astonished and horrified, at the parts that were not the same. Her slightly parted mouth revealed teeth that had sharpened, almost into fangs, her fingers were now clawed, and her wing-like fins looked larger, more jagged and darker than before. But the most jarring change of all was on her head. In place of her once long, lush red hair were serpentine tails. They weren't snakes, exactly, not like Medusa's, not with heads, but scaled tails hung down her back, bright red as freshly spilled blood.

"Yes, we were cursed too," Stheno said, reading Medusa's silence though her eyes were still closed. "But not as much as you. Tales of you have spread far across the seas."

"It's really you," Medusa said, breathless. "Why didn't you come sooner?" She felt suddenly like a child again, shrinking, drifting on a merciless sea, calling for her sisters to help against the waves.

"Father forbid it. He didn't want … any trouble. But he doesn't see the big deal in us being changed. He didn't argue against your curse or the parts that we bore. He hasn't made Poseidon pay."

"Of course not," Medusa said bitterly.

"But Mother … Mother is proud of you for surviving this. She thinks, with your snakes, you are even more beautiful."

"How can she know?"

"Athena," Stheno said, her lips coiling as if she wanted to spit, "warned her that she can never look upon you or she will be turned to stone. Still, she visited once, while you slept, and gazed over you."

Medusa couldn't believe it. A sorrowful longing gripped her. How could this curse have ever more layers? Was she not already in the depths of suffering? And how could she turn a god to stone? Could the curse really hold such power? Or had Athena made an empty threat? Answering that question would risk too much.

"That is her punishment, to never look into your eyes again," Stheno said. "Poseidon celebrates this as a victory. He always wanted vengeance on her, ever since she refused him. And Father shows no mercy on Mother."

"So how did you come?"

"I came despite them. Euryale is not as … ready. But for me, it's been long enough. I know you're hunted. I'm here now, to help you."

A chill spread over her skin, as if entering warmth from the cold. Medusa was stunned, sure this could still be a dream. But there she was, her fierce sister.

"But how," Medusa asked. "How can I not turn you to stone?"

"We are the same," Stheno said. "Born of the same womb, we are what they call gorgons."

Then Stheno began to open her eyes.

"No," Medusa shouted in horror, shutting her own eyes as fast as she could.

But it was too late. They had made solid eye contact, if only for a fleeting moment. But that was all it took. She waited in dread for the agonizing cry, the loss of warmth as her sister turned, her soul fleeing as her body turned to ashen rock.

But instead, a warm hand touched her cheek, settling on her chin.

"Medusa," she whispered. "Open your eyes." That sound of her voice, still animated, was the softest warmth she had ever felt. Still, she couldn't trust it. Maybe she hadn't been looking directly at her?

"You're too much for me to risk," Medusa said, tears spilling out from her closed eyelids. "I've already lost everything."

Stheno wiped her tears away, caressing her cheek.

"You can't lose me," Stheno said. "It's fear, Medusa, fear that petrifies your onlookers. Without that, they wouldn't turn to stone. What they see in your eyes, your rage, turns them. But I have that same rage as you. I'm not afraid."

Medusa let the words settle. She couldn't be sure what those men saw before they turned. No one would ever know. But there was always that look of terror, forever frozen to capture their last moment. Stheno *was* different and the closest thing to Medusa's own heart as anything in existence. She needed to trust her, if only for the chance to be whole again.

Holding her breath, Medusa opened her eyes.

Her gaze fell directly into Stheno's sea ivy colored eyes, like an answer to a long buried question that ate at her soul. Medusa had given up on ever being seen this way again but hadn't realized what the loss had truly cost her, until now, when the emptiness filled. Fear dispelled, and Stheno looked on, cursed and changed, yes, but still alive, at least as much as one who never dies could be. Finally, Medusa was seen.

She pulled her sister into an embrace.

Emma awoke the following morning with a sense of serenity, bathing in that final exchange of Medusa and her sister. Then the details of the previous night came hurling back. The memory of her fight with Cain, the roaring flames, and the terrorized girls flashed in her mind. She shivered in the chill of morning but quieted those memories, warmed by Michelle's presence beside her. Bright sunlight streamed through the window, and Emma moved to get up, her body aching.

"Are you all right?" Michelle whispered. Emma turned and found Michelle's eyes alert.

"How long have you been up?" she asked.

Michelle smiled. "Someone had to fend off your parents from disturbing you," she said. Emma laughed a little, and the dark memories lifted.

"But I do have classes to teach," she said, suddenly sounding rather formal.

Emma nodded, sitting up.

"Are you okay?" Michelle asked.

Emma nodded, not wanting her to worry. "Just tired," she said. She was so thoroughly tired. But she felt other things too. She wanted Michelle to stay but wasn't sure how to say it.

"Well, you did bring down an empire." Emma's cheeks warmed at Michelle's admiring smile.

She felt a swell of pride at what she had done, something far greater than she ever imagined she would.

"Thank you," Emma said, wishing Michelle would come back to her side. But Emma also needed time alone to process what had happened. "By the way, I owe you a new earpiece," she said, and Michelle laughed.

"I'll see you soon."

Emma's stomach fluttered at the promise. Their gazes locked and Michelle's warmth lured her closer, pulsing through her. Later, she told herself, and serenity settled over her even as Michelle shifted to leave. Something told her there would be time for them soon.

When she left, Emma stared at the sheets that still held her shape, the air cooling in her absence. Emma made her way to the kitchen, her limbs nimble again, the bruises already fading. Triumph bolstered her step. She had defeated an enemy, ancient and powerful. The fear of being hunted waned, not only because Cain was gone, but because she now knew she could defend against anything.

But a more thorough calmness remained just out of reach. Danny was still dying. The thought tightened into a pit in her core. She noticed the day's newspaper, the front page article sprawled over the kitchen counter.

FBI Exposes Poseidon Co. in Case of Kidnapped Girls.

Below the title was a picture of the headquarters up in smoke. She scanned the lines, her pulse rising again, and when she turned the page, she found a picture of herself. It was a blurry one, the cameras capturing her scales as they were fading from orange to black, like embers in the night. The caption read, "The mysterious Serpentina was seen carrying the children out of the fire. Her role is still under investigation, as she fled the scene before capture." Not entirely true, she thought, but maybe the FBI didn't want to look bad. At least the article didn't call for her arrest.

She wondered when the investigation might bring law enforcement to her doorstep. She had sworn to expose the truth once she got out, to expose Poseidon. But the events appeared to prove that truth already, maybe even more strongly than her claim ever could. Still, there might come a time when she would have to speak.

Her eyes stopped scanning at the sight of Pria's name. *So she decided to wake up in time for the reporters*, Emma thought, her jaw tightening.

"I was terrified," said Pria, the oldest one of the girls kidnapped. "But this amazing creature saved my life. She moved like no human I've ever seen. I only wish I knew who she was so I could thank her."

Emma scoffed. *Oh, you thanked me all right.* She wondered if Pria returned home to fall into Jason's arms, looking for the warmth and comfort Emma had once found there. A spike of rage jabbed at her stomach. But she swallowed it, remembering that Medusa, despite an even greater betrayal, had not been a monster and deserved better than to be framed as one by history. Emma had done the right thing, and she would uphold Medusa's legacy, use her gifts for good. Her heart was shattered from the betrayal, but the pieces were merging back together. A comforting softness enveloped her chest as she recalled her dream, the sister who had come to join Medusa, and the warmth that had blossomed in her soul because of it.

From an outsider's perspective, Emma's life still appeared in shambles, with Danny sick, the loss of her best friend and her boyfriend, and her failing grades in school. Yet she burrowed beneath the loss, grasping for that glow of triumph. Six girls were free because of her, and they had a chance at a future now.

She had lost track of what day it was until she checked the newspaper date. It was the week before Thanksgiving. She wondered if her family would crowd around Danny's hospital bed to eat turkey together or if he could even eat.

Emma moved the paper aside and found a letter beneath it, addressed with her name. She ran her fingers over it, her pulse quickening. It was the kind of large envelope reserved for important things, and when she saw the address, her heart stopped. It was from Columbia.

Emma slid the thick paper from the envelope and began to read. Her eyes widened and she nearly dropped the page.

An early acceptance letter.

She had been accepted to Columbia based on "merit and faculty recommendation." She read on, her eyes eating up the words. The circumstances were described as "nonconventional" and her matriculation would still depend on her "completion of high school graduation requirements." But this ... this was unexpected. She almost couldn't believe it.

Then, in the penultimate paragraph, she read, "Under exceptional circumstances, Dr. Belken has reserved a portion of his laboratory and remainder of his grant money to you for future research, if you choose to accept."

She was speechless, rereading the lines several times. She thought about Dr. Belken, foreseeing his own fall yet taking the time to arrange *this*. Perhaps, even in his death, this last attempt to mend what he had done made Emma swell with sadness and gratitude.

She finished the final paragraph. "This is an unforeseen transfer," it read. "It does not elude our attention that as a high school student without complete training, you will require significant oversight, which will be assigned. Please email us at your earliest convenience so we can arrange a meeting to discuss more details."

It was signed by the dean of students and the director of research at Columbia University.

This was *unheard* of. She would have a chance to pursue her own research. Emma was so excited she jumped from her stool, eager to tell ... *who?* Jason and Pria were gone. And after what her parents had expressed, they would be less than enthusiastic and might not even want her to attend. Maybe she could tell Danny or Michelle. But somehow, she felt hollow, her happiness like an insult to all the bad things that had happened and were still happening. But *something* had worked in her favor.

28

She brought the letter to her room, thinking about it as she gathered stray objects that belonged to Jason and tossed them into a cardboard box. There wasn't much—a few T-shirts, soccer shorts, some of his old assignments, and a letter he wrote her once, which she resisted the urge to reread. Then she crouched to collect the scattered beads from his broken bracelet. The smooth, cool weight of them that had once been so pleasant, so ripe with promise, now seemed to pierce into her palm.

She carried the box outside. It was a long walk to Jason's house, but she needed it. It gave her time to remember everything from beginning to end—their first kiss, the way his body felt, his laughter that would echo in her heart long after he said goodbye. Her steps were heavy as she arrived at his front stairs. She sensed motion, activity in the house, but she blocked it out and turned swiftly, wanting to avoid any confrontation.

But she had barely made it down the driveway before she heard her name.

"Emma?" He stumbled into the box.

She shut her eyes, wincing. She hated how she could smell his scent, even from so far away, and hated how potent and painful the sound of his voice had become. She didn't want to see him, but she wouldn't run. Not this time.

He was standing on his steps, keys in hand. He had been in a hurry. She could tell by his tousled hair and wrinkled shirt that lay unbuttoned at the top. Then he glanced at his car. Even now, he was looking to get away.

"You're going to see her, aren't you?" It dawned on her.

"I mean, she almost died last night, Emma…"

It riled her. As if she should feel bad? Or cruel for not encouraging him to go to her? But at least he answered her question honestly. He *was* going to her.

For a split second, an image flashed of him turning to stone. That pulse of anger, was it a fear or a fantasy?

"Why didn't you just break up with me?"

"Hey," he said, his voice softening. He looked down at the box, and she hoped he saw the broken bracelet. "Can we talk about it some other—"

"No! Because this is the last time I'm talking to you." A painful wave stole her breath because she meant it.

The words seemed to sting him more than Emma expected.

"Wait." He waved his hand as if in refusal.

"If you liked her so much, why didn't you break up with me?"

"I tried, but you were so busy." His words were clumsy.

"Bullshit. You know where I live. If you really wanted to, you could've told me." A part of her caved with guilt. She *had* blocked him off. But she had no intention to make excuses for him now.

"If you really wanted to, if you actually respected me, you would have."

"You didn't respect me either then," he said. "My time, my commitment."

She scoffed.

"Were you ever committed to me?" he asked. "Really committed?"

Emma challenged him with a glare. How could he even think to say that? After what he had done.

He stepped down the first stair, checking around as if self-conscious of being heard.

"How long, Jason? How long were you guys hooking up?"

He hesitated. "It wasn't long, it was just, we were talking a little … then after the Halloween party—"

Emma held up her hand. "No, actually, I don't want to know." Tears stung the corner of her eyes. Her throat constricted and she had to pause.

"I'm sorry," he said, sounding so solemn she almost laughed. Did he think he could take any of this back?

"My best friend!?" Emma shouted. "It had to be her?"

"It's not like that," he said.

"Screw you!"

"I made a mistake!" He approached her, but Emma stepped back, holding her hand up in warning. She really could do it, she thought, she really could turn him to stone. "I made a mistake," he repeated. "Pria just—"

"Don't blame her."

"You're right," he said, now reverting passively, something she used to think was respect but was perhaps just a trick or avoidance. At least there was pain in his eyes, proof that she meant something to him, that he wasn't a sociopath and this hurt him too. But it was not much of a consolation. Her heart hardened.

"But she's not right for me," he continued. "She doesn't mean anything to me. You're the one I love."

Idiot, you're going to see her now. He was still so handsome, she thought, with his broad, muscled shoulders, chiseled jawline and deep eyes. She once thought she found a world for them inside those eyes, but now they held only an echo of emptiness. It was no longer his touch that she wanted, but another, softer one, the one that brought her home the night before.

"I was just … I was confused," he finished.

"You still are. But I'm not, Jason. It's over."

Emma's steps were lighter as she left him behind.

She was new. As she walked, she recalled the serpents that had encircled her the previous night. Her heart fluttered. The fear that had plagued her transformation now faded, and she already missed their coiled, scaly bodies, extensions of herself. For that one moment, when she was wholly transformed, she could feel her full power and was not afraid. She yearned for them again, to know those serpents, their shape, weight, and sound, embracing them as Medusa finally had.

She found her dad in the kitchen when she returned.

"How was your night?" he asked.

Emma nearly laughed. *If he only knew.* "I had the weirdest dream," she said.

"I think you had a letter this morning."

Emma was quick to answer. "Yeah, I got it."

"Anything interesting?" he said, and Emma's mind swirled. She hadn't figured out how to tell him yet, and it didn't feel like the right time.

"We'll see." But as she answered, a scent wafted to her nose, catching her full attention. It came from her bedroom, beckoning her up the stairs. She followed its trail, and when she opened her door, she was greeted by a cloud of scent. Her nose burrowed through to its source, and Emma almost gasped. There, in the dirt beside her cactus, three red blossoms grew, their soft petals cradling golden-crowned centers.

She stepped toward the pot, inhaling deeply. The scent carried the same notes as her blood, mixed with ever more elusive layers. It smelled at one instant like a dewy beach at dawn, then in another, like honeyed blossoms baked in summer sun, changing into rain-soaked moss, soft green buds peeking through frost, and wheat fields waving in an autumn breeze. Each note flickered like a mysterious flame, morphing from one to another, immersing and alluring her.

She wondered how a thousand people hadn't found this perfumed flower when it emitted this intoxicating scent. It seemed to change into whatever she wanted, like an extension of her imagination.

The stairs creaked as her dad climbed up behind her. "You all right?" he asked, standing in the entrance to her bedroom, seeming a bit puzzled as he watched her leaning over the plant.

"What does it smell like to you?" she asked.

"What? I don't smell anything," he said.

She spun to face him in disbelief, sure he was playing a trick.

"You don't smell it?"

"No," he said. "Just the same house smell. Anyway, I'm heading back to the hospital, but Mom will be home soon."

Emma nodded, her heart sinking as she imagined what awaited her family at the hospital. She felt a bit faint as her senses swarmed with the flower's fragrance. As he left, she knelt before the dirt, cradling a blossom in her hand. She knew what she wanted to do.

Emma stepped into Danny's sunlit room during afternoon visiting hours. Her brother smiled, and she was thankful to find him awake. She rushed forward and hugged him, aware that so much had happened since the last time she'd seen him. But for him, it must have been the same old routine of hospital meals, needles, and transfusions. She felt his skeleton in her arms.

"Did you make that?" Emma asked, pointing at a Lego snake sitting on the table by the window. He nodded.

"Last week. But Mommy mostly made it." The words took all his energy, and he slumped lower into his sheets.

"I love it," she whispered. Then she brushed the hair out of his face and sat closely on the bed.

"Danny," she whispered. "What are you the most afraid of?"

She wasn't sure he had the might to answer, but softly, he murmured, "Being away from Mommy and Daddy and you."

She wanted to take his tiny hand and tell him they would always be together, but she couldn't promise that. Tears welled in her eyes.

Emma had seen her mom at home before she left for the hospital. She had sat down, her face more tired and worn than she'd ever seen it. "They think Danny only has a few days left," she said. Her voice cracked as she finished the sentence. Emma had hung her head and felt tears drip from her eyes and onto her palms. It couldn't be the end already. When he was sick, there was still a chance he would make it, a chance he could get better. But death…

She looked at her little brother.

"What if there was another thing to try," Emma said, "that was still not proven and might have risks but could save you? Would you want to try it?"

He nodded. "Yes. But they said there's nothing to try."

Emma nodded. She knew if she tried to speak, her voice would crack with tears.

There were so many reasons not to do what she planned, when she picked the flower from her bedroom and placed a single drop of her venom into its delicate center. How could she play a god? She didn't know the right amount, the proper preparation, or the full extent of risks. What if it offered no benefit at all? Or what if it made him worse? There was the chance that it would work, and then what? Was the potential immortality a benefit or a curse? *You can't appreciate life without death... men were not meant to live forever.* What if they wanted to study his blood then, chase him like they had her? But he was going to die otherwise. That was the alternative.

Then came the words of the woman on Crete. If she remembered them right, he would be sterile and ... aggressive. What if he turned into a version of the villain she had just defeated, a *predator*? No, she wouldn't let that happen. He was young, and she could intervene, somehow. She could help him, teach him what was right and wrong. Still, all those risks, all those sacrifices, faded to dust in the face of his imminent death. It was unfair, to rob him at such a young age, of all he could be. To have this chance seemed a million times more valuable than watching him die and withholding a cure. He would thank her one day, wouldn't he?

"I brought you something," she said, and she brought the flower out of her pocket. "It's to eat."

"They said I can't eat anything."

"You can eat this," she said. "It's allowed. It's medicinal."

He eyed her reluctantly. "Is it a vegetable?" he said, and she smiled a little.

"More like a fruit," she answered and dropped it in his palm. As he studied it, she prepared a cup of water, holding her breath. She tried not to think about all this moment could mean, because the weight of it threatened to crush her.

He chewed the petals and swallowed, washing it down with water, the muscles in his neck rippling beneath frail skin. Emma exhaled, afraid of what might happen. But nothing seemed to change, and a few minutes later, Danny drifted off to sleep.

A nurse came in and gently reminded her that visiting hours were over but said she could stay in the waiting room until the next shift started. Emma walked there numbly and began to pace back and forth. Maybe she hadn't done it right. She had been afraid to get her hopes up anyway. Maybe this was for the best. But how could death be best?

Finally, Emma crumbled into a plastic chair, holding her head in her hands. She wasn't sure how much time had passed before a doctor entered.

"Are you Danny's family member?" he asked. She straightened from the chair.

"Yes," she said, holding her breath.

"I'm his oncologist," he said, and she couldn't read the look on his face but was sure she hadn't seen it before. He looked *incredulous*.

"What is it?" Emma asked.

"His lab work," he said. "Of course we're repeating it to make sure, but all of his blood counts have suddenly … returned to *normal*." He appeared to grapple for words. "I've never seen anything like this."

Emma almost lunged forward to embrace him. She didn't need to wait for the repeat. Maybe it wouldn't make sense to them, but she knew what was happening. It was working.

"And he's, well, he's getting his energy back," he said. "Suddenly it seems." But his face didn't look as happy as she thought it should for such a finding. Maybe he was still baffled.

Just then, both of Emma's parents rushed into the waiting room, breathless.

"We came right away," her dad said. "Can we see him?" The doctor nodded urgently and gestured for them to follow. She watched her parents' eager footsteps race down the hall. This would be everything they hoped for. She had given them this gift. She lingered there, reveling in it.

Just then, the hospital's PA system came to life. "Code gray," it announced. "Children's hospital, room twenty-three."

She almost filtered it out as background noise, but she stopped herself. *Twenty-three.*

That was *Danny's room.*

"Code gray, children's hospital, room twenty-three," it repeated. Emma froze.

She heard the shuffling of feet as nurses and security ran by. Something crashed to the floor upstairs. Code gray, the nurse had once explained, was a behavioral code, often necessitating restraints.

Her mind raced to the only conclusion. She was afraid to move, her heart pounding in her ribcage. But she followed the trail of staff, sensing the new, intense heat radiating from her brother's room as they neared. A nurse ran past her, carrying padded restraints, and Emma's skin prickled as she peered, wide-eyed, into the chaos of Danny's room.

THE END

ACKNOWLEDGEMENTS

Serpentina was first born in my imagination as a child. Before she had a name, she existed as a reincarnation of Medusa, the mythical woman I spent hours reading about in Sloatsburg's public library. She morphed into a fearless heroine with the powers of a snake. She was my daydream on long car rides in our family's van, when I stared out the window imagining her swinging through the forest branches with unstoppable speed. She was the agile fighter I would envision when I competed in sports. I wrote stories of her adventures in composition notebooks and drew pictures of her in strong, flexible poses that embodied female defiance.

She faded as I got older, but never left my mind. She always lingered there, through middle school, high school, medical school and then residency training. She would pop into the forefront in moments I let my imagination wander from the stress or difficulty of the day, and I would tell myself I needed to write her story, for real this time. But maybe I wasn't ready to.

My mom's untimely passing was the unexpected impetus to finally write this story. I waded through a fog of grief, unsure what to do, until I picked up my pen and began to write. This novel became my return to childhood and a reflection of the woman I had become. This will always be writing's greatest gift, and I hope to share the solace it offered me.

I am so grateful for the support and encouragement of my family in my writing endeavors, especially my siblings Sarah, Mary, Johnny, and Hannah, who are willing and enthusiastic readers of even my early drafts. I will always remember Sarah's written critiques, which she reviewed with me page by page, and how we found so many things to laugh through. I also must thank my dad for his helpful information regarding technical aspects I consulted him on while writing this. And I owe a special thank you to my husband Martin, for his enthusiasm for this story as well as his honest critique.

Serpentina could not have been brought to life without the amazingly talented artist, Zohra Mekki, who took my basic design sketch and created a stunning cover, all while completing a semester abroad study in Italy. She is a pleasure to work with and a creative, skilled artist I am lucky to have found.

I continue to be incredibly grateful for my friends Viktoriya and Mercedes, who I first met at a writing conference in Manhattan, and who have provided support and feedback through the writing, editing, and querying process ever since.

I would also like to thank the editing professionals who fine-tuned this novel and offered expert advice. My first editor, Roisin Heycock, created an uplifting and collaborative environment to improve my early draft. I also valued my consultation with Molly Cusick, who offered encouraging feedback on my novel's opening chapter. And I appreciate Karen Robinson's final proofread.

ABOUT THE AUTHOR

Faith grew up in Sloatsburg, NY and studied theater and art history as well as medicine at Stony Brook University, where she earned her MD to become a psychiatrist. Her love for stories and creative writing continues to grow and *SERPENTINA* is her third novel. Her second novel, *Where Ashes Reign*, was published by an indie press in 2021, and her short story, "Pygmalion" was published in the summer 2019 issue of Mad Scientist Journal. When she's not writing or practicing medicine, she enjoys traveling, trying different types of green tea, and seeing how many plants she can fit in her apartment.